The

Fire Golem

by

Bethany A. Beeler

ISBN: 978-1698535272
Beautiful Buddha Books

Other works by Bethany A. Beeler

TransQuality: How Trans Experience Affirms the World

Gods of Rome

The Smoking Inn (Vol. 2 in *The Chronicles of Diana Atestesso*)

Yanter

How to NOT *Know Your Trans: A Memoir*

The Fire Golem (Vol. 1 in *The Chronicles of Diana Atestesso*)

Mirrororrim

Maria (of the angels)

Above the Stars (forthcoming)

Brighton's Bluff (forthcoming)

L & the League of Short-Order Cooks (forthcoming)

The Engine of the Avenging Angels (forthcoming)

Freeland (Vol. 3 in *The Chronicles of Diana Atestesso*) (forthcoming)

Caerdwain (Vol. 4 in *The Chronicles of Diana Atestesso*) (forthcoming)

The Bishop Tripped (forthcoming)

Master of the Universe (forthcoming)

For information on Bethany's paintings and novels, visit

http://bethanybeeler.com

Table of Contents

for Albie

The fire still burns

Remember what you must do
when they undervalue you,
when they think
your softness is your weakness,
when they treat your kindness
like it is their advantage.

You awaken
every dragon,
every wolf,
every monster
that sleeps inside of you
and you remind them
what hell looks like
when it wears the skin
of a gentle human.

—"Fire"/Nikita Gill

And the old, old question:
what kind of person will you now become?
More to the point,
what kind of woman will you now become?

—Sharon Blackie from *If Women Rose Rooted*

Prologue

The fire roared a finality, the heat of the engulfed house burning her bleeding cheeks. It was done.

Then a dark blot reared in the flames and stepped toward her.

Part I

Diana

Hair is grey and the fires are burning
So many dreams on the shelf
You say I wanted you to be proud
I always wanted that myself
—"Winter," Tori Amos

"C'mon, Di'! You can't spend a year in that musty old house! Just sell it as is and we'll split the money," harangued her brother.

"Brad, the place is worth three times as much as what the ugly-house buyers quoted you, and—"

"Di', you're a nurse. You don't know shit about real estate. The house'll get what the market says, no matter how much you fancy it up!"

"Oh, and *you're* the house flipper, Mr. Georgetown condo? Structurally, the place is more than sound, and mountain tourism poises some rich Pittsburgh doctor to buy it as a winter ski lodge and a summer rafting haven for the family. And I'm *not* a nurse, dammit, but nursing school professor with a PhD. Y'know, I *am* capable of sticking out a grad degree or two, unlike some siblings I know."

"You can have all the grad degrees you want, Di'—I'll always make five times as much as you do. No amount of academia or DIY know-how is gonna make the old place anything but a drafty Victorian relic. Even when my Bobby and Stacy were kids it gave 'em the creeps. It's maybe fun for one night of ghost stories and memories in the middle of summer, but you're talking about spending four seasons there, Di'. *Alone.* Do you remember the relentless snow? The heating bills Dad bitched about?"

"It's called a 'sabbatical,' Brad. I'm *supposed* to be alone, so I can work on my projects. I haven't published anything since Luna was ..." Diana's voice caught, and a silence muffled Brad's side of the phone.

"Uh, yeah," grunted Brad, "About that ... any news?"

She let the silence weigh on him. "Only now do you bother to ask about her."

"Look, I'm sorry, okay? It's just ... that it's been so long ..."

"Three years, two months, twenty-two days, and—" She looked at the time on her phone. "—nine hours, give or take a few minutes. But who's counting?"

"I know, I know, alright? Isn't it time to, um, think about ... maybe—"

"'Moving on?!'" she snapped. "Like Luna is a relic CD you dump in the thrift-store box?"

"You always were the hermit holed up in her third-floor bedroom reading, reading, reading, and listening, listening, listening to God knows what! So, yeah, as a matter of fact, I *am* asking whether it's time to move on. You've not heard a thing since the day she was abducted. By now, she's probably fluent in Mexican or Guatemalan or wherever he took her. I mean, it can't be that bad, can it? He *is* her father—"

She threw her phone across the office and heard it thud a hole in the gypsum board then crash to the floor where she saw that its screen was cracked and dark. Her office phone rang. She waited seven rings before sighing and picking it up.

"You *hung up* on me, Di'?"

"My name is 'Diana.' We aren't kids anymore, and I won't put up with your shit."

"Y'know, I might actually be concerned that my little sister *is* acting like a kid and gonna hole up for a year of her life in a place that she swore up and down she'd never go back to. That's no way to put your life back together! Besides, half the things in that cavern of a house are mine, goddammit—my interest has a say in the matter. I've paid the lion's share of the insurance, tax, and property management on the place. Even with the bottom-of-the-barrel price that the ugly-house people are offering, both of us will make a tidy sum. Can't you put the pieces back together with 150 grand?"

"Trust me, Brad, the profit I'll sell it for will remunerate your gracious humanitarian sacrifice. If you don't remember, *I* got the house in the will; you got the cars, half the furniture, and their IRA. Silly me for thinking that you ever actually cared about your little sister and your kidnapped niece beyond a return on your investment."

She heard his sigh on the other end of the line. "Wills can be contested, even this long after probate. Even if they couldn't, I have the money to bring a lawsuit. The fact that I haven't—*and haven't said* anything till now about the way you've handled things in your life—should speak to how I feel about you and my niece. It's your choice, Princess Diana, if you wanna spend a year in a place, your fondest description of which, I recall, was 'a fucking hellhole,' be my guest. But a year, Sis. A year. If I get even a hint you're up there stewing in a puddle of alcohol or oxycontin, I'll have you served quicker than you can push a needle."

He was gone.

∞ ∞ ∞

"Joseph" read the name on his work shirt, right under the cable-company logo.

"Just need you to sign here, Ms. Atestesso," he said in a slight Texas twang and handed her a clipboard.

"No money's due now, Joseph?" She liked to address service people by the names displayed on their shirts, even though her housemate, the grad-anthropology one, insisted it was patronizing and unasked for.

"Dee, the company puts the rep's name on the shirt or the badge. But you never first asked them whether you had the right to address them by name," Sara had preached after Dee had first-name addressed a checker at the grocery.

"Geez, Sara," Diana had sighed, "It's just a momentary transaction, and it might help them have a better day."

"Did you ever just haul off and call any of your patients by their first name without permission?" Sara had retorted.

"That's different, Sar'! It's not like they had "Hello, My Name Is …" badges on their hospital gowns." She'd been beginning to second-guess her decision to share a home with three other grad students, the oldest of which was five years her junior. Being nagged by adorable young people was not all it was cracked up to be.

"Only because the hospital didn't *make* them wear name patches! I bet you went in, checked their full name and date of birth against their hospital wrist band, then asked, 'I'm your nurse, Diana. How would you like me to call you, Mr. Smith?'"

"A hospital is a completely different situation, Sar'. We had protocol to follow."

"What's good for protocol in a hospital oughta be a standard for a service professional. We owe each other that respect." Rounding off her point with a wink and waggle of her tongue, she hoisted her backpack and headed to class.

"You don't owe me a thing, Ms —"

"Call me, Diana," she said and extended her hand.

He shook it."Yeah, my given first name's 'Joseph,' but everybody calls me by my last name, 'Clay.'"

Diana handed back the signed clipboard. "And, really, no money's due now, Joseph-Who-Goes-By-Clay?" He was cute and seemed a few years advanced from the ubiquitous undergrad working his way through college that peopled Denton, TX. She felt no wedding ring as she shook his hand, but the cable company might have a no-jewelry policy (though, apparently, that didn't extend to his captive-bead earrings).

"Nope. They're having a deal for free install this month. Even if they woulda charged you, it would be in your first bill, Diana-Who-Thank-God-Isn't-A-Sorority-Brat."

She smiled. This one had some wit. "If my looks didn't give away my age, you would've already concluded that sorority sisters don't live in a ranch-style rental."

"Your looks are more than fine by me, with a sense of humor, to boot," he winked, mischief in his gaze. She didn't usually go for the blonde-and-steely-blue-eyes types.

"Make a girl blush. Am I your last call of the day?"

"Wish I could say that, Diana, but I still have one more to go, and I don't look forward to it—I know the address. Neighborhood full of pier-n'-beam foundations. That under-wiring's a bitch to access. I'll be sliding on my back in dirt underneath the house with a three-inch clearance from my face, if I'm lucky."

"Ugh! And the bugs and what not!"

"Nah, it's a hoity-toity neck-of-the woods, where the professors have to stay up-to-date on their pest control with the other Professor Joneses."

"I'm a doctoral candidate at TWU," she said, now a little curious. "I might know who you're going to see, to give you a heads-up if they're worse than sorority sisters."

A winning smile lit the corner of his mouth. "Really? I'd be obliged." He thumbed a page on his clipboard. "Lessee … it's a 'Dr. Professor Grieve.' You know 'im?"

"She's a 'her,' and I could've told you before you said her full name that, if they use the 'Dr.' prefix, they're bound to be pretentious as hell. This one, though, doesn't need the prefix to be a pill. We call her 'Dr. Grievous,' but not to her face; she's unfortunately on my PhD committee, though she's outnumbered by humane colleagues. Good luck with that one."

Clay rubbed his brow with the back of his hand. "Shit. Heat, crawling under a foundation, and a tight-ass all wrapped in one. Must've done something to upset the Karma Bitch."

"Just greet her as *Dr.* Grieves every step of the way, and you'll have her eating out of your hand—that is, until you make a mistake," Diana laughed.

"I ain't the mistake-maker," he said. "I'm supposed to be the mistake-fixer—this is her third poor-reception call of the month. Could be anything, really, but my guess is that it's something to do with the electrical on these old retro-fitted, elm-lined houses. Gingerbread on the outside but a bunch of aging infrastructure on the inside that the last occupant just patched over to sell the place. Make the kitchen and bathrooms look nice, and a buyer'll look past the issues brought up in the inspection 'most every time."

Diana raised her eyebrow. "You know a thing or two about construction, Clay. Just so happens it's a hobby of mine."

"I'm glad to fit the T-square in your esteem, Diana-the-House-Fixer-Gettin'-a-PhD. Let's just say that the cable service industry ain't my first bull in the rodeo."

She smiled. "I'd like to hear more about that, Clay-the-Bull-Rider but preferably not on a night after you've traversed the ass-bottom of an old home."

It was his turn to raise an eyebrow, but only for a flicker that wasn't evidenced in his reply "Tomorrow I'm off. I was gonna do some fixing-up at my place, but if you're telling me that you prefer I keep my perspiration to a minimum, I'll do only indoor fixing."

He wrote on a corner of a clipboard page and tore it off. "Here's my number, but if Dr. Grievous is half as bad as you say, don't expect me to be home, feed the pooch, and showered earlier than nine. I don't keep voicemail."

"You're different, Clay," she smiled. "And I'm looking for some different. It's a date. I'll call you with details. I pick the place, and we dutch the bill. I don't do one-night or first-night stands. Cool your jets and talk to me, and we might have a good time."

That one usually led to no phone pick-ups. Maybe Clay would be different.

"Sounds like the calm night I'm in need of," he winked back and turned to the door. "Gotta haul ass, Diana, so I won't be late for Dr. Grievous."

As he stepped out the door with a jaunt towards his truck, she yelled, "Make sure you're not trying to be so damn cute that you forget and call her 'Dr. Grievous'! You may not take that shower till eleven!"

∞ ∞ ∞

Selene Grieve was giving no ground. She never did. That's what friends and mentors do.

"No, I'm not going to let you rethink this, Dr. Atestesso. You must take sabbatical one way or another."

"Selene, please, cut the bullshit formalities. None of this is being recorded."

"We must always follow protocol, Diana, regardless of whether we're being documented. So, too, we will follow the protocol of your sabbatical. You must take it."

Diana sighed. "I know that, Selene, but nothing says that I have to take it at my family home in the Southwestern Pennsylvania Appalachian Mountains."

Dr. Grieve grimaced in the faintest approximation of a smirk Diana had ever seen from her Dean. "I don't believe I ever stipulated where and how you take your sabbatical, just that you return from it refreshed and in a position to publish and advance your career and, of course, the corresponding fortunes of the TWU College of Nursing."

"But, Selene, I have no contingency plan. My apartment is already sub-leased out, and both of us know what housing is like in this town since UNT started upping its enrollment year-after-year. At this late date, if I don't go to PA, where do I go? I might as well *not* sabbatical."

"Then, if you have no local housing," Dr. Grieve sighed, rather self-satisfied, "Your staying here instead of taking sabbatical is moot."

"So, you're forcing me to take housing in DFW, 60 miles away!"

"That would be your choice, Diana, but you know that no CON faculty live outside of Denton County. We encourage local ownership of the program."

"I would then be the black sheep of the College. Why should I even worry about publishing then? I would already be perishing in yours, if not the College Senate's, esteem."

Dr. Grieve folded her hands. "That is one of the choices we have to make in the profession, Dr. Atestesso."

Diana threw her hands in the air. "Okay, I give up! Why are you so hell-bent on my taking sabbatical in Pennsylvania?"

Again, Dr. Grieve evidenced what anyone else would've sworn was a burp but Dee knew was a smile. "Have you had lunch, Dr. Atestesso?"

"No, but I'm not hungry. My stomach has been doing flips all morning."

"Then all the more reason to settle it with a long-overdue meal. Am I right in recalling that you are definitely *not* a breakfast champion?"

"God, no, Selene! The thought of anything on my stomach except the requisite java makes me nauseous."

"At least we agree on one thing today. Breakfast is noisome. But the term is 'nauseated,' not 'nauseous.'" Come. I'm taking you to lunch."

Selene wouldn't allow any discussion of pertinent matters until she had seen to it that Dee had ordered a full lunch. Finally, after the server had taken their order, Diana bore in. "Alright, Selene, we've got to settle this."

"Very well. Allow me to make myself clear." Dr. Grieve cleared her throat. "Something that is 'nauseous' inspires or induces nausea. If one experiences the unfortunate discomfort of nausea, then one is 'nauseated'—that is, one does not inspire or induce nausea in another but rather has had it induced in them."

Diana just stared at her. "Please tell me that the diagnosis of autism was unknown to your pediatrician when you were young, otherwise they might have compensated for it!"

Dr. Grieve stared Diana down—then burst into a belly laugh. "Oh, Diana! You have a one-of-a-kind sense of humor! *And* your buttons are so delightfully *press-able!*"

It was Diana's turn to grimace … until she couldn't hold back her own laugh. "Okay, okay! I get it. I've been wound-up lately."

"Diana, you've been wound-up ever since dear Luna was abducted. You've had your moments in which you've been able to forget that horrid cavity in your life. But they're just that—mere moments. It's a slavery that every one of your decisions, thoughts, hopes, and dreams are held in ransom, quite literally. However, despite your wearing your buttons on your sleeve, you've borne up under pressures and grief that I can hardly imagine, even though I'm Luna's godmother. Which returns me to *why* your sabbatical is so necessary, and why it should be in your old homestead."

"I know, I know. I'm just having second thoughts … and third, fourth, and infinite thoughts."

"May I ask what is spurring those?"

"Of course. I share everything with you. If not for you in my life when Clay had gone off the deep end, I'd have lost my position and any passion for what I do. So … it's my brother, Brad."

"Is he still riding you about his having had to take care of your mother's internment?"

"Not that usual axe he grinds, though he somehow forgets that I was the one who nursed Dad after the strokes, all the way to his death, and saw to his burial while Brad spent his good sweet time in Orlando playing a stupid bowl game. No, this time, he's saying he doesn't think my taking sabbatical at the old home is a good idea."

Selene frowned. "On what grounds?"

"Believe me, I took with a grain of salt his concerns about his financial portfolio. Not that he wasn't a help in paying the property taxes and other incidentals when things with Clay went nuts. I just hate it when he pulls the older-brother card and talks down to me about my decision-making and life like ... I ...”

“—owe him some accounting.”

“Exactly!” said Dee, pounding her fist on the table. “He’s even started implying I have an oxycontin addiction.”

“Did you inform him that his niece’s godmother is not just your Dean but also anal-retentively obsessive about your physical and mental well-being all the way down to grilling you about every prescription you take, even if it’s antibiotics for a sinus infection?”

“Well, he *does* know you’re a nurse, so ...”

Selene waved her hand, almost toppling the salads the server was setting down before them. “Regardless, his intimations are groundless.”

“But that’s not the point. He’s *never* taken me seriously, and when I announce a decision like this as a courtesy to him, he uses even that small leverage to underline that he’s never taken me seriously!”

Selene paused her fork. “Why should his taking you seriously matter?”

Diana toyed with her croutons before adamantly shoving a huge bite of chicken, lettuce, and raspberry vinaigrette into her mouth. “Well, *[munch]* he’s threatening a lawsuit to ‘protect his interests.’ *[Chew]* I don’t need, on top of trying to get published and renovating the house, the pressure of ... *[swallow]* having to prove myself to him!”

“Who, really, is the person you’re trying to prove something to?”

Diana paused long enough for a tear to dot her cheek.

“Yourself, Diana?”

Dee looked away and tried to tongue a piece of arugula from between two molars while holding back the floodgates. She picked up a napkin, blowing her nose. After a long pause, she dabbed away another tear. "It's like ... ever since *he* took her from me, he's hung around like a ghost, haunting every movement, every thought of mine. He *violated* me, and Lord knows what he's doing to Luna." She looked up at Selene like she were gazing for the first time at a mirror. "I ... I used to *believe* in myself, y'know? And it isn't right that he can do this to me, after all I went through, getting out of that hell-hole in the mountains and the shit I went through there, then working my ass off to earn a doctorate and tenured position. I second-guess everything now ..."

Selene didn't look at her but spoke nonetheless. "Including whether you should take sabbatical there. And it's not because of Bradley's not taking you seriously. You yourself said he's never taken you seriously, so this is not a new development. Might I ask, are your misgivings because you feel like you'd be abandoning Luna?"

"I've said that all along, but you assured me that her ever-vigilant godmother would ride herd on the Patrol, the FBI, and the Rangers, though I doubt any of them are pursuing the case as a priority, it's been so long."

"Speaking of which, did you get the notarized documents to them?"

"Everyone but the FBI; I'm setting aside tomorrow morning to drive to the field office in-person. All of them need to know that you'll be my point person here. They can talk to you as if they're talking to me."

"Rest assured, Diana, I'll impress upon them that the statute of limitations doesn't run out on a missing-child case."

Dee sighed. "That's the other thing! She was *abducted*—why do they treat it as a missing-child case, like she was somehow mislaid? Clay's been missing since two years before he stole Luna. Can't they make the connection?"

Selene reached out a hand to squeeze Dee's. "I'm sure they've made the connection. But they know they're dealing with one of their own. Different set of rules, Diana. They look after each other. And until the FBI has solid evidence that state lines were crossed, they'll be anything but proactive. They've higher-media-profile cases to chase, the sons of bitches!"

Dee looked up. That was a seismic outburst compared to Dr. Grieve's normally Vulcan demeanor. The good Dean apparently noticed Dee's noticing. "It's just that my long-passed daddy was a helluva Texas Ranger who wouldn't stand for such lollygagging on the part of any law enforcement. I'm sure you know he broke the Malachi Dallas scandal."

Squeezing her hand back, Dee smiled. "Someone's mentioned it a few times. Wish I could be as proud of my father."

"You need only be proud of *you,* dear! You're an incredibly strong and resourceful bulwark. You never wished Clay's depravations on yourself—nor should you blame yourself for falling for him in the first place. It wasn't all bad. In fact, as I remember, he got your mind off your doctoral project enough that you didn't obsess it into something useless. I remember your laughter, especially when Luna was born. Like you, I can't understand how something wicked your way came. But you owe it yourself to return to where it all began, and to face that house, to stare it down to the ground and make it life-giving."

∞ ∞ ∞

It *had* been good.

The first date hadn't been like a date at all but rather like two long-lost friends rekindling a dormant relationship. He couldn't have planned it.

"Okay," she said. "Be honest with me, because you were flirting with me from the second I opened the door—and I am *not* full of myself. Do you always play the 'Aw, shucks, Ma'am, I bet you say that to all the cable guys' role, or is that, shucks, Ma'am, really you?"

"It's pretty much me, but I was also pouring it on thick once I knew you weren't an undergrad bimbo."

"Bimbo? Wow, you know how to charm a lady with word-choice."

He smiled and toyed with his tableware set-up as they waited for their fare—Pizza Hut was prosaic and innocuous enough to let him know that she wasn't trying too hard, nor that he needed to. Besides, there was the next-door arcade where she hoped to go after the meal.

"I'm no academic," he said. "But I don't have a chip on my shoulder about it. You can learn lots of things without haunting a classroom. Like Nike says, 'Just do it.' Well, I do it, but I don't need polysyllabic words to prove I've done it."

"It's okay," she grinned. "I'm not saying that intelligence and curiosity are moral prerequisites. But they can be a turn-on, especially if the bearer doesn't wear a tweed blazer with elbow patches."

Clay sported a Rangers' tee that showed his muscles and stray tats. "I like the challenge of a woman with spark, and sparks come in a variety and mixture of forms. I've met lots who're smart, with no pushback or gumption. Others are just audaciously stupid, their spark alone not enough to set you aflame."

Dee pursed her lips. "And where, at first glance and first words, do I fall on that spectrum?"

He apprised her for what became a few uncomfortable seconds. "You promise to be the kind of challenge I live for."

She might've left right at that moment. She should have, and everything would've been different. But something paused her It wasn't second-guessing. She'd like to think it was her answering the challenge.

"I *promise* to be? What makes you think we're a go from here?"

"I admire strategy even more than a challenge," he winked, then glanced at the server who was bringing their pepperoni- and-mushroom deep-dish, "You make me strategize. I'm willing to believe I do the same to you … or at least pique your interest in that department."

"Care for anything else?" said the perky server generously emptying her pockets of parmesan and red-pepper packets.

Clay peered up at her and answered before Dee could. "I think I have my hands full with this one."

The server laughed. "Clay, you're such a card!"

Dee raised her eyebrow. "You're a regular?"

He was already biting into a slice, though she could see from the steam that it had to be scorching his mouth. Only after he'd chewed and swallowed and she'd gotten her own slice onto the plate did he reply. "Let's just say I know people in low places. No shame in that, is there?"

"No, I suppose not," she nodded and dumped a packet of red pepper on her pizza.

"You *are* a handful," he pointed at the red pepper. "I never could abide spice. Gives me hives and diarrhea."

"Again, you *are* a charmer. But you won't faze me. I'm a registered nurse—I've seen all there is to see in the gross and freaky department."

"Have you?" he raised an eyebrow. "Maybe that's *your* challenge. 'Cuz I can give you a crash-course in freaky."

She bit into her piece and said mid-chew, waving a hand, "I said I could use some 'different.' I've already lived enough freaky to last a lifetime."

"Have you?" he again quizzed, gulping down a huge bolt. "It's in my mind that most folks don't know what freaky really is. I'll tell you my story some time and let you be the judge. Let's have some fun tonight, instead."

∞ ∞ ∞

Dee didn't move in with him for a year. Part of it was simply that she didn't want to leave her housemates in a lease-lurch. But part of it was a second sense she didn't always listen to. It wasn't until she'd felt more comfortable in her relationship with her doctoral committee and had developed a not-so-grievous relationship with Dr. Grieve, that she deemed herself on firm enough footing to contemplate the move.

She enjoyed her independence. But, like anyone might, she also liked being loved and appreciated. Clay *was* different—enough to overlook the oddities that didn't always square.

"Whaddya mean 'some things don't square,' Dee?" Shelby, her grad-bio-chem housemate asked. "It's not like you to not do your research—and I'm talking about more than just your thesis."

"I'm not sure," Dee mused. "It's this whole 'I grew up an orphan' story. Yeah, I know he didn't have the best of upbringings—and maybe that's it. You'd expect him to be, well, more fucked up."

"Like it's almost too good to be true?"

"Exactly." Dee combed her fingers through her hair. "It's not that I don't believe him—I mean, how do you make up a story like that?"

Shelby squinted an eye. "Is he close about other aspects of his life—say, his bank account, his credit cards, his job? Run ins with the law?"

"Well, no. He's always been totally up-front when he does or doesn't have the money or time for us to do something together. He doesn't use a debit card, just carries cash. He says he banks at the telecom credit union, and I've no reason to think he doesn't, though I've never seen a checkbook or statements lying around his place. Seems like he's just pretty simple and basic about that kind of thing. It's not like I've run a background check on him."

"Maybe you ought to," sniffed Shelby.

"Shelb', I'd hardly know where to start, and isn't that a breach of trust, as in, 'Okay, I'm piqued by the idea of us shacking up and all, but can you give me your social and a few references?' That's not something a relationship allows."

"Hmm. It ought to, especially if you have a reason to suspect anything."

"That's just it, Shelb'—I *should* have no reason to suspect him. So why do I?"

Shelby looked hard at her. "The question really is, Dee, why aren't you giving yourself *permission* to? Or, better yet, why don't you simply ask him yourself?"

"What? I'm supposed to say, 'Hey, I really want this to work, but I deserve to know more about you before I make this big step'?"

"Don't you deserve that?"

Diana sighed. "I suppose I do, but how do I say that without endangering what I've got? I'm tired of playing the field, and I really want to start adulting, Shelb'. Other people my age are married with kids, they have a direction, a trajectory for their lives, they're building a house of the future together with someone else. Don't I deserve *that?*"

"I suppose you do, if that's your dream. But what about the house of the *present?* What does the Diana occupant of *that* domicile deserve?"

Diana shook her head. "Isn't this maybe your bias talking, Shelb'? You've never liked Clay, never opened the door to him."

"Wasn't my door to open. I'm not the person to give relationship advice—just a single, lesbian, bio-chem geek who has no clue, nor is terribly concerned, about a house of the future. I dunno, maybe I'm too young to know better. But I know this—he *does* seem too good to be true, and I say that with no envy whatsoever, and not 'cuz I'm a lesbian or have designs on you, Dee. (Sorry, you're more the lipstick-lesbian type, and I prefer butch with a tiny soft side.) Yeah, I don't warm to him, but that's got nothing to do with whether you should move in with him."

"I know I should step carefully here, and in my moments alone, I see that clearly. But when I'm with him, well, I enjoy my life—something I've never allowed myself to do. Is it wrong to make a decision like that based on what I feel?"

"It's not like feeling has to be opposed to reason or prudence, Dee, or even that it has to be your motive exclusive of reasoning. Look, I'm a scientist, and there's a really easy way to method this out. My high-school ex and I are on good terms still, even though I broke it to him that I'm queer. He took it pretty well, actually, 'cuz it softened the sting of the breakup. He's a cyber-analyst for a massive detective agency in Fort Worth and owes me a favor or two. Why don't I have him run a background check—financial, employment, and criminal on Mr. Clay? All it'll cost you is the price of running the actual report. Jeff'll do the analysis for free as a favor to me. If it brings up any warning flags, he'll be sure to note 'em."

∞ ∞ ∞

Clay's lovemaking was harsh that night, and, for the first time, unsatisfying to her.

"What's the matter?" he asked, standing by the bed and hoisting on his drawers.

"Oh, nothing."

"C'mon, Di', I know that pensive look. Something's wrong. I wanna know."

"Well … for one thing, it was kinda rough tonight. You don't normally make me hurt."

He pulled on his shirt. "I was rough? I'm sorry, babe. Had a hard-ass day. My dispatch manager was being a real prick."

"Were you thinking of them, then, when you were ramming it home just now?"

He laughed and jumped back into bed with her, stroking her face. "C'mon, you can't say it didn't turn you on, Di'. You like it when I take control."

"As a matter of fact, I don't." As a matter of fact, it scared her. "And you know I don't like it when you call me 'Di'."

"Aw," he said, rubbing her shoulder, "It's my pet name for you, that no one else calls you by."

She turned to him. "There's a reason for that, y'know—I've told people *not* to call me that."

He stopped the rubbing. "But I'm different, baby. That's what you like about me—I'm your different. Oughta afford me a little privilege."

"And I don't like it rough. I made that clear from the beginning."

He smirked. "Your body says otherwise, Di. It's the wettest

you've been in a long time, like cutting butter with a hot knife."

It scared her now how that comment sent chills through her … and simultaneously made her wet. She fought it. "Is that what I am to you?" she flared. "A piece of meat? The butter pat to stab when you've had a bad day?"

He sat up. "Hey, hey, hey, baby! Who's the one who's had the bad day? Who's the one taking her own issues out on her love? I need to tame the tigress."

She jumped out of bed and stared at him like he was an intruder. He saw the look in her eyes and color rushed to his face. But only for an instant. His voice was back in control. "Whoa, sweetie! I am so sorry. I was just playin' around like I do, pushing your buttons there. I didn't know you were that touchy. I am so sorry. Come back to bed. We don't have to make love again, for as long as you like. And when we do, I promise it'll be gentle. I overstepped my bounds, and I shouldn't have presumed. A guy can sometimes take an angel for granted, y'know? And I just did, but I've no excuse."

She paused.

"Baby, c'mon, it's me, remember? Clay All the Way? We're moving in together next month. Two against the world. You're his challenge. You might recall he's the one who brings you flowers and devotes his life to you? And, well, I was gonna save this surprise for when you moved in …"

Diana sat down, her heart skipping.

"There we go," he whispered reassuringly, caressing her arm. "I thought you might be having second thoughts about moving in, 'cuz it's a big step, and, well, I'm pretty much a bum cable guy who has no future …"

"Stop it!" she protested. "You know none of that matters to me, and I hate hearing you say that about yourself. I've got my own career, and I don't predicate our relationship on what you can provide for me. You're more to me than that, Clay."

He sighed. "It's a guy thing, babe—it's important for me to know I can provide. And there's no future for me in a job where I'll always be a grunt. But you know how you've told me to chase a dream, 'cept I didn't think I had a dream to chase? Well, a few months ago, I got pulled over by Highway Patrol—" He soothed the look of alarm in her face. "Don't worry, he didn't give me a ticket. I was in the cable van, and I charmed my way through, saying I was late for an appointment, which I was. Seemed like a decent guy, like someone who saw a kinship in me. Weird, huh?

"So I worked up the gumption to flat out ask him what it takes to be in the Patrol. Believe it or not, he smiled and gave me his card, with a web address and recruitment number on the back. Turns out I don't need a college degree, just at least a GED and 60 college credits, which you know I've got in spades from my jacking around with criminal justice in community college. One thing led to another after several phone calls, *lots* of research online, and an ass-load of interviews. Turns out, I'm cut out for this. In fact, I'm a natural! At least that's what their physical readiness exam and their screening and psych tests say. So, the big surprise is that I start academy in June! Already turned in my notice with the cable-company salt mine!"

She was flabbergasted. "Is it here in Denton?"

"Naw, I gotta spend 23 weeks at the Academy in Austin. But they'll have openings in the Denton area where I can serve my 12-month probationary duty, then I'm a full-fledged Texas State Highway Patrolman!"

"What? But that's less than a month after we're supposed to move in together. I mean, what's the point of my moving in if you're not gonna be here for six months?"

"It's not like that, babe! After the first two months, I get two weekends leave per month, plus holidays. We'll see each other.

Besides, Blackjack'll keep you company!"

"Oh! So, I'm moving in to take care of your pit bull while you jaunt off to Police Academy? How convenient."

Clay looked crestfallen. "Geez, Diana. I … I thought this'd make you happy. It's a position of authority, and respect. After what I've been through, I think it'd do me some good to see myself in that light."

Diana was horribly conflicted. She was supposed to be proud of him, wasn't she? So why did she feel torn? Was she that selfish that she couldn't flex enough in this relationship to let him grow … especially after she'd encouraged him to do just that?

But no, no! What would this do to the relationship? They hadn't experienced distance or absence. And Clay was an uncontrollable flirt—no telling what damage he could do with the ladies of Austin. And … being the live-in or someday-wife of a Trooper? Waiting for him to come home alive after each and every patrol? Waiting for the inevitable phone call or knock at the door—"Mrs. Clay, something's happened …"

And how could she follow him if he were stationed somewhere outside of Denton or the Metroplex? Yes, Selene had intimated that a tenure-track position was opening in the College of Nursing that would be perfect, but there was no guarantee Dee would get tenure. If Dee didn't, she would have to look for a teaching position possibly anywhere in the nation. They didn't grow on trees. If she did make tenure, that would restrict his ability to move or to be promoted to a position in, say, Austin. She did *not* want a long-term Interstate-35 relationship.

"And I know what you're thinking, Di', 'cuz I've thought it through myself, even inquired with the recruiters about this and every eventuality. The Patrol is flexible in placement and stationing. They *have* to be—it's not like they have lines of dudes begging to put their lives on the line every shift. I told them I'm anchored to you, baby. Where you go, I go. Where you get a teaching job, I'll be a trooper, even if it's out-of-state, 'cuz there's all sorts of transfer and state-to-state reciprocation programs. This country values its law enforcement.

"And I know, too, that it would be hard on you. I didn't spring this on you willy-nilly—I'll care for my safety because I'll always have *you* to come home to. I'll make it damn near impossible for an assailant to step in between what you and I and our kids will have."

What could she say? That she'd initiated a background check on him? That, even after a year, she had more questions than answers about him? To do that would be to admit to herself that there was no point in this relationship. That there never had been. She couldn't step across that threshold.

∞ ∞ ∞

"I'll drop you the full PDF so you can read it in detail," said Jeff, sitting at their kitchen table, a sheath of papers in front of him. "But it's clean as a whistle."

"Really?" Diana was surprised but, oddly, not relieved.

Shelby was standing beside Jeff, looking over his shoulder. "Tell her the rest, Jeff."

"What 'rest'?" Dee asked. "What else is there?"

"It's quite literally nothing," Jeff shrugged. "And that's what's eating me."

"Eating you?"

"He means what you and I thought, Dee—it feels too good to be true."

"Yeah, something like that, but, in more technical parlance, I'd call it the opposite of an orgy of evidence."

Diana cocked her head. "You lost me with the Law-and-Order-SVU dialogue."

"It's actually kinda like that, Diana," said Jeff. "You know how a glut of evidence at a crime scene can tip a frame up? In Clay's case, we have the flip side—this report is, well, too damn spanking empty."

"What tells you that? A hunch?" Dee asked.

"Experience. Reports like this aren't just rarities—they're impossible. You'd have to be living off-the-grid since childhood to this very day to have a background this sparse. Yes, we have his social. That was nothing for me to find and cross check against his current address and employment to ensure we've got the right Joseph Clay. You'd be surprised how many of 'em there are in Texas alone, which at first got me wondering if it's an alias, but his name checks out with his docs from the Station Creek Kids Ranch. Aside from that stuff, his GED and community-college transcripts, driver's license, his last three 1040-EZ returns, and his current employer, Mr. Joseph Clay (with no middle name, thank you) has literally nothing else to demonstrate his civilizational fingerprint. Damn, you expect a traffic citation or two, medical records, or at least an emergency-room visit, a car registration, a deeper job history, late utility payments (or utility payments at all!), credit pulls on his credit report. I can't even find that he registered for the draft. All his community college payments must've been in cash because he literally has no electronic payment records. Hell, you should have SSN hits for more than just your current job. Was he a migrant farm worker?"

"No, but did Shelby tell you about his past? He was abandoned by his mom at a young age, and he has no clue who his dad is—his mom never told him. Being brought up at an orphans' ranch in the wooly wilds of Texas doesn't exactly train you to establish a credit rating. He thinks power companies are a rip-off since deregulation, so he runs a generator and mounts solar panels. He doesn't own a car —just uses his cable-company van. He's, well, *different*."

"Yeah, Shelb' told me all of that, and I took it into consideration in my investigation. Look, I did a helluva lot more digging than I normally would've for a favor and the cost of pulling a report. The sheer lack of anything made me curious as fuck. You just don't see this—unless someone intends to fabricate a past."

"Is that what you're saying—that this is made up?"

"That's just it," shrugged Jeff. "I wish I *could* definitively say that. But this all could be totally legit. The necessaries are all there to not arouse the suspicion that it's doctored … and that's what has me second-guessing—if I wanted to create the perception that this was legit and beyond scrutiny, I'd have done it exactly this way. How smart is this guy?"

Dee paused. "The records should show that he didn't stick with community college. But he's smart enough to keep me on my toes. It's rare to find any subject he doesn't know at least a modicum about—even nursing. I've given him novels and philosophy to read that are at the edge of *my* abilities—and I've had a beyond-post-grad reading level since I was tested back in junior high. Not only can he read it at a vicious pace but he can converse about it beyond just having a Will-Hunting photographic-memory recall."

Jeff mused over this. "Then he's more than intelligent enough to pull off a fraud of this caliber, if that's what it is. But why would he need to? Say he has a minimalist past and is lives off-the-grid. His report would show something more than this, some semblance of being a human being and not the digital equivalent of a ghost."

"Shit," whispered Shelby. "This is creepy as fuck."

Diana felt like a deer in the headlights. "You don't think that he's in a drug cartel or the NSA or a foreign agent?"

"Hollywood saves that shit for shows like *Blacklist*," Jeff countered. "Besides, classified security rankings give off their own secretive pheromones that're easy to read. You run into brick walls and roadblocks that can't be explained in any other way but the privileges of national security. Your Joseph Clay offers no brick walls—just maddeningly empty rooms and hallways that lead back to the front door, like you've never seen the inside of the house. It's so damn good that I almost can't see how it *could* be fabricated."

Diana pulled a beer from the fridge and collapsed into a kitchen chair, staring at the two of them. "What am I supposed to do now? It's like I'm worse off than if we'd never done the check. It's not that I'm ungrateful, Jeff. You've dug deeper than I ever expected. But how do I act on this besides saying, 'Sorry, babe. I'm just not ready for this commitment'? The poor guy's predicated his State-Trooper career move on our relationship being a reality."

"Don't thank me, Diana. It got to be a thing I just had to pursue … to nowhere, it seems. He does have pulls on his records from the State Highway Patrol. Depends on how desperate they are for recruits as to whether they heed the alarm bells I hear. Whatever you do, I wouldn't tell him you had this background work done. If it's a fake, he's already astute enough to know someone's checking on him, and if he is up to some skullduggery, you don't want to be the one who shines the flashlight under whatever he's up to."

"Great!" lamented Diana. "And if he's the real deal, how much more of a distrusting bitch will I look like if I tell him that his background records seem too good to be true?"

"There *is* another route that's been the most obvious move from the beginning," Shelby offered. "You could just ask him to tell you more about his past. If he makes up elaborate shit that doesn't square with the sparseness of these records, at least you'll know he's lying."

Diana looked at her. "And if his story *does* square with it?"

"Then," mumbled Jeff, "You've got to decide whether you can share life with a mystery man."

∞ ∞ ∞

Diana moved in with Clay a month later, on a Saturday. He insisted that she get none of her housemates or colleagues to help. He wanted to do it all. "This is our life together, baby. I promise to take care of you all the way, starting now."

He was good to his word, getting her moved in by 3pm that day, much earlier than she thought they'd take and not one cross word between them, which seemed a minor miracle, given the North Texas late-May heat and humidity.

Clay brought her a beer as they sat down for a post-move rest in the living room of the double-wide, about which she was craving to ask how he'd afforded on a cable-guy's pay. She shooed away the question. Dee had committed herself to not prying. All it had gotten her were misgivings and mystery about his background check. Wasn't his dogged faithfulness to his promises proof enough? She'd also resigned herself to his becoming a Trooper. He didn't need her permission for a career choice, and she'd always resolved that, no matter what relationship she'd ever pursue, she was *not* going to rely on her partner's income. Besides, all the rounds of interviews for her tenure-track position had gone perfectly—and Selene had done everything but blatantly tell her that she'd created the position for Diana. Once she got tenure, they would *not* be living in a double-wide 15 miles out-of-town. The place wasn't even in Denton County proper, but just across the line in wild and wooly Forrest County. She'd enjoyed the privacy, but she couldn't see herself spending long periods of time in the place, given that there was literally no one living within a mile of them. The ghostly yips of coyotes in the night resembled what she thought a banshee might sound. The place was nice enough.

Clay was not a prototypical bachelor but had kept the interior and exterior pristine, probably because there was hardly anything to take care of. Diana's moved-in furniture was three times as much as Clay owned. He'd very sweetly set up the extra bedroom as an office for her, but if she was going to do any work from there, she'd have to see if they could get satellite here in the boonies or pay for a hot-spot. Despite being a cable-company grunt, Clay didn't own a TV, let alone satellite. The cable lines halted seven miles back down the road. Lack of television and internet were minor issues, as she'd never been a TV junkie and would do most of her work at the university. Another plus outweighing Clay's unknowns was that he wasn't a sports addict. Sure, if he could score free tickets to a UNT basketball or football game, he'd go, but he mostly enjoyed reading and hunkering down with Blackjack. Up to this point, Clay had done all his internet surfing on his cable-company phone and the tablet they'd provided. Now that they were adulting, both with solid jobs, they'd each be able to buy new laptops.

"Thanks for the beer and for doing all the work, sweetie!" she said, honestly grateful.

"Hey, thank *you* for kissin' the frog! I'm lucky to be dating you in the first place—your moving in transforms this joint into a palace. I am one happy Highway-Patrolman-to-be!"

Speaking of palaces, the living room didn't smell like dog. She assumed he'd done an extra-intense job of cleaning the place. "Honey, it's hot outside and we're done moving. We should let Blackjack in, poor guy!"

He smiled. "Don't have to."

"He's inside? It's not like him to not bowl me over with doggy kisses. Did you lock him in a room? Let him out. I'm surprised he's not whining."

"You've been in all the rooms today. No lock up. *And* the

place doesn't smell like dog."

"I noticed that. Did you put him up with one of the guys you work with?"

"Nope again. He's gone."

"What?" Dee rose out her seat. "Did he run away?"

"You're batting a thousand with the nopes, Di'. Like I said, he's gone."

Why was he making a game of this? "Clay, I'm pretty sure a beast that size doesn't just teleport into thin air. What did you do with him?"

Clay swigged the beer, a cat-that-ate-the-canary grin at the corner of his mouth. "Got rid of him."

"What?"

"Yep. He's gone, babe. I knew you'd be surprised!"

"But, Clay, you *love* that dog. Before we met, he was the only companion you had!"

"I love you more, Di'."

"What's that supposed to mean? It was never a contest, nor is it like, if you love me, you can't love him."

Clay tipped his beer to her. "You said you didn't want the burden of taking care of him while I'm at Academy. Your wish is my command, love."

"I never said to get rid of him! I wouldn't ask you to do that, like I'm some sort of princess."

"Ah, but you are, babe. You're *my* princess. We're starting a life together. Out with the old, in with the new!"

She was flabbergasted. "Clay, Blackjack wasn't a pile of clothes you haul to the thrift store when you get a new wardrobe! He was your friend."

"But he's nothing compared to you, Di'."

"Dammit, Clay, I'm not 'Di,' I've told you that, *and* I've told you that I'm perfectly fine with Blackjack. He was like my own whenever I came over here. I don't know what could've made you think I wanted him gone. You didn't even talk to me about it!"

Clay tilted his head. "But *you* had talked to me about it—and you were right. I'd gone off half-cocked and took that Highway-Patrol bait. I had no right to assume you'd just take care of him while I was gone, like it was a done deal."

"Jesus, Clay! That didn't mean I was making an ultimatum! He's family."

He tipped a finger. "He's a dog, Diana. *You're* family. Besides, he made the place smell. Really, I can't believe you're making a fuss over this. I thought you'd be relieved, happy even. Seems like I can't make a go of getting anything right about this move-in."

"I didn't say that, Clay! You've made this an easy move. I just don't want to be the reason Blackjack's gone, like it was him or me. You know I'm not that way."

Clay sighed and put down his beer. "Yeah, I know you aren't, baby, but I wanted everything to be perfect. I don't want even the slightest thing to put us at odds. You mean everything to me."

She wanted to pull out her hair. Clay was no idiot. He *had* to have known that she never meant for Blackjack to be gone. If she didn't know better, she'd swear Clay had premeditated this whole thing, like he wanted to get into her head. But that was crazy—he'd use the *dog* to manipulate her? All this second-guessing came from the unknowns at which she'd hesitated to the point of getting a detective to check out Clay. Her cheeks reddened at the thought of it. Clay had no one in this world but her. Maybe he was just now learning the balancing act that was love, no matter how smart and witty he was. She might be talking to a part of him that was indeed at the emotional development of a young boy putting his mother on a pedestal—except in Clay's case, his mother had abandoned him.

She took his hand. "I know I mean a lot to you, Clay. And you mean so much to me that I've woven my life with yours. This news about Blackjack is just abrupt, you know? I never want you to think I'd hold my love like a gun to your head. You aren't responsible for making me happy. But you *are* responsible for maintaining your own happiness, and Blackjack is part of that."

She squeezed his hand, a tear in her eye, then raised it to her lips, kissing it. "Let's welcome him back, Clay. Let's go get him and let him know he has a home here—*our* home and his."

Clay looked down for what seemed an eternity. "Babe, I can't."

"What do you mean? I told you it's alright. I *want* him to be part of our family."

"Babe," he shook his head, "I can't. He's gone."

"What? Did you give him to someone or take him to a shelter? Surely we can get him back. They'd understand!"

"Babe, I took him to a field north of Sanger and put a bullet in his head."

∞ ∞ ∞

They held each other that night, both exhausted.

That move-in day hadn't gone so flawlessly.

His revelation had literally been too much for Diana to process. She'd headed for the door—to go somewhere, anywhere, to try to put back into place the shrapnel. She had to leave. She had to get air, light, earth under her toes.

He chased her, but she'd been out the door and in her car before he'd bolted out. Pounding on the car windows, he yelled, "What does this mean, Di'? That we're done? You can't have it that way!"

What? *Done?!* Who'd said they were done? She felt like she was watching some other couple fight. She knew the girl wasn't leaving—the poor thing just needed some space to clear her head and reassemble the scattered fragments in a field north of Sanger. She wasn't *leaving*—she just needed to lie at the bottom of the Mariana Trench, waiting for the pieces of the wreck to drift down, where she could reframe it in the dark and quiet.

"Nobody leaves me, Di'! *NOBODY!!*"

The car was already pulling away, gravel flying. She'd drive, maybe to the Red River, to sit on the bank and watch Blackjack's corpse drift bye. So she could see it. So she could bury it in a place that made sense.

∞ ∞ ∞

When she'd returned, all her things were in the front yard, in piles. As she'd exited the car, she noticed a kerosene can by her couch. Clay wasn't there.

Then the door of the double-wide opened to something already set afire. Shirt torn, sweat pouring down his face, his chest and arms red with welts, like he'd beaten himself, he carried a long-wand lighter.

Then he saw her and halted. The lighter dropped to the dust. He eyed her like she were a heat mirage.

"I wasn't leaving you, Clay," she murmured. "I just needed the space, to process. Don't ever do something like that again for me, Clay. The price is too high."

∞ ∞ ∞

As they held each other in bed, both smelling of the body wash and shampoo they'd shared in the shower together, she shook her head. They'd been both sweaty messes, having to move all her things back inside in 85-degree humid-night Texas heat. The hauling of things had worked the demon out of her, like she were carrying pieces of Blackjack and her life, fixing them into a home—this time, one *she* had a role in assembling. Clay was just too played-out to do it alone, and she wouldn't hear of it.

She'd said nothing to him, just grabbed the first things that came to hand and dragged them back into her new home. After all, a home was just a space to occupy while you lived your life. Double-wide or old coal-baron's Victorian mountain mansion, homes were cavities to temporarily hold her while she became her.

At first, he'd just watched her carry things in, like he wasn't seeing what he was seeing. Finally, when she'd hoisted a box of books, his shadow fell across her. "Don't you ever leave me again, Di'."

She never paused. Just made to move around him. He stepped into her path. "I mean it, Di'. Don't ever do it again."

Diana shoved the box into his abraded arms. "Christ, Clay! You were gonna burn everything I own?"

"Everything *we* own," he whispered. And it was true. In her disorientation, she hadn't noticed that the entire place was empty. His shit was out here, too. She scanned the scene like a smart-phone panorama pic till he curved back into the field of her vision.

Sweat or tears rolled down his cheeks, his chest heaving. She grabbed the box from him and set it on her couch—*their* couch. "Clay, what possessed you?"

He looked down and started sobbing. "It's a demon," he

shuddered. "You can't leave me, babe, you can't. It brings him out. I'm not myself. Please, you gotta stay. You gotta bear with me."

She took him into her arms. They talked till sundown, sitting on her couch in the great outdoors, the scene making her both weep and laugh. "What a couple of fuckheads," she'd giggled. "Look at us—Ma and Pa Kettle sitting out on the furniture, along with a nice refrigerator for the kids to play in!"

At her laughter, a look of relief washed his face, and the old Clay was back. "Shucks, Ma'am, iffin' I knew you wanted kids that bad, I'd've ridden bareback last time we fucked."

Her cackles were heightened by his tickling of her and she of him till they both collapsed into the sweat-damp couch cushions, Diana then fishing two Lone Stars out of the still-chilled fridge.

"Jesus," she burped after they'd shotgunned both, "You look like shit. Have you been moving large objects all day?"

He shook his head and grabbed two waters from the fridge. "Naw, babe, this is my life, and I'm livin' it large! Burning the candle at both ends and all our livelihoods to boot!" They clinked their plastic bottles and sipped and laughed till the sun had set.

∞ ∞ ∞

"Why'd you do it, Clay?" she asked, stroking his hair as they lay in bed, too tired to fuck but too enervated to sleep. "He was just a dog."

"I know," he whispered in drips. "I knew it the moment I put the gun to his head. But the trigger was pulled before I could stop it. You can't imagine the mess. I knew I was wrong, with every shovel-full of his grave. I wanted you to be happy."

"I am, Sweetie," she cooed. "I am. You don't need to do

things to make me love you or stay with you. I thought my moving in proved that. I'm here now, Babe."

"I thought for sure you were gone. I was between Hell and a cauldron, Diana. Here I'd done what I thought I had to do to make this right, make things perfect. And you were leaving 'cuz I did it. Did the right thing, which suddenly was wrong."

"Relationships aren't like that, Clay. They're two people. You can't supply the happiness of the other one. Give of yourself, yes. But don't let the expectations create an idol that blinds you from seeing the real person you love. I'm real, Clay, and I'm here. I came back. I'm here for the long haul. I just needed space to breathe so I could wrap my heart around what you'd done. I'm not worth that, Clay. Always ask me, please. Don't ever do something like that again. Ask me if I'm happy. Ask me if I'm angry. I won't leave."

∞ ∞ ∞

When, after six semesters, she was awarded tenure, she left work early to drive home to the double-wide to tell Clay, but when she pulled in, his patrol car wasn't there. This was supposed to be his day off. Checking her phone, she saw Selene's congratulations message—hardly necessary since she had been the one to deliver the good news. "I am proud to have you continue to bolster the quality of education at the finest nursing school in the country. Your work in neonatal care is groundbreaking, and I can't wait to see it published in book form. It could become a required text. But you, too, should be proud of this achievement. At 30 years of age, you have finished what I at the same age was only starting out towards. I'm more than proud of you, Diana—I'm continually amazed."

Selene didn't know where the period key was when it came to text messages. But Diana nonetheless warmed mightily to the praise, which further thrilled her at the prospect of breaking the news to Clay. He'd probably gone to Lowe's or the electronics store or some other errand. He never left notes or messages for those minor departures.

Dee tried his Trooper cell, but he clearly had it off. She'd taught him the art of work-life separation. Days off were days off. Period. She knew he wanted to get ahead, to impress, to ascend from Patrol into command or investigative ranks, but that would mean a move to Austin, something her tenure had now headed off at the pass. He could transfer from Patrol, into detective work in North Texas, using Denton as his base. It wasn't like the rural meth-lab trade had subsided to any degree, though he said drug work was boring, needless, and dangerous.

His cell went to voicemail. "Officer Joseph Clay of the Texas Highway Patrol. Leave name and number, and I'll respond when duty allows."

"Where are you, ya big oaf?" she giggled. "Come home! I got off teaching early and bought some sirloins and corn-on-the-cob. Your belly usually has a way of getting you to the plate quicker than duty allows. Come home ASAP! Dinner's at five, and if you aren't here, I'll give your steak to Goliath."

As she opened the door, Goliath, their Jack Russell Terrorist, as Clay called him, bolted out the door. Jesus, hadn't Clay let him out to pee? Then again, Clay hadn't been terrifically charmed by Golly when she'd brought him home six months ago, a gift of Selene, whose nephew bred Jacks. "Jack Russells are ADHD on steroids, Di'," Clay had grumbled. "He's gonna be up our asses every two seconds, and, dammit, after the shit I see on Highway, I just wanna come home to you and some sedation."

"You don't even know him, Clay," she'd pshawed. "They're a perfect breed for the country. He can roam out here to his heart's content, racing out all that energy, won't you, Golly-noozums?"

"'Golly-what-the-fuck'?"

"'Golly-noozums'! Short for 'Goliath,' which is what I named him!" She suspected that Goliath's not being Clay's idea explained his less-than-warm reception

"Is that little fucker house-trained? I don't want him pissing on my carpet."

"*Our* carpet, Officer Grumpy Ass. How could you not love this little face?" She held Goliath to Clay's cheek for kisses, but Clay was out of his chair faster than Goliath could lick.

"Ugh, because his breath smells like seven different kinds of ass is how!"

"He's just a juvenile and the perfect age for training. Haven't you noticed all the dogs on shows and ads are Jacks? They're the smartest breed there is."

"That's just Dr. Crazy's nephew's way of getting off his hands a mutt he can't sell, and you fell for it."

"Despite what Mr. Grumpy-Ass thinks, Golly, we are going to train you to be smarter at coming home on time than *he* is."

Clay shook his head and looked at Goliath like the creature carried leprosy. He'd not been keen on dogs since Blackjack. "Train him not to come near me unless I want him near me. And I *ain't* gonna clean up after him or feed him."

Some of her joy was snuffed. "I didn't say you had to. I'll train him to act like you don't exist, if that's what you want. Jesus, who pissed in your Cheerios today that you can't see some fun and love in this? It's like we've got a baby now."

"Exactly what I mean—a hassle we don't need when both of us are working so hard to get ahead. Just train him to be wary of me, if he knows what's good for him. Jesus, *'Goliath!'* What a dumb-ass name for a pint-size dirt grubber."

I might train him to chomp your tiny balls, you lunkhead, she'd groused to herself. Despite his initial reluctance, Clay relented to allow Goliath to stay in the house, but he would never let him onto the bed with them. Clay went ballistic when, during one of his overnight shifts, she'd snuggled with Golly on a night when a blue norther came through. The next night, Clay had found white and brown hair on the bed that must've clung despite her meticulously cleaning the sheets and comforter.

"That little shit *ain't* our kid, Diana, and if he were, I'd teach him to respect private space! Keep the bedroom door closed, dammit, so he can't sneak onto my bed!"

"He didn't 'sneak,' dammit!" she'd fired back. "God, you're a tight-ass motherfucker! I was *cold* and persuaded him to come up and keep me warm. Y'know, this was *my* bed that I moved here before you decided to put everything we own under your surveillance, Office Clay-feet. This is *our* home—not your patrol. And I and Goliath aren't your perps to interrogate!"

His arm had flinched at her flare of temper. He'd tried to hide it, but she saw it and stepped back, Goliath growling.

Clay snapped a glare at the two of them. "That little fucker has always hated me, Di'. You *use* him to piss me off, and maybe one day you'll go too far."

Despite her fear, she stepped toward him, Golly still growling. "What's that supposed to mean? Is bwave Ocifer Cway-feet afwaid?"

The back of his hand mashed her mouth, leaving stars in her vision. Golly was out of her arms and hanging by his teeth from Clay's wrist, Clay screaming and clutching his mace. He sprayed Goliath square in the eyes till the poor thing let go, snuffling and tearing down the hall, pawing desperately at his muzzle.

Dee bowled into Clay with everything she had, hurtling him back through the open bathroom doorway, where he slipped and cracked his head on the tub. Her adrenaline was pumping through her eyeballs as she saw Clay clutch at his holster while he tried to get up. But he crashed into the wall and grabbed at the tub to right himself. By the time he was able to get to his feet and feel the blood dripping from the back of his head, Diana had his issue pistol aimed square at his face, a look of menace in her eyes.

He stared at her blearily like she was a vision of terror and stumbled out of the double-wide, into his car. She didn't see him for five days.

∞ ∞ ∞

It hadn't been the first time he'd hit her. She wanted it to be the last time.

"I need to report domestic battery," she'd said, heart in her mouth, to name-badged Sherri at the Forrest County Sheriff's Office.

The computer-entry of the details was perfunctory until Diana gave the name of the assailant. "My domestic partner, Officer Joseph Clay of the Denton Area Division of the State Highway Patrol."

Sherri paused. Only for a second. But Diana saw. Once the intake was done, she found herself sitting an incredibly long time in the waiting area, despite its being a slow Tuesday, with no one else in the room. Finally, the door was opened by a portly Deputy Tubbs. "Mrs. Clay?"

"It's Atestesso. Dr. Diana Atestesso."

He peered down at his clipboard. "Oh, yeah. My apologies, Professor. Would you mind if we talked in my office?"

Dee felt watched by the various Sheriff's personnel as she followed the Deputy through a small maze of cubicles towards an office. Tubbs looked over his shoulder. "Can I get you a coffee or a soda?"

"No, thank you."

"Alright. If you'd just take a seat here, I'll close the door for privacy."

She sat down on the other side of his desk while he wedged himself behind his computer and scanned the screen. "You're wishing to report domestic battery, is that correct, Ma'am?"

"That's sadly correct, Deputy Tubbs."

"I'm sorry to hear that, Ma'am." He glanced at her for a passing second, then gazed at his clipboard again. Not looking up, he said, "Did Sherri tell ya about the Denton Area Abuse Resource Center, Ma'am?"

"Yes, she did, but I have resources of my own. I just want to report this and let the justice system do its job."

"Well, Ma'am, that's what's tough in this situation—for domestic abuse cases, the wheels of justice grind awful slow. I just wanna make sure you have every help you need during this time."

"Thanks for your concern, Deputy Tubbs. I'm not unaware of the exigencies of domestic battery. I want to see this through."

He reclined in his chair, his badge glinting from the overhead fluorescents and paged through first the computer file, then the clipboard. "Says here that the purported incident occurred three nights ago, is that correct, Ma'am?"

"Friday night, to be exact."

"Any reason why ya waited till now to report?"

"My partner hasn't been home for nearly four days now. I have reason to believe he might be wary of my reporting this, so I had to pick the most opportune time to leave the house. I've called in sick to my job—it wouldn't do to teach classes with a bruised cheek and a fat lip."

His eyes lifted from the clipboard, paused over her for an

uncomfortable time, then looked back to the clipboard. "Didja report to an emergency room for your injuries?"

"Deputy Tubbs, I'm a professor of nursing and an RN. That my injuries required no emergency treatment doesn't make them any less injuries suffered at the hand of my partner."

He shifted in his chair. "I was looking for some outside confirmation of the time and degree of your injuries and to make sure ya received adequate care."

"And, I'm sure," said Diana, "Looking for some reason to believe that what I'm reporting is true."

He put down the clipboard, lifted a pen off his desk, and started clicking it. "Ma'am, as an officer of the law, it's my duty to not be biased, for or against anybody, but to enforce the law. What I believe ain't the point. I'm just gathering info here."

She felt a despondency and fatigue leaden her chest. "And of course," she sighed, "There most definitely wouldn't be any bias when a fellow law enforcement officer is involved."

The clicking stopped. Tubbs lifted the clipboard again, ruffling through its pages till he perused one for so long she wondered if he even still acknowledged her presence in the room. Only when the silence and disengagement had become nearly unbearable did he put down the clipboard and press forward in the chair, resting his elbows on the desk and clasping his hands. "Mrs. Clay, can I be honest with you?"

He didn't wait for her answer.

"Domestic fracases are hard to pin down, let alone prosecute, 'cuz they can be 'he-said/she-said' scenarios. I can see you're injured, and I can't know what you're suffering inside, Ma'am. But Forrest County's as rural as they come. We don't have nearly the staff Denton does, and our DA don't make headlines prosecuting domestic disputes but rather putting meth-producers behind bars. What you're asking for is a long haul with a hard-to-figure outcome. You might wanna just go home, heal up, and see if you and Trooper Clay can come to some consensus on household peace. Otherwise, you're in for a lot more pain and a whole lotta disappointment."

"Mr. Tubbs, are you saying that you're not going to pursue this and that I should just go home and shut up?"

"Mrs. Clay—"

"—*Dr.* Atestesso."

"Ma'am, what I'm saying is that Trooper Clay is a fellow law enforcement officer, and that, when you're counting on another gun having your back, it covers a multitude of sins."

She stared at him. "How good-ol'-boy of you."

"We have two female officers on staff here, Professor, and I guarantee they feel the same way. Like any of us, they wanna get home safe to their families."

"Even if one of their family members batters them?"

He sighed. "Honestly, Ma'am, I've seen a hundred domestic disputes if I've seen one. They're never clear-cut, never just one party to blame."

She narrowed her eyes. "Which then exonerates any police officer involved in such a dispute?"

"Ma'am, your husband—"

"—My live-in partner."

"—is a twice-decorated Highway Patrolman in just two years on-the-job. We look after each other because we have to. And the DA'll look after him, too. It's for the greater good."

A tear pooled in the corner of her eye, but she refused to break down. "What about *my* good?"

"For that matter, Ma'am, Trooper Clay himself suffered

injuries—" He paged through the clipboard. "Some blunt-force trauma to the cranium and lacerations to his wrist. Sounds like as as good was given to him, and then some."

"He'd just belted me and maced my dog who was instinctively defending me! Plus, he was armed! How do you know anything about his injuries, as I reported nothing about them at intake because I had no idea what they might be, he fled the home so quickly?"

Tubbs folded his hands together. "Like I said, Mrs. Clay, we look out for one another. Putting your life on the line every time you set foot out the door carries with it some privileges."

"Like beating the shit out of loved ones?"

"Okay, okay. Look, you can pursue this, if you're hell-bent on it, but it won't go well, I promise you. That's not a threat—just a reality. Believe it or not, I'm telling you more than I oughta because I feel for you. But I also gotta be able to go home to my own family after my shift is done, which isn't always a given. So, you can fight this tooth and nail, to little or nil outcome, or you have an alternative."

"Which is?"

"Like I said, we look after each other. This won't go un-noted in the ranks and in the Highway-Patrol superintendency, Mrs. Clay. There'll be repercussions that oughta take care of this."

"So that's it? The blue brotherhood'll 'take care' of it? How am I to know anything will truly be 'noted with repercussions'? How am *I* able to go home without knowing whether it'll cost me *my* life?"

He stared at her. "Ma'am, go home and make up with your husband. This thing'll see itself through."

∞ ∞ ∞

She went back to work on Wednesday. Holing up the rest of Tuesday at Barnes & Noble, she'd booked a pet-friendly AirBnB after alighting home to retrieve Golly. Her bruises had healed enough that foundation and lipstick covered them. After Clay had run, she'd flushed out Goliath's eyes with contact saline solution and cradled him in her bed. He never whimpered, never cowered. In fact, once she'd managed to purge the mace and he got a night of sleep, Golly was up and ready the next morning to bag possums. If only she could be that unsinkable.

She'd taken Golly to work with her on Wednesday, and her students were thrilled to meet him. It brought her the only smile she could muster after days of uncontrollable anxiety. The question of returning home gnawed her. Revealing it to Selene in more detail than "Clay was wrestling with depression" was out of the question. Diana had tried telling someone about the abuse—the Sheriff's Department. What good had it done her? Aside from sharing her outrage and offering Diana a place to stay, what could Selene do? Dee would have to return to double-wide ranch at some point, even if only to pack her things for good. Wrestling with her fear of going home was a pining for Clay that humiliated her. How could she want to be with him after what he'd done? His temper was hair-trigger, and it hadn't been the only time she'd seen murder in his eyes. Her determination that this had to be the end of them was being eroded by the grief of losing what they had together. But what did they have if it could be shattered in a nanosecond by the Clay she didn't know inside the Clay she *thought* she knew? Dee could only imagine Selene's disdain if she'd confessed such conflicting thoughts, but another voice in her mind chastened her for thinking Selene could ever be so sanctimonious. Selene was her friend, her mentor, the one rock in her life besides Clay. The awareness that her relationship with Clay was so insular, that neither of them had many close outside friends, made her feel like she were standing atop the sand foundation that was

Clay, as the tide rose.

Along with the anxiety and longing, was an obstinance that refused to cede ground to the bastard. It was her home, damn it! She felt stubborn, too, about their relationship. What was it if it couldn't weather crises? He needed her. She needed him. She couldn't shake the conviction that they were meant to be, no matter the challenges.

She stood outside herself, watching a hopelessly dramatic and lovelorn teen make a mountain out of a molehill. So he'd lost his temper—that didn't make him a domestic abuser. Besides, she already knew Clay barely tolerated Goliath, and she'd nonetheless kept pushing the envelope.

But, oh, for Christ's sake! It was her bed and her home, too! She could damn well let Goliath sleep wherever the fuck he wanted. Did any of that justify battery?

She was a tenure-track professor, after all—students looked to her for guidance, much like she looked to Selene. How could one incident so easily derail her? No, she had to reclaim her home. Anyway, for all she knew, Clay was gone for good.

∞ ∞ ∞

His patrol car was in their gravel driveway when she got home that night.

Diana didn't turn off the Civic's ignition, even though Golly's tail was wagging so hard in anticipation of being home that he was nearly bruising her arm. The outdoor lights and the living room and kitchen lights were on, but she couldn't see Clay moving inside. Was he waiting to attack or booby-trapping the place? Might he have demolished everything and be lurking in the wreckage? She should call 911 … and tell the dispatcher what? That her live-in was home? Insanely, the scene from *The Shining* when Jack Nicholson yells "Here's Johnny!!" played through her mind. She still had Clay's Patrol-issue pistol in her purse.

"No!" she said aloud to the escalation of what-ifs. "No more violence. If he's gonna kill you, Dee, he's gonna do it. But Goddammit, this is your home and your life and your relationship. It's worth standing up for!"

She was mad enough now to exit the car, but she'd be damned if she'd take Goliath in for another macing or worse. Before her indignation could subside, she slammed the car door, locking it with her key fob, and marched up the front steps, almost yelling "Here's Diana!" The front door was unlocked. She thrust it open till it banged against the wall. Clay was sitting on the couch, rubbing his brow, not looking up.

She didn't say anything, just stood on the threshold, breathing fiercely through her nostrils, tensed and ready.

He still didn't look up. Just shook his head, too ashamed to look her in the eye. He was in civvy clothes, his hair combed but still wet from what she assumed had been a shower, judging by the shampoo, after-shave, and soap smells wafting down the hallway. An opened bottle of Lone Star was on the table, maybe one sip of it drunk.

"What?" she said at a loss. "If I'd changed the locks, were you going to break down the door?"

"Naw," he mumbled lamely, "I used the key."

When he looked up at her, she could see rings of sleeplessness under his eyes. His wrist bore a clean dressing.

"I hope you had to get stitches, you bastard—in your wrist *and* your fucking wrecked head."

"Diana, I'm … so sorry."

She stayed in the doorway. The car was running. She gripped the key between her fingers in case she needed to stab out his eye. "Sorry's not good enough." She rubbed away her make-up to reveal the ugly yellow remains of her bruises. "It won't take away this or the memory of it I'll live with the rest of my life. And you maced a little dog!"

"I know sorry's not good enough, Diana, but I gotta start somewhere."

"You start where *I* tell you to start!!" she hollered. The air rang with echoes, and she drilled her eyes into him, to see if his anger flared.

But he hung his head. "Okay. Where should I start?"

She didn't turn off the car and didn't budge from the doorway, the pistol weighing her handbag.

"You can start by telling me what the fuck possessed you to *hit me*, Clay! You had a moment there, you fucking bastard, when you could've stopped yourself. I saw you flinch the first time, but, Christ! I don't care if I had spit in your face, you had that moment of truth where you could've grasped that hitting me was unthinkable! In no universe is that ever acceptable! But you went there! Do you know what I've been through the last five days? Do you have any idea of the fear and self-loathing? Of worrying about you even as I hated you even as I was terrified of you? *You!!* My friend, my lover, my partner—two against the world, like we always say! You were gone, you cunt! And something took your place that I will never see again, or so help me God, I will *leave* you Clay! You ripped my dignity and safety from me, you sonofabitch. I won't *ever* let you have it back again!"

She broke into tears and hated herself for it. "And what about *us*, Clay? Did you even think for a second about us when you belted the shit out of my face and blinded a helpless animal?"

Her chest heaved with sobs, as she dropped the handbag. He was up to comfort her, but she raised her key hand. "No!! No, you bastard! You don't get to hold me or comfort me from the pain *you* caused! You just get to live with it, you prick, until I trust you again, *if* I ever trust you!!"

Diana was out the door and into the car but not before she'd grabbed a cinder block and tossed it through the front windshield of his cruiser. Let the bastard try to chase her down now. He stood in the doorway, looking forlorn. She drove beyond the Red River, deep into Oklahoma before she came home that night.

∞ ∞ ∞

She smoked a cigarette at the kitchen table, Clay still on the couch like he'd never left it the whole time she'd been gone. Her back was to him. "Where were you the past five days?" she'd demanded, swigging the rest of her Lone Star. He hated when she smoked. The carton of Marlboro Lights sat on the kitchen table in clear view. Got them from an all-night Sinclair station in Ardmore. Hell, *she* hated when she smoked, but it felt liberating to spend *her* money on something he despised.

"I stayed with Bru," he mumbled.

"Bru?"

"Yeah, you know, Dave Brushevski, Highway veteran. Remember I told you he and his wife had separated two months ago? I didn't have anywhere else to go, and it was late. He was pretty understanding, considering I woke him up, and he had a shift the next morning."

"Did you do your shift?"

He shook his head and ran his fingers across his scalp. "Called in sick for Saturday. Thought it might kill my chances of ever advancing, but I just couldn't go in."

"So you just slummed around this Bru-whatzit's house?"

"Yeah," he mumbled. "Brushevski, but we call him 'Bru.'

Decent guy. His place ain't the Waldorf Astoria, but I couldn't be choosy. He finally convinced me to go to the Captain about what I'd done, which I did bright-and-early Monday. Boy, I was scared."

"Good," she said, grinding out the cigarette. "I hope you shit yourself till you were dehydrated."

"Diana, I know I've got no room to ask it, but can you at least come into the living room so I can see your face and try to expl—nope. Cancel that. There's no explaining, and you can sit where you damn well please. I got no right."

She contemplated lighting another Marlboro. Instead, she fished a Lone Star from the fridge and set it in front of him on the coffee table beside the now warm one he'd not drunk more than a sip of. Then she picked up Goliath from the easy chair with Clay's butt-groove in it and sat down with Golly on her lap. "I'm here now," she said. "Make sure you look me in the eye while you explain."

∞ ∞ ∞

That had been then, 18 months ago, and this was now, when both of them had matured, she thought, and had started coming into their own. She'd just made tenure, and he was distinguished enough to be contemplating assignments of his choosing.

Clay hadn't so much as flinched the few times since then that they'd argued. While he never quite resigned himself to the dog, he at least allowed that this was Goliath's home, too.

Dee had pulled the sirloins from the oven and let them rest 15 minutes before she put them in the cast iron skillet where the salt-and-pepper crust sizzled aromatically. The asparagus was now in the oven, and the salad in the fridge, waiting for the Hidden Valley Ranch dressing. She'd decanted the Malbec, and it now sat on the kitchen table, which was decked out with candles and cloth napkins. Tonight would be special. Tonight felt like home. Real home.

He pulled up at 4:54 and waltzed in with roses. Did he already know? Didn't act like it. Just did his usual—pecked her on the cheek, but with an I-know-something-you-don't-know twinkle in his eye. "Roses for my blossom," he said. "And *sous vide* sirloins for us?"

She smiled. "The white-trash version. We can't afford a *sous vide* infusion machine."

He winked. "Maybe not right at this moment, baby. But could be in our future."

For the last 18 months, he'd gone to therapy. It's what his Captain had demanded. Clay hadn't been officially put on probationary status, but he'd been given notice that an untoward instance of any sort would be permanently reflected in his record. At least that's what Clay reported of the blue brotherhood's response. Diana had suggested couples counseling, but Clay had begged her off it. "I'm the one who's fucked up, baby. Why should you be dragged into my nightmare?"

"It's not a nightmare—it's one of those for-better/for-worse things. We share even the hard stuff, babe," she'd told him.

"Captain says my Patrol's benefits covers my therapy, and I took it he meant this is *my* thing to see through. I can do couples counseling on top of it, but do you see an opening in either of our schedules to afford that?"

So he'd been true-blue, never missing a therapy session nor a single day of duty, pulling extra hours to do security for charity events or to run rural funeral processions. His dedication had earned him overtime that burgeoned their savings—hopefully for a down payment on a home in Denton, she dreamt.

Although he didn't tolerate doggie kisses, his occasional run-ins with Golly didn't escalate into macings but actually some laughs. One time, when she'd made peppered pork chops, Clay's had slipped off his plate as he'd carried it into the living room. Goliath was on it in a lightning strike, but the pepper (something he'd been sensitive to ever since the macing) made him dog-hack. As Clay shot to the carpet to retrieve what might remain, he stuck his hand in dog snot, even as Golly hacked on him. "Son of a bitch! There's mucus on the carpet and …" he reached his hand behind his head, "… and mucus on my neck! And it's not even my mucus!"

Without missing a beat, Dee had giggled, "Sounds like a country-western song—'I got mucus on my carpet, I got mucus on my neck, and it aaaaiiiinn't myyyy mucuuus!'"

Clay had paused for an instant in which Diana thought he'd blow his top at being the butt of a joke sourced from Golly's snot. Then he laughed. "Okay, Patsy Cline, you got any more o' them thar poke chops to replace this gnarled one that I definitely ain't gonna eat?"

∞ ∞ ∞

The sirloins had turned out perfectly. As they munched their salad after the main course, Diana looked for an opening to broach her good news with him. "So, you were talking about the future, sweetie. It could be sooner than we guess."

He raised an eyebrow. "Yeah, for just breaking 30, we've done pretty well for ourselves. Everything's coming up roses."

"So where do you see us in five years, hon'?" she asked.

He gazed around their home. "I'd like to think we'd be here—but it'd be bigger and better, and not a double-wide. I own the land outright. Maybe we could build something more permanent."

"Or buy something a little closer to our jobs, in an established neighborhood. I know the A to Zs of construction

53

and remodeling thanks to the dad I had. Of course, I don't want Mom to pass any time soon, but she's not going to live forever and her health's never been good. Her lawyer told me that Daddy left me the house in his will. I think I could sell it for a decent amount. We might even be able to buy a home in a settled Denton neighborhood with cash, and use this place as a country refuge, or even rent it."

His eyes twinkled. "You've always been my challenge—the challenge to summon the best of me, babe. I like the sound of all the 'us' words you're using. Let's have 'em bring out the best of us." From somewhere behind the vase of roses, he slid a ring box to her fingertips.

Diana nearly dropped her fork. She looked up at him aghast. He nodded "Go on, baby." As she creaked it open and gasped, tears welling to her eyes, he whispered, "Would you seal the bond to truly make us Two Against the World?"

She was hugging him so hard, she nearly toppled them to the floor. "Oh my God! Clay! Yes, yes, yes, *yes!!!*"

As she squeezed him, he wheezed out, "I'll take that as a definite maybe."

"Oh my God, oh my God!" she trilled, ring on her finger, hands to her mouth. "I've got some news for you, too!"

"Now hang on, Sweetheart, I ain't done."

She looked at him. What could top this?

"You're not only looking at your pending husband but also at *Lieutenant* Joseph Clay of the newly formed Cyber Crimes Division of the Texas Highway Patrol, based right here in Denton. I'll be making nearly twice my old pay *and* doing something I love!"

"What?" she screamed. "You mean Professor Burt got the funding?"

"Double the amount and years he'd asked for," Clay smiled a big toothy grin. "Seems the Legislature is big on law enforcement this year."

"OMG!! Congratulations, you crew-cut cyberpunk Patrol-officer genius!!!" she squealed. "And, babe, you won't believe this, but, today, *I made tenure!!*"

His mouth dropped. "When it rains sunshine, it pours!!" he crowed. "Let's pour two more glasses of Malbec to toast this!!"

∞ ∞ ∞

As Clay snored beside her, she stroked the tips of his buzzcut. Maybe now that he was an officer, he'd ease up enough to grow his hair back to the wavy lux of his pre-Academy days. Soon to be off patrol for good! No more gnawing at the back of her stomach that, tonight, he might not come back alive. No more dragged-out, easily irritated Clay who brought home the haunted eyes of having seen the worst humanity could offer. Maybe they could get a pittie, to replace Blackjack.

Dee gazed at his sleeping face. What a little boy he looked when he slept, his guard finally down. Slumber was the only time she'd ever seen him without an edge, not keeping the world at arms length in a death grip. Could he be a laid-back papa?

Oh, she knew it wouldn't happen right away. The new job would consume him, she was sure. And she wouldn't hold him as strictly to being home on time because burning the midnight oil would be the means of making the Cyber Division a permanent reality—and his rise in the ranks to a position commensurate with his talent, intelligence, and ambition. Five decorations hadn't been enough for him. Nor had four raises in pay, a new patrol SUV outfitted with all the latest, and two-time Patrol Officer of the Year for the Cross Timbers Region. Why was he so restless? Maybe he'd finally take the teensiest lull to appreciate and enjoy what he'd accomplished.

A year ago, six months after they'd made up and after he'd started therapy, he'd come home with the first gleam in his eye since before the incident. He didn't usually talk about patrol events, as he tried to spare her and didn't want to rehash the horrors he daily processed. But tonight, the armor was cracked open enough for him to tell her about a UNT professor he'd pulled over before ending his shift.

"Thought it was the usual prof, but he wasn't in a rusty station wagon (though the deans and president types can afford Beemers). This one was in a Crown Vic that looked like it might've seen police service. Doing 80 in that new construction zone on 381 outside of Kaffrey. Lots of douches just love to open it up on that stretch, and I assumed he'd noticed no workers, and so thought he didn't have to ease the lead foot between the orange signs. Like picking ripe berries. His license ran through clean, and he was mannerly and calm like he'd been through this before. Easy ticket-and-defensive-driving to keep the insurance rates down. Car looked pristine and drug-free. Dude was clean-cut and nicely dressed. Seemed so nonplussed that he chatted me up, not even batting an eye at the ticket."

"At least he didn't give you grief like some of the rich brats do," she'd said.

"No, he didn't give that vibe at all. Asked me about my experience in Patrol and my plans, which I thought an odd topic of conversation. Turns out, he's a rare breed—police-alum (Fort Worth) with advanced degrees in, get this, computer science, cyber security, and criminology. That perked up my ears. In fact, he specializes in courses designed to attract UNT cyber geeks to dual-major in criminal justice, with the carrot-on-the-stick of easy employability in the field with their degrees."

"That *is* different," she noted.

"Oh yeah. So I asked him if he'd ever entertained the prospect of involving existing Highway personnel in a joint academic-law enforcement venture, you know, putting two heads together instead of operating in isolation. Apparently, that's the gospel he's been preaching to a lot of deaf ears, so he asked me about my interests and connections. You know, babe, all those hours I spend on the laptop ain't devoted to porn."

She smiled. "Never crossed my mind."

"I mean, why would I go on the web for stew meat when I got filet mignon right here, am I right?"

"Jesus, Clay, you're a card."

"You know I mean it, babe. Anyway, I told him about the work I've been doing on my own and at the Division office on the dark web, tracking drug and auto-theft rings, not to mention the biggest scourge, human traffickers. Texas pavement isn't the primary highway for those scumbags—it's the internet. Turns out, I wasn't talking Swahili but his *lingua franca*. I'd already torn up his ticket, so he wasn't just playing nice with me, 'cuz he gave me not only his card but an appointment to meet with him on Monday for lunch."

"But Clay, you and I were going to take my lunchtime to go look at houses in Denton."

"I know, babe, but we ain't ready monetarily nor schedule-wise to take on buying a house right now. I agreed to it at first because I wanted to encourage you, but, when push comes to shove, to be honest—my therapist keeps emphasizing that I be open with you about my feelings and preferences—I'm not ready. I just get this feeling there's a brass ring out there I need to grab for all the tumblers to fall into place for us."

"Clay, you never had to humor me if you didn't want a house right now, and I can see your wanting us to be in a surer position. But we could spend the next ten years saying 'Now's not the right time.' Don't our lives have to start somewhere, sometime?"

"Babe, the adventure is right *now*. We've got some*thing* really special, right at this moment, that I don't want to ruin by piling on our backs a house that we may not be ready for. Hell, we've still got one more year in our twenties. That heavy stuff can wait a little longer, can't it?"

She'd acquiesced then, and, as she stared at his sleeping form tonight, she had to admit he'd been right. Living in the moment, seizing the brass rings in front of them had come to fruition, all in one fell swoop. Her belly rollercoaster-plunged with all that had happened over the last seven hours since Selene had granted her tenure. Truly, the adventure was right now, and she resolved to make the earliest possible arrangements with Dr. King to have her IUD removed. She rolled over to him and began nibbling his ear. She knew he'd be waking early to serve one of his final shifts on patrol, but he never said no to lovemaking.

∞ ∞ ∞

Afterward, while he slept and she washed up, Diana pondered their sex life. It had been fun before they'd moved in together, she guessed—well, obviously fun for him. Clay could be imaginative and always wanted to do more than the conventional missionary position. When they were just dating, though, they'd hadn't the responsibilities and calendars they had now, and could spend the time and energy to, *a la* Fleetwood Mac, make loving fun, at least for him.

For her, sex had always been a curtain across the doorway she wasn't eager to pull back. Maybe feint at it or hold a conversation through it, but to draw it open was to invite something she knew involved more than she wanted. People are weird about sex, she thought. Yes, she knew there were women who had as active and adventurous sexcapades as some men, maybe even more so. But for Dee, it too often felt like a chore that, though she hadn't chosen it for herself, had been only somewhat interesting at its best. She could almost say that, given her druthers, she rather binge-watch *Star Trek: Voyager* versus the hepped-up expectation-laden prospects of "performing" in bed. And that was just it—even at its best, she felt she *performed* sex. At its worst, that it was performed *on* her, that she had been *done* and that the doing had little or nothing to do with whether she was vested in it. The physical sensations could be pleasant, and, emotionally, when it was someone you loved, it could be tremendously satisfying to give yourself to them. Clay's eyes usually lit up like Christmas trees at the very prospect of lovemaking, and, for that reason alone, she enjoyed those encounters, even if it wasn't the actual sex that fueled her fulfillment.

She didn't think herself a passive mannequin during sex, and Clay certainly expressed no dissatisfaction. But he always wanted more and sometimes didn't listen to her objections. He'd annoyingly push the envelope under the assumption that he could give her a whole new world of experience when it was exactly that experience she didn't want—not because she necessarily found it objectionable but precisely *because* she didn't want it. The more he forced it, the more excited he got but the more scared she got, recalling the time she was nearly date-raped as a freshman when her roommate drunkenly barged in, killing the hideous ambitions of the Junior who'd pinned her to the bed. It also reminded her of incidents that lurked the basement of her memories.

For whatever reason—and she didn't like to talk about it, though sex seemed an endlessly fascinating subject for him—Clay was lately interested in analingus. She normally made sure she was clean before they had sex, but her nurse's training made her squeamish about the hygiene of that one act. In her more indulgent and slightly buzzed interludes, she'd acquiesce. It was *his* tongue, his risk, and she wouldn't kiss him after he did it, but he never minded. The sensation was okay but never enough to justify his excitement about it and his entering such a private place. I mean, it was a relationship after all, but was there literally nothing off-limits? Yet, it thrilled him, and, with the advances he'd been making in therapy and the growing stability of their home life, she'd let him do it more, so that he had started taking it for granted, not even asking her. Two months ago, when they'd been heavily buzzed on beer while she was having her period, they'd nonetheless got to kissing and petting, and he was on her, even though he knew it couldn't go to what he'd consider completion. He'd kissed down her stomach, past her navel, then grabbed her by the hips, turning her over and burying his face in her cheeks. Okay. Whatever, she thought. She even cooed and grunted, thinking that he might be able to rub out his cock against the sheets. Cleaning up with a washcloth and a damp spot on the bed would be worth the night ending quicker and her getting some sleep, she was so tired.

He kept at it, and, eventually, the beer made her doze. She woke with a nauseating jolt when she felt his cock between her cheeks. "Clay! What the fuck're you doin'?" she slurred.

"'S'okay, baby. I got lube. I'm gonna make you feel good."

She felt a blunt pain in her bottom, as he'd missed the mark and pounded her perineum. She swatted back at him. "Clay, dammit! Stop it! You're drunk!"

"No, Di'," he said, panting. "*You're* drunk—and finally loose enough to have some fun."

He bent down and massaged her asshole with his finger. At first, she hated the invasion but there was something about it that felt good, even though she didn't want it.

"Clay, stop it! I just wanna sleep. Leave my butt alone!"

"In good time, baby. First, let me show you the light."

She did indeed see light—lightning shots of pain as he forced himself into her. Tearing, searing, ripping bolts of agony.

"Clay!!!" she screamed, but it seemed to make him ram harder. "You're hurting me!!! Oh God!! It hurts so bad!!"

"You'll get used to it, honey," he panted, "Till you'll love it. But there's always that first time."

She screamed bloody murder till he jammed her head into the pillow so she couldn't breathe. At that moment, his body spasmed, his hips thrusting so that she thought he'd split her open. Then he slowed, and she felt his dick go flaccid as her sphincter pushed it out, a wetness trickling between her cheeks. Before she could understand what had happened, she heard the shower go on. As steam pushed out the bathroom, she turned on the light to see blood and semen on the sheets. All she could remember after that was clawing at herself and the sheets with a soapy washrag, then crying herself to sleep, never hearing when he came to bed.

∞ ∞ ∞

He said nothing to her about it the next morning nor any time after that, which she preferred. The next week, she was enveloped in a fog of semi-delirium, wondering if it really had happened. But the stain on the sheets (that she next morning tore off the bed after he'd left for patrol and set aflame in the trash-burn bin out back) and the lingering rectal pain, plus the expulsion of semen when she went to the bathroom told her the humiliating truth.

But she still loved him. She told herself they'd both been drunk and in the moment. It hadn't been the first time he'd ever been rough in bed, and she'd let him tongue her there, so maybe he thought she was game. But after that, she made sure not to drink more than two beers or one cocktail when intimacy might be in the offing, and she monitored his alcohol intake, as well. On the occasions he was wanting to party, she made sure he had enough that he'd just drift into sleep.

Increasingly, she found reasons not to share the bed with him, pleading a bad back for which the couch alone would provide comfort or that his snoring was keeping her up. Thankfully, his job got extra busy for a couple of weeks, as did her teaching, which left them both too tired to bother with sex. When he got impatient at the lack of bedroom activity, she just sucked him off, pleading 'woman's problems,' though the whole idea of having to appease him that way made her feel like a whore.

But tonight, the night of her tenure, his promotion, and their engagement, he'd been gentle, and she'd been relaxed, even a little aroused. She could see herself as his wife, easing into an intimacy like this, one in which they were both at peace and sure of their positions in the world, ready to really start life as parents.

∞ ∞ ∞

Luna was born almost 12 months later and nine after their wedding day. Brad had called Diana, "Fertile Myrtle."

"Runs in the family, Sis, at least on Mom's side. Dad was an only child, but Mom was the middle of seven and grandma the oldest of ten. You gonna raise an army for Clay?"

She sighed. "I'm lucky we have Luna. Clay took a long while to warm up to the idea of being a dad."

That was an understatement. He'd responded to the news of Diana's pregnancy a lot more harshly than he had the introduction of Goliath. She hadn't exactly told him that she'd had her IUD removed. Apparently, he'd taken for granted that she'd been on the pill, and she didn't disabuse him of that notion, then or now.

"But, Christ, you were using birth control, weren't you, Di'?"

"Yes, I was," she lied. "But fat chance you'd ever notice. What am I, your fuck machine?"

He'd raised his hands to his forehead. "Isn't that shit supposed to be infallible?"

"It's a drug, Clay—a hormone. It's not the Pope, though I daresay it's got a better track record. It's 99-percent effective, but there's that 1% …"

"Jesus, what a time to win the lottery!" He'd slapped the arms of the easy chair in exasperation.

"Yeah, gee, poor Noozums, what an imposition this must be on you," she'd tossed back. "Don't let it hold you back, Geronimo. I'm sure you'll be about as participative in helping me to term and rearing our child as you are hands-on with our contraception."

His unblinking stare lingered on her a little too intensely, making her stomach flip, which didn't help her morning sickness, though it was past nine at night. "Don't mock me, Di'. I've got responsibilities. Things in Cyber are at a critical point. I *can't* spare the time to do the parenthood thing." His gaze passed off her, to the floor, where Golly lay, chewing his newest toy. "Now's not the time for your sarcasm, Di'—or for a child. We can just terminate it."

"It?" she demanded. *"It'* is a girl, Clay! Your daughter! I've had my first sonogram. Did you think I was gaining weight? Or that my stomach problems were the beginnings of an ulcer from worrying over your needs?"

He rose from his chair, and Goliath growled, but Clay ignored it. He wasn't in uniform, but he was as big and fit as ever, something he'd never tired of seeing to. She backed away and stumbled to her seat on the couch, hating herself for crying in front of him. "I thought you'd be happy, Clay. This cements our relationship even more. Yet, you curse it worse than if I gone out and spent our savings on a Mercedes."

He wasn't moved. "You lied to me, Di'. You *had* to know about this, and you kept it secret. You *wanted* a baby, and you *knew* I wasn't ready for it."

"When *will* you be ready for it?" she lashed out. His arm twitched, but she didn't hesitate. His therapy sessions had stopped (if he'd ever done them) a few weeks before their union with the Justice of the Peace. "You still aren't ready for a house! Your work will *always* be 'too much'! Go ahead and beat the shit out of me—maybe you can make me miscarry. But you'd better kill me, you bastard, because if I live, I *will* leave you!"

He glowered over her like her threat was a negotiable offer. She didn't care. She'd felt their daughter in her. She knew that he'd come around once he would hold little Luna. Right now, his job and the potential of getting a house, as well as the new car they'd had to buy were clouding his vision. Goliath's rising growl now distracted him. "What do you want, you little fucker?" he said in a vulpine voice and calmly kicked the dog so hard that it lifted Golly into the air, smashing the lamp on the side table.

"Jesus Christ, Clay!" she rushed to clutch Goliath, and a good thing that was, as her unfazed guardian was scrambling to launch himself onto Clay.

"NO!" Clay yelled in a voice of command, not to the dog, not to her, but to some power of the cosmos that threatened to snatch all from his control. "It will *not* be this way!" he bellowed to the gods. "It doesn't work this way!"

He trod out the door to wage a war to prove just that.

He didn't return till 1am. They made love, Clay insisting it be back door, to "ensure her lies didn't matter." It became the regular way they made their bed together.

∞ ∞ ∞

All that mattered to her was carrying Luna to term. Selene saw the rings under Diana's eyes and constantly inquired about hers and the baby's health. Diana explained it away as what her ob-gyn had termed a "typically tough first pregnancy," which was indeed true but didn't lessen the pain of lying to her one friend and guide.

Diana lied a lot these days—to Clay, to her doctor about the home situation, to herself about being constantly exhausted and prone to despair, despite the immense hope that the birth of their daughter presaged. Nothing was as she'd expected—and who should know better than an obstetric and neonatal nursing expert? But life with Clay had never been text-book. It could be, she admitted in the moments in which she wasn't lying to herself, a hell.

But, at other times, he could be so … so … *Clay*. Sweet, more than charming. That wasn't an act, she knew.

"Clay," she'd dared to ask the previous night after their lovemaking, "Honey, why are you fighting so hard against becoming a papa?" She spooned closer to him.

Silence. But she didn't grow afraid, as, instead of stiffening, he heaved a sigh like he'd let down Atlas' burden. "Baby," she whispered. "It's okay. I know it's not easy. I'm scared, too, but it can be an adventure—*our* adventure, together. Or," she kissed his neck, "A challenge even tougher than me."

She felt him take in a long breath. "Being a kid was a nightmare, Diana. And I don't wanna go back," his voice trembled, "I've been trying to outrun my past every second I'm alive."

She pulled him closer. "It doesn't have to be that way with us and Luna. In fact, it's our chance to right your childhood. Baby, we can't erase that nightmare, but we can shape a dream that makes it shrink in comparison. I promise you, babe, I don't want a brood of kids. Just Luna. 'Cuz, well, you know, I didn't exactly have a picture-perfect childhood either."

He squeezed her hand that hung over his chest. "Diana, I'm not making this a competition. I suppose we all have our childhoods. But my mom left me on a street corner in Kaffrey and gave me no clue she was leaving. I just looked up, four years old, and she wasn't there. Like someone had snatched her away. Aren't you afraid that, even if we don't do something evil like that to Luna, that we'll still abandon her a thousand other ways?"

"I'm scared, too, baby," she'd breathed. "Deathly scared—and not of the pain of giving birth. That's the beginning. I'm scared as much as you are at our ability to fuck this up. But I also know that you and I together, with Luna, are more than the sum of our parts."

Diana felt a kick inside her. "There! Do you feel her, Clay? Luna's telling us she's not afraid and that we don't need to be afraid. To do like you did when you first asked me out, then when you asked me to move in, then when you asked me to marry you—to dare it. Clay, honey, you've always dared with me. That's why you're *my* challenge."

She turned him to her and cradled his forehead between her breasts, taking his hand with a force greater than any fist he'd ever raised to her and placing it on her belly. "Clay, this is us. Life isn't a bunch of shards and abandonments. It's bigger than the two of us, and bigger than any of our striving to make it perfect."

She felt his tears trickle down her chest, then his shudders. As he fell asleep, she dreamt, if for a small time, that he might believe.

∞ ∞ ∞

Her labor lasted twenty hours, Clay rarely leaving her side. His holding Luna for the first time was like watching a naked person cuddle a porcupine. But Dee never corrected or goaded him. Clay could be terrifying, she knew. But she wanted him to be him, even with Luna. At least at that time of peace.

And it was, for a year. A time when the two of them seemed effortless in their love for each other, and in their rearing of Luna. As difficult as her pregnancy had been, postpartum carried with it none of the miseries that too often happened to other mothers, other families. Luna was healthy, and breastfeeding was a delight. Clay even volunteered to do nighttime feedings, warming her refrigerated breast milk and cradling Luna in the rocker that occupied the space where Diana's one-time home-office chair had been, gently returning their daughter to the cradle where Diana's computer desk had been. Clay was hyper-vigilant about the potential of SIDS, sneaking out of their bed to stand watch at Luna's bedside, despite the fact that he'd bought a police-grade baby-monitor system that gauged the child's most silent passage of gas.

Diana's recovery was a quick bounce-back that she'd not anticipated, given the utter fatigue and sickness of pregnancy. That wasn't the only thing that was bouncing. Luna grew at nearly the 75th weight percentile of babies her age. The College of Nursing's paid family-leave was generous. Even after that, throughout Luna's infancy, Selene generously offered to sub Diana's classes or run Diana's practicums at Luna's slightest sniffle.

Their jobs were as consuming as ever, but Diana could sense that maybe Luna put Clay's outlook into perspective, tempering his dogged ambition. They were so busy with their lives that looking for a home was seemingly impossible. At least that's what Clay maintained, and Diana was so content with the peace that Luna brought to their family that she didn't press the issue. So it was a double-wide in the middle of nowhere. So what if it was solely in Clay's name, just like the land? Two less hassles for Diana, and, at least with this place, Clay was happy to do most of the maintenance chores required, though she'd found herself quite a little bit lately having to mow the lawn, as things had heated up recently for Clay at Cyber.

"Think about it, Di'," he'd reasoned. "If we move into an old Denton neighborhood, there's so much city crap to follow. If we move to a new subdivision, dollars to donuts there's a homeowners' association that's tight-ass on 80 bajillion things you have to do to keep your place consistent with the 'neighborhood aesthetic'—i.e., make your birdhouse conform to everyone else's so you can maintain resale values. Old or new, association or not, Denton's got grass-length limits. One busybody neighbor, and you're either cited or have to mow your lawn right there and then. Out here, hell, let it grow knee-high."

"I know, babe," she'd acquiesced. "Still, when it gets knee-high, how am I supposed to see a copperhead that strays near Luna? Also, Clay, the schools. Denton will give her the best opportunities."

"Luna's tough as a rhino, aren't you?" he said, clambering to all fours and play-butting Luna's head. The two fell into a giggly knot, from which Clay emerged with their one-year-old in his lap and his hair tousled. "*You* would bite the copperhead, wouldn't you?" he said to Luna. "And snake-hunting's a way for that dog to earn his keep."

"He specializes in possums, and I don't wanna think what a venomous snake might do to him if he's not quick enough."

"C'mon, Di'! The little bastard's—oops, sorry for the language, Lun'—er, bugger's tenacious. He'll turn anything from an onion to a semi into splinters." Golly was curled up in his doggy bed, singularly nonplussed by the epithets hurled his way. "And the schools? Di', we're saving so much money not paying a mortgage that we can send her to Immaculate Conception, and, later, a top-notch college-prep academy in DFW! You drive right past Immaculate Conception to get to work."

"Gee, how convenient that it's my work schedule that'll have to revolve around the school's. Plus, I'm not too keen on Catholicism. You know I left that behind a long time ago."

"Okay, okay. I'll shuttle the little butter tub when you can't, and things have changed, Di'. Hell, even Jews and atheists send their kids there. Burt does, and he's both, though he'll never admit to the Jew part."

"What might be good for your boss—well, *one* of your bosses—isn't necessarily a go for Luna."

Clay waved it away. "We got three years to think about it. She's still a little honeybun, and I'm gonna enjoy her that way," he said, picking up a toy and nuzzling it into Luna's belly. She pushed it away, but he kept at it, rubbing it in her face. "Whatsa matter, Boo-Boo Lu? Ain't this your favorite?"

"She's getting tired, babe," Diana said, reaching out to take Luna. "She gets fussy when she's sleepy."

"My butter-baby get fussy?" asked Clay. "We'll just see about that." He tossed away the toy and curled his fingers into claws. "The vulture's coming for little Luna!" he said in a high-pitched squeal—well, at least as high-pitched as Clay could get, which sounded like a creaking rusty gate on reverb. "The vulture's gonna peck your double chin, ya little fatty."

"Clay, hon', stop it. She's just got baby fat, and she doesn't like what you're doing."

Clay laughed. "If she's tubby, it's 'cuz she feeds off those luscious boobs of her momma, don't you, Miss Chunky?" The vulture tickled her face, Luna pushing it away.

"Here, Clay, give her to me. It's time to put her down for the night. We have a bedtime ritual that helps her get to sleep."

"Well, Daddy's home, and all rituals are on-hold."

Luna started fussing. "I don't get it," grumbled Clay. "I did this to her last week, and she belly-laughed. Be consistent, you little brat."

"Clay! She's a baby! And she's tired. There's such a thing as too much Daddy."

"Oh, and I suppose there's never too much Mommy."

Diana reached for Luna. "Jesus, Clay, it's not a contest. Sometimes it's just too much Luna for Luna."

Clay pulled Luna out of Dee's grasp, which made Luna cry. "No way. She's gotta learn the rules. Daddy's in charge."

"Clay, she's too young. Now, unless you wanna change her and figure out how to get her to stop crying and go to sleep, give her to me. I'm not playing tug of war with our child."

"Wouldn't be a contest," smirked Clay, rising to take Luna to the changing table in her bedroom. Diana shook her head, waiting for the inevitable need for her intervention. But Clay was dogged tonight. For 15 minutes, she heard him wrestling with Luna, the changing table, diapers, and ointment. Luna's cries only became more plaintive, so Dee walked down the hall to the bedroom doorway.

"Dammit, you little brat! Stay still!" She saw him lift Luna's legs to spank her bottom.

"Clay! Don't spank her! She couldn't possibly have any idea what it means!" Diana rushed to the changing table, but Clay had scooped up Luna, her diaper falling off in the process.

"Oh no you don't!" he said. "I said I was gonna put her to bed, and so I am."

"At least let me get her a new diaper. Jeez, Clay, how do you eff up adhesive tabs?"

"What do you want from me?" he yelled above Luna's crying, which was growing frantic. She might never get to sleep. "I work at a computer all day. I'm not the baby expert you seem to be. If you're so damn smart, why's she crying when I got the shitty diaper off her and cleaned her up?"

"She's over-stimulated, Clay, and swinging her up like you just did isn't helping."

"What? Are you saying I don't get to have a role in her parenting?"

"Jesus, Clay, I didn't mean anything of the sort! She needs to calm down to be able to fall asleep!"

"Maybe she just needs to cry herself to sleep. If Mommy always has to hypnotize her to get her to sleep, how spoiled is that?"

Diana just looked at him. "Are you serious? Christ, Clay, she's barely one year old. Now, please, let me have her."

By this time, Luna's crying was at the hysterical point, her sobs now hyperventilating heaves, her face red, snot and spit running down it.

"Nope," said Clay. "She's just gonna hafta learn the hard way." Then he unceremoniously dumped Luna into her crib, where she scrambled furiously to pull herself up, reaching out to them. Clay pushed her face, back to her seat. Diana lunged to take Luna, but Clay yanked Dee by the hair out of the room, shutting off the light, and slamming the door. Luna's screams were desperate, high-pitched gurgles. Diana went for the door, but he stood in front of it, raising his fist.

Diana yelled, "Joseph Andrew Clay!! Don't you dare!!!"

Fist paused mid-air, his face fell. He stared at her, dropped his arm, then walked past her to the living room, where he collapsed into the easy chair.

∞ ∞ ∞

"Clay, why is life such a battle for you?" she asked, cuddling him on the couch. She'd finally gotten Luna to sleep after putting on a new diaper, wiping her tears, and feeding her. When the exhausted Luna fell asleep, Diana walked to the living room where Clay was silently weeping, his hand over his eyes. Dee pulled back his hand and gently laid the sleeping Luna in his arms. "Your daughter loves you, Clay, as much as she's able. Just let yourself be with her, baby."

He gazed up at Diana with tear-swollen eyes, seemingly more an infant than their daughter. She knelt and laid her head on his shoulder, her own tears trickling down her cheeks. Later, the two of them tiptoed into Luna's room and put her to bed.

Clay now stared at the floor trying to summon an answer to the question she'd asked. "I've … never had it easy," he finally whispered.

She stroked his arm. "Clay, I love you—don't you believe that? Can't you be easy with that?"

"I *want* to be," he murmured. "I wanna be like everyone else—with a normal life, taking things the way normal people do."

Dee gave a wry grin. "As if you and I could ever be normal. How *do* normal people take things?"

"Normal people are in control, Di'. They don't worry about everything falling apart, like it's hanging by a thread."

"But, Clay, you *aren't* hanging by a thread—Luna and I are steel-cables. Whether you can see it or not, *you* connect me to everything I love. I don't want normal. But I desperately want you to be happy."

He peered into her brown eyes, as if she were a mirage that would dissipate. "Why did you call me 'Andrew'?"

"What?"

"Earlier … when I was losing it, you yelled, 'Joseph Andrew Clay!' Why did you give me a middle name? Mom never gave me a middle name. I'm just insane Joseph Clay."

She kissed him on the cheek. "Honey, you're not insane. And I don't know why I yelled that. Maybe *I* was the one searching for control. That's what I used to yell at my brother when I couldn't take anymore tickling—'Bradley Andrew Atestesso, you stop it right now! I can't *breathe!*'"

Clay snickered. "You had a safety word with your brother?"

She play slapped him. "We may have grown up in Appalachia, but we weren't incestuous BDSMers, you perv! It was the same thing Mom would yell when he was in trouble, or about to be. Stopped him in his tracks. That's at least when Mom still had her mind, which didn't last long."

"I never had a middle name, Diana, and you gave me one. I mean, I'm not gonna legally change my name, but I like the sound of 'Joseph Andrew Clay.' You've named me."

"I want to name the wish that would charm you into believing the happiness you have, right here, right now, babe."

He looked down at the floor. "Easier said than done, huh? It's my golem."

"Like Gollum in *The Lord of the Rings?*"

"Hell, if I'm a character in a book, I'm one of the boys who doesn't survive in *Lord of the Flies.*"

"Now I *will* put my foot down on that one, Joseph Andrew Clay. We may live in the middle of bum-fuck nowhere, but it's by choice, and I happen to regard it as a lot more hopeful than a desert island where you die. Now back to my question, what do you mean by 'Gollum'?"

"Not 'Gollum,' my precious," he hissed, making her poke him. "Naw, the *Golem.*"

"Apparently, I'm a sheltered barefoot belle who's lived under a rock in Appalachia and North Texas. What the hell is a golem?"

"*The* Golem," he whispered, his eyes locking onto something only he could see. Then he answered her quizzical look. "Y'know, the old Jewish myth."

"Enlighten me."

He sighed, then paused for a long while, dredging up a beast from the depths that tenaciously refused to surface. "I was at Station Creek Ranch, the boys and girls home, after Mom … y'know … left me in Kaffrey. It was the local Christian fundie equivalent of an orphanage."

"Of course I know about that. You stayed there till you were 17. What's it got to do with golems?"

"Most of the people there were decent, I guess, even though they could be preachy. Hellfire and brimstone, and how Jesus was your one gateway to happiness and eternal reward. I don't believe their bullshit now, but when you're a little kid, it could make a dent in your imagination. After a while, I let it go in one ear and out the other, especially when the older kids told me what was really what, and I started to read stuff I could access past their dial-up-internet fundie filter."

"Again, I know that stuff, and it helps explain in part why you chose to have an anything-but-normal life with an anything-but-normal challenge like me."

He shook his head and roused a tiny smile that quickly snuffed out. "Yeah, you're a challenge for sure, baby. But you ain't the Golem."

"Sooooo, anywhoo, explain how a Jewish myth crept into a fanatically evangelical orphanage," she prodded.

"It was the damnedest thing, Di'. Right under all those fundies' noses. They had this old dorm-charge lady who'd watch the house overnight five times a week. Guess she was supplementing her social security, 'cuz I'm pretty sure they paid

her under-the-table. She was old as fuck, and, get this—a
holocaust survivor. We'd freak out at the stuff she'd tell us
about the Nazis, and those were her bedtime stories for us. You
can imagine I didn't sleep too well after those reminiscences.
Hell, I rarely slept well the first two years I was at Station Creek.
She'd see me restless or getting up to go to the bathroom or get
a drink of water half-a-dozen times, so she'd pull me aside.
Scared the fuck out of me once, but she meant well. She'd
sometimes cradle me. She never told us straight up, but I get the
idea that those goddamn Nazis sterilized her. Ain't sure. Most
nights she could lullaby me to sleep. I'd wake up next morning
in my bed like some space angel had transported me there.

"She was there forever, and when I got a little older, my
restlessness had less to do with being a lonely kid and more
about mischief. I never dared play a prank on *her*, but I was
always apt to make life practical-joke hell for other kids. Paced
the boredom of the place. She caught me one night warm-
dipping a newbie to get him to piss the bed in his sleep.

"Woo-ie! She lit into me in a hissing whisper, with that
Polish/Yiddish accent of hers. Then she all of a sudden stopped
and took me by the arm into the cubbyhole that was her
makeshift office where she could have some privacy or a
midnight snooze once she'd made sure we were asleep. She
wasn't happy with me, maybe 'cuz I'd spooked her with my
hijinks.

"She poured me a cup of coffee from an old percolator on a
hot plate. My eyes got wide at *that*. We weren't ever allowed
coffee, or even soda. I'd thought it a religious thing back then,
but I figure they didn't want us to be antsy 24/7. It's a wonder
they didn't spike our cafeteria punch with Xanax.

"'Go ahead, *Vilda Chaya*,' she said. Still don't know what that
means, but maybe it's Yiddish for 'little prick.' 'Drink de coffee
vhile is hot. So, Boychick, you like de mischief, eh?'

"I nodded my head even though I'd just burnt my tongue on

her coffee. It tasted so bitter and daring to be drinking it with Mrs. Bubbefski. 'I tell you story I learnt from my grandmama about a boychick who liked de mischief.

"'Vonce upon ze time dere vas a spoilt brat, who make ze trouble for all his village. Vas into everything, sneaking around. Dey hate him. Von day, his mama shpank him,' she said. 'He ran avay very angry and say he make her and de village pay!

"'He run to a forest. He not zo brave now, little boychick. A man come from de trees and boychick make to run but de man vas quick and snatch de boychick ear. De boy cry like baby but man no let go. "Vat you do in my forest, Boychick?" he say.

"''Please," cry boychick, "I run 'vay because no von love me. Whole village hate me. I too small to make dem pay."

"''Ah!" laugh de man, who vas vizard. "I vonce like you but now I have craft and magic. I give you secret. Go make find de tree vit de vhite star on it. Ze soil under dis tree is magic. Breathe deep, boychick, and blow on ze dirt and shpit on it and shape de dirt and you have magic to make dem pay. No more puny boychick!"

"''Thank you, Rabbi Mazek," say de boychick and go make find de tree. Boychick look day and night but no find star tree, so boychick sit down and cry. When he look up, he see de tree vif de vhite star. He dig and scrape till hands hurt. Zen he find clay, and take deep breath and blow it on clay, and he shpit on it and mix it vit his hands till he fall asleep. Vhen he wake, boychick see big clay man stand over him. He hear boy cry about how his village and mama hate him, and clay man pick up boychick and take him home. "Dis my Golem!" say boychick. "My magic, my craft!" And Golem kill de villagers who hate boychick and beat mama so she make cry and serve boychick vhatever he vant.

"'Boychick happy for vhile, but soon, all de village run avay, to be far from boychick and Golem. His mama cry till she die.

Boychick so lonely, but Golem stay vif him till boychick sick of Golem. But Golem no go avay. Boychick try to run, but Golem alvays dere. Boychick try kill Golem but Golem laugh. Boychick try kill himself—but Golem no let. Boychick grow old, old, older den vizard he meet in forest, but no die, till he so weak, and Golem pick him up like feather and swallow him. Now boychick is Golem who eat boychicks who like de mischief. All boychicks who vant craft but can't control magic or demselves, dey is dinner for Golem. You von of dem, Boychick?'

"My coffee was cold, but it was enough. I didn't sleep that night and hardly any the next. I went around like a nervous hare, Diana, jumping at any sound. The next time I saw Mrs. Bubbefski, she winked at me and grinned. 'How is de Golem, Boychick?'

"I suppose she told that horror story to every misbehaving kid at Station Creek, but none of us talked about it. Most just brushed it off, I guess, as the tale of a crazy old woman to keep them in line. But it still haunts me, Diana. 'Cuz, what if I *am* the Golem?"

"Joseph Andrew Clay, you don't still believe that literal old-wives' tale, do you? Golems don't stalk North Texas, eating little boys or full-grown State Highway Patrol Lieutenants."

Clay stared back into space. "I know you're right, Di'. But what if *I'm* the Golem? What if I got eaten long ago, before I knew it was happening? Moms don't leave their kids, unless there's something monstrous about them. What if I've all along been the Golem? You've seen it come out, haven't you?"

Diana stroked his brow. "Sadly, some mothers *do* leave their kids, and not because their kids are monsters. And there's more than one way to abandon your child. Your mom chose a street corner in a small North Texas town. Mine left me without ever leaving the house. You're strong, Joseph Andrew Clay. You're not like your mother, and you're certainly not some dirt monster from Jewish-folk-tale hell. You're my husband, and you're the father of our child. Those are magic roles that kick the ass of any old hag woman's crazy tale. I care *about* you, and you care for and about us, Clay. With Luna, we're *three* against the world."

∞ ∞ ∞

"Mama! When's Daddy home?" demanded Luna, who was every bit as precocious as Diana had remembered herself being before Mom had withdrawn into a hole, leaving Diana vulnerable, lonely, and achingly self-doubting. No doubts about two-and-a-half-year-old Luna, though. She was a daddy's girl. But Daddy had been keeping late hours at the Cyber Division, where the taut grimace on Clay's face every night said all was not well.

"Sweetie, I'm sorry, but Daddy's not coming home before you're in bed."

"I stay up!"

"But, honey, if you stay up, how will I read *Where the Wild Things Are* and *Mike Mulligan and His Steam Shovel* to you? They're your bedtime books."

The pensive frown on Luna's cherub face evidenced what a devil's bargain this posed. "Maybeeeee," she danced around in a circle, "We read Monster End Book again and again and again and I stay up and Daddy do Mullgun Shovel and Wild Tings and do de voices when he come home!" The genius of her plan caused her to jump up and down on the sofa, inspiring Golly to jump beside her with his pull toy. If only Luna's arm could develop quickly enough to throw Golly's ball further than a potato chip—*that* would keep the both of them occupied for hours *and* tire them out. Bedtime would then be no issue with or without Daddy.

"Honey, you remember? Golly chewed your *The Monster at the End of This Book*. I ordered another one from Amazon, but they haven't shipped it yet."

"Ship, Ship, Ship! BOAT! BOAT, BOAT, BOAT, BOAT, *BOOOOAAATTT!!!* Can I take a bath wif da BOAT?"

Whoops. Luna's vocabulary was outdone only by her associative reasoning. Lately, the mention of anything nautical was making Luna the most water-logged and scrubbed toddler this side of the Red River. "You took a bath last night, Sweetie. But, okay, since Daddy isn't coming home till late, I promise you time in the bath with Boat—"

"YAAAAAYYYYYY!!!!" The carpet would have a donut-shaped burn if Luna continued to orbit her joy.

"—but *only* if you promise *not* to invite Golly into the bath this time, *and* we read *either* Mike Mulligan *or* Wild Things for bedtime, but *not* both."

Luna halted to consider her negotiating position viz-a-vis this offer, hand on her chin. Her moon-size hazel eyes looked up. "Two Wild Tings?"

Dee smiled and nodded. "Deal. We'll read *Wild Things* twice tonight." With any luck, Luna's bath and circle orbits would tire her out enough that just one reading of *Wild Things* would accomplish its sure-fire soporifics. Diana knew she herself was tired enough for it to put herself to sleep mid-read.

"Two YAAAAAYYYYYYS!!!!" Luna was again orbiting, this time with both hands in the air, tossing victory signs, which made her resemble an old photo of Richard Nixon at his high-water mark. Thank goodness she didn't have Tricky Dick's ski-slope nose or his amoral proclivities.

Unfortunately, getting her little one to sleep necessitated three readings of the Gospel According to Wild Things. Diana had sadly underestimated the caloric energy of half a can of SpaghettiOs.

Clay didn't get home till 11pm, three hours after Luna had

fallen asleep. The down time had been anything-but for Diana, as she'd had to process the evals of her students' Standardized-Patient Sims from the last two days. She was almost cross-eyed tabulating the results into the grading app. Clay trudged in looking as exhausted as she felt. At least she didn't have to get up until Luna did. Clay would again have to be at Cyber by 6am. Diana's first class on Thursdays wasn't till 10am.

"Hey, Baby," she said and kissed him on the cheek. "You're a sight for sore eyes—and I really mean it. My eyes are bleary from grading."

He collapsed at the kitchen table while Dee heated the rest of Luna's Spaghettios for Clay. She went to pull a Lone Star from the fridge, but he waved his hand at it. "Can't do beer tonight," he rubbed his eyes. "I still have work to finish up. I couldn't stand being in that place a second longer."

"You sure I can't make you a sandwich, honey? How can you stand Luna's menu choices?"

"My stomach's in knots. Lately, Spaghettios are the only thing that doesn't roil my gut."

"Did you not eat lunch again?"

"No time," sighed Clay.

"Clay, you've had rings under your eyes for three weeks. Don't your bosses have any concept of exhaustion?"

"Better to ask if they understand the concept of being understaffed."

The microwave dinged, and she retrieved the SpaghettiOs, setting them before Clay as she sat down with him. "Clay, it's time we reconsidered the idea I talked about a month ago. We don't *need* two incomes. I don't have to have a home in town. We can use our savings to give you a break. Think of what we'll save in daycare. Luna would love the chance to see you more often." In recent days, it had been more a matter of Luna's seeing him at all.

Clay wearily shook his head. "I can't sponge off you like that, Di'. I have dignity."

"It's not sponging, and your dignity be damned—what about your physical and mental health? You come home twice as drained from this than you ever did on patrol. I don't understand why they're grinding you into the ground."

He shoveled a spoonful into his mouth. "Because I'm the only one who can do it. The cases are intense right now—kiddie-porn *and* three human-trafficking rings, and some of it involves office-holding muckety-mucks in DFW. Goddamn slime-ball hypocrites. Even if Burt *would* okay a new-hire or two, I simply can't spare the time to train them *and* do my work. This ain't as teachable as fry-cooking."

"Why can't Burt train them?"

Clay waved his spoon in figure eights. "'Cuz grand-ass Professor Burt is too busy courting Austin muckety-mucks to get more money for the program. The aforementioned DFW ones may be getting wise to our being on their trail, and they're working hard to erase our line item in the upcoming Patrol budget. So, Burtie is yet again out of town. Even if he was here, training'ld get him in over his head, and I'd have to retrain 'em to undo the stupid-ass things he'd show them. Burt's the talk-and glamor side of the operation. He can wow the purse-string holders with fancy descriptions, the actual workings of which he doesn't know a damn thing. That's for Lieutenant Behind-the-Scenes-Grunt-Ass Clay to do while Burt collects the accolades."

Diana laid her hand on his. "But didn't you tell the Captain about the situation?"

"Hell, the Captain knows even less about the workings than bright-boy Burt does. Sure, Captain enjoys the credit of his department's getting a job done, but you just can't explain to him the work behind it. Completely opaque to him. When I tried telling him that Burt is overworking me, Captain said, 'Lieutenant, what would you have me do? Yes, I could land you in your choice of assignments, but we don't have anyone to replace you in Cyber. This has been your baby since you came up with the idea and signed its dotted line.'"

"What about HR or Internal Affairs or an ombudsperson? Clay, you've gotta have some recourse."

He shoveled in the last mouthful and shook his head. "Di', it would be career suicide for me to take this outside ranks. There's no such thing as confidentiality, no matter what HR or IA promise. Besides, I still care about the work. It's important enough that I want to see it through."

"Can't you talk to Burt directly, then, the next time he's in town?"

"I've tried countless times, Di'. He plays it coy, 'cuz he knows he's got me where he wants me—making him look good while I slave away. He ain't gonna kill the cash cow. But if the sonofabitch doesn't watch it, things might bite him in the ass."

Dee furrowed her brow. "What does *that* mean?"

"It means," said a drooping Clay, "that while I'm the only one who knows the workings of what we do, I also know where the bodies are buried. I'm not to that point yet, Diana, but don't push a man who knows too much *and* knows how to cover his tracks."

"I don't understand."

"Let's just say that, before I met you, baby, I had to do some stuff to survive. If I hadn't, you and I wouldn't be sitting under this roof. Only I know about it, and I prefer to keep it that way. But don't push a man."

He went into Luna's room to kiss her on the head, and Diana wasn't able to have more than a passing conversation with him till that weekend. By then, something had changed in Clay.

∞ ∞ ∞

"I can't describe it, Selene ..." whispered Diana, as Luna, in her Iron Man Halloween costume, toddled about Selene's living room, putting every dwarf-attainable piece of porcelain into peril. Auntie Selene didn't care. She'd either buy more, or, if it was something sturdier than porcelain or too big for Luna to ingest, she'd give it to Luna for good. Thus, Luna's bedroom was festooned with knickknacks and curiosities that would make a curio-shop proprietor slaver. That, and, tonight, after touring Selene's neighborhood at sundown, she'd come home with so much candy that it would take a year to dole it out to her, just in time for next Halloween with Auntie Selene.

"... He's just ... brooding."

Selene stole a glance at Luna as she cuddled a glass unicorn from the end table. "He's always brooded, dear. Then, in a nanosecond he's manic. I've told you that if he'd had a decent therapist when he'd bothered going to one (and that was under duress) that professional, if they were worth a damn, would have post-haste referred him to a psychiatrist for a bi-polar diagnosis."

"It's different this time. Something's simmering under the lid, and he's not letting me near the stove. Just a cursory 'Hi, Di,' and a peck on the cheek when he comes home. When I ask about his day, he says 'The usual. Nothing to write home about'—when last week it sounded like he would've hired a hit man to take out Burt. I ask him pointed questions about the Cyber understaffing situation, but *whoosh!* an iron door slams shut. 'I was just blowing off steam last week, babe. Burt'll see the light, eventually.' But Clay's so withdrawn, like he's constantly mulling over something."

"He's ruminating, Diana—and I don't mean in a benign sense. 'Ruminating' as in obsessing in a specific way, strategizing intricate scenarios in a mental universe that only he can see but which is much more real to him than his spouse and child are. Thus he misses the treasure right in front of him."

Dee looked down at her cup of tea and McVittie's biscuits (Selene's go-to for tea-time). "I know he hasn't been your favorite of late—"

"He's been on my feces list for quite some time because I can see past his superficial interactions when the three of you are with me. I don't know whether he's plotting or if it's just so out of his control that it's now autonomic, but violence lurks under the gossamer-thin patina of his daily functioning. I can only imagine what you face at home."

That cut a little too close to the quick. "No, he's sweet at home—at least he was before this *Rain Man/Slingblade* tribute show. Luna's wild about him."

"And so are all of us when we intuit that others demand our most winsome show-of-self in order to love us. I did it with my father, and you did it with yours. It's one reason we're sisters in spirit. Not every girl has, as the contemporary parlance would coin it, 'daddy issues,' but for those of us who do, it's a tight-wire *tour de force*."

"Is college administration so consuming that you have to apply your psychiatric nursing credentials at tea-time?"

Selene laughed an unsinkable-Molly-Brown guffaw. "You know me well, Diana. Suffice it to say I employ those skills at not just any tea-time—only at those with the ones I love. You are family, Diana. You'll always have a place here in your need."

Selene's gaze became penetrating—not as if she were prying for information—but as if she were staring out of Dee's reflection in the mirror. "Diana, I've seen this before. You must be prepared. Have a bag packed for you and Luna. Or, better yet, on your next visit, bring your necessaries here, so Joseph won't suspect. Yes, I know this would be the first place he'd come, but Joseph knows that my brother is a retired chief of police always on bat-signal alert for his only sister. What Joseph *doesn't* know is that my state-champion skeet-shooting trophies are yet in the attic. I practice my Glock at the range on a weekly basis."

∞ ∞ ∞

Clay's taciturn moodiness about his job persisted well into the holidays. Luna seemed to be the only antidote, but that was taken only sparingly, as Clay maintained, if not increased, his long hours. After Thanksgiving, he begged off coming home at 5pm to watch Luna on Wednesday nights so Diana could teach her once-a-week evening Neonatal course. Thankfully, after Turkey Day, there was only one more session and the final, so Dee apologetically dropped Luna at Auntie Selene's sitting service.

"Really, dear," said Selene, holding Luna and kootchy-cooing her, "I *look for* chances to babysit your daughter. No sorries necessary. Matters are coming to a head for Joseph. I've the guest room arranged, with a few new plushies in it for our little collector here." Selene set Luna on her feet and shooed her into the living room.

"I don't believe in my heart," said Diana, making sure Luna was out of earshot, "that it could ever come to my leaving him. What kind of bitch would that make me? He's under intense pressure—"

"All of it self-inflicted, and your sentiment also misses the point that *you* are under intense pressure … courtesy of Joseph Clay. Dearheart, I'm not trying to pry you two apart. Indeed, early in your relationship, I saw Joseph as a healthy yin to your yang. But I've since seen other sides of him—and you. You're carrying wounds, Diana, and you know you can't hide those from me. It's your business and your choice, I realize. But I will not stand idle as you suffer potential outrage." Selene waved back the protests Dee was mustering. "Dee, honey, the holidays are uber-stressful on those who are normally adjusted—if such a population exists. For a person as wound up as Joseph, they're an absolute hell that he hasn't the faculties to control. You will be on the receiving end, no matter how much you love him and sacrifice for him. Even if I'm wrong, which I hope I am, better safe than sorry."

From the living room behind Selene who stood with Dee in the entryway came a crash. "Oh no! Luna!" hollered Diana, but Selene pushed her out the door.

"It's not anything I can't handle. After all, I'm a nurse, and, by my watch, you'll be late for your final course session. Now, go! That's a Dean-of-Nursing order!"

∞ ∞ ∞

"Clay, it'll be a nice time," soothed Diana as they drove, dressed to the nines, to his office holiday party, in one of the small ballrooms at the Vineyard Hotel, old downtown Denton. "For once, you can enjoy your colleagues in a non-work environment. And we rarely take the opportunity to dress up and go out. It's kinda romantic."

"If I'd wanted to see my colleagues outside of work, don't you think we'd have already hobnobbed with Burtie before this?"

"We used to, in your early months at Cyber."

"That was then, Di', this is now."

"But I don't understand. You told me the other day that, as of the New Year, you'll be training three new staff members. So Burt must've secured the funds. Otherwise, how could y'all afford the Vineyard for this holiday shindig?"

"It's Burt's opportunity to gloat over his triumph."

"And it's your triumph, too. Burt couldn't have spent so

much time out-of-town to raise the capital if you hadn't held down the fort and cracked one of the human-trafficking cases."

Clay clenched his teeth. "There's this thing about unsung heroes, Di'—nobody sings about them when the band is playing someone else's anthem. That's okay. Turn of the year, there's gonna be more changes than just three new staff for Lieutenant Flunky here to train."

"Such as what?"

"Let's just say that the time isn't ripe for revelation, but I've been working on more than what Burt thinks."

"Dammit, Clay! How am I supposed to enjoy this party, which is just as much your celebration as Burt's, if you seed me with cryptic bullshit like that? I feel like I'll have to walk on eggshells with everyone."

He smiled out the corner of his mouth. "Baby, you're standing on the firm ground that I've been preparing. Just wait for it to happen. I won't let you down."

∞ ∞ ∞

The letdown came near the end of the party, when a few of the celebrants were shuttling out, and Diana was looking forward to a post-party drink with Clay at their favorite nightspot. But Professor Burt had cornered them at their table, just as they were getting ready to leave.

"Good evening, you two!" said Burt, sitting across from them. "We haven't had the chance to talk the entire evening, and now you're escaping? Let's toast—non-alcoholic, mind you; we *are* officers of the law—everything we've worked so hard for!"

"Sláinte," said Clay, with a tight smile gripping his face as he raised his ginger ale. Diana had successfully steered the two of them clear of Burt the whole night, which wasn't hard, considering that any time she looked Burt's way, he was in close *tête-à-tête* with muckety-mucks and Division higher-ups. Every now and then, he'd look their way, as if keeping an eye on the two of them. For his part, Clay simmered a slow burn she could smell the fumes of. His eyes seemed to always be in the direction of Burt's voice, when that one's tones rose above his whispered conversations.

"Why don't we get together more, Lieutenant?" laughed Burt.

"It's been hard to pin you down for more than a five minute chat between gallivants, Professor."

Burt smiled wryly and looked at Dee. "He's right, you know. It's a good thing I'm single because, if I had a wife and family, they would hardly recognize me, I've been gone so much."

"So much," murmured Clay.

"Wait a minute," paused Dee. "Wasn't Burt married, with kids at Immaculate Conception?" A fireball descended into Diana's stomach. "Clay's just fatigued, Professor. It's been quite a load for him, and our baby has missed him due to the long hours he's worked."

The Professor looked intently at her. "Diana, I've always seen you as a delightful and earnest soul. I have some things to say to your husband that I would spare you hearing. I want to give you the chance to not bear the brunt of them."

Diana clutched her husband's hand. "No, Professor. I'd like to stay. You see, Clay and I have always seen ourselves as two against the world."

The Professor paused and looked down, pondering. "Joseph, do you want her to hear what I have to say?"

Clay didn't flinch. "I thought this was a party."

"It was supposed to be," said Burt, "Until we gained wind of certain things that make this moment have to be difficult business instead of celebration."

Clay stared through Burt for what felt like an eternity. "Burt, you think you can break me, don't you? But you simply don't know me at all."

Burt sighed and glanced around him at the other attendees still there. "On the contrary, Joseph. I know things about you I wish I'd never known. Dr. Atestesso, I implore you—please, spare yourself this. There are better ways to hear such things."

Diana squeezed Clay's hand. "I'm here for good, Professor."

Burt looked mournful, then raised his hand to get the attention of Captain Herschel and three other Lieutenants. One-by-one, they looked up from the conversations they were having and formed a perimeter around Burt, Diana, and Clay.

"What is this, a star chamber?" asked Dee.

"It's not any kind of court, Diana," said Burt, looking down as if in shame and shaking his head. "I wish it didn't exist at all. It's about safety and ending this thing in as dignified a way as your husband will allow. Joseph, you can spare her and all of us, if you'll just cooperate."

"Are you firing him?" Diana said aghast. "At a Christmas party? Are you Ebenezer fucking Scrooge?"

Clay let go of her hand. "No, Dr. Don't let him do this to you. He can't fire me, given what I can deliver to the DA and FBI about *him*. And I'm not just any whistleblower, Burt. I'm your worst nightmare."

Burt looked embarrassed and singularly uncomfortable. "Lieutenant, this isn't Hollywood, despite what you might be imagining. You can't know the pain I—we—all of us at Cyber and Highway Patrol—feel about this."

"Know?" demanded Clay. "I know a lot more about you

than you think."

Diana interceded. "Is this how you treat a decorated officer who's held together the Division while you've traipsed about taking the credit for yourself? I used to be proud of Clay's being Cyber, but now I'm not so sure."

Professor Burt stared at her aghast. "Diana, you—has he told you nothing?"

"Di', no!" Clay tried to hold her back.

"*Told* me? He didn't have to *tell* me anything, Burt. I saw it in our daughter's eyes night after night when I told her that daddy wasn't going to be home to tuck her in. I saw it in Clay's drooping shoulders and hollowed-out eyes—"

"Diana!" muttered Clay, "This isn't your battle!"

"I saw it and felt it in our bedroom when he wasn't there because he was hunched over a computer at Cyber or our home, which used to be a haven for him. He's told me that he's overworked and that Cyber's understaffed and that you and Herschel have slammed the door in his face at what seem very reasonable requests for help or even for a goddamn break!"

Burt slumped back in his chair, amazed, and stared at Clay. "You've told her nothing?"

Diana looked back and forth from Clay to Burt.

"You lied to your own wife that your long hours were due to incessant work on Cyber's behalf?"

"Go ahead, Burt," said Clay, eyeing the battery of officers now around them. "Dig your grave, you bastard, with every word in front of my wife and these witnesses. I've got so much dirt on you, you'll never dig out of the mudslide."

Burt took off his glasses and rubbed his eyes. Two uniformed and armed Denton municipal officers had joined the cordon. "My God," he said, hands trembling as he put his glasses back on. "Clay, what have you done?"

"His duty!" quipped Dee.

"Diana," pled Burt, "Do the two of you have separate checking accounts? How could you not know?"

"What?" asked Diana, feeling like the floor was slipping from under her feet.

"That's what they do, Di'. They try to hit you in the weak spot by freezing your bank account. But I was already ahead of them, wasn't I, Burt?"

Burt pounded his fist on the table. "Enough of this, Lieutenant! And I address you in that erstwhile term to preserve what little dignity you have remaining. I sadly and painfully inform you that your half-pay probationary period is at an end. You are summarily dismissed from all Highway Patrol engagement, responsibilities, and employment. We've tonight impounded from your driveway the Patrol vehicle that you refused to surrender. Refusing to turn in your Patrol-issue computers, firearms, badge, and other equipment you possess, as well as the Division funds you have managed to electronically secret, will result in no little jail time. If we cannot end this amicably, please tell me that you'll end it without a prison term, because, in my heart, I can't believe that you, my one-time friend, have done this out of malice and premeditation but out of what I pray is an altered mental state, if such can be prayed for."

Clay had leapt across the table before Dee could move. He was on Burt, punching, then choking him before the muni detail could subdue and handcuff him. As they hauled him away, he sobbed, "Don't believe anything they tell you, Diana! They can't do this to me. They don't know what I've got on them. Believe me, Di'! Don't ever leave me! *Ever!*"

∞ ∞ ∞

Burt drove her, at her request, to Selene's, where Luna was staying the night. He didn't say anything to her, though it wouldn't have mattered, because she couldn't hear anything over Clay's last words that still boomed in her mind. Behind them, Captain Herschel was driving her car.

At the doorway, Burt paused. "Diana, I have no idea how bewildered you must be. I know you're reeling. I haven't stopped reeling since *I* discovered what I thought couldn't be. If not for yourself, at least for me, then, please let me try to make sense of all this for you."

Diana was stripped of moorings. Adrift. Flotsam on the flood. She nodded her head and entered the living room, where a robe-clad Selene met her and Burt. The three sank into chair and sofa cushions, and Burt told Diana things she couldn't hear, would die from hearing. She said no word, Selene's arm around her shoulder and her own responsive grasp of Selene's hand reassuring herself that she hadn't gone catatonic and that she was absorbing this information. She was being informed. Re-formed. De-formed. Un-formed. Lost.

"Diana, I thought you knew of Clay's suspension and half-pay probationary leave. He hasn't been in our offices since the week before Halloween." Diana focused on Burt's swelling bloody lip, watching it emit sounds that undid her.

"I've no idea what you know, so I'll tell you all. You might not be able to believe it. I hardly believe it myself.

"When I met and worked with Clay on setting up Cyber, he was as decorated and dedicated a Patrol-person as there was in all of Highway. It was my great fortune that he lived in the Denton area and so respected his duties that he pulled me over for speeding. If acorns spring mighty oaks, that's how Cyber germinated.

"He was instrumental in getting the Division rolling. I simply couldn't have done it myself. Those accolades are as clearly reflected in his record as is the decline I'm about to relate to you. The sheer amount of work Clay did was astonishing, truly the work of any three other personnel. It was so prodigious that it pushed my belief. I didn't question it then, I was so intent on the good that Cyber could accomplish. I had a vision for what it could be, and Clay seemed ideally attuned to making all our dreams a reality. His computer and web coding talents are such that he could easily be working for any world-class intelligence and investigative organization in the world. All this from an autodidact. I couldn't believe it at first. However, every genius and special talent bears their own style and mark. The technical details of it are too much to explain, but, suffice it to say, that the mark Joseph leaves is totally unique—ersatz, even. No one with formal training would accomplish things the way he does, doing double- and triple-work where a simple few keystrokes would've sufficed, and, in other areas, making inroads so intuitive, original, and ingenious that they revolutionize stifling protocols and procedures. A keen art historian can, in few seconds, tell an original Bruegel or a Rembrandt from a copy that would convince crown princes. There are few, if any, talents like your husband in cyber work, anywhere on this planet.

"In fact, he was *too* good. The pieces fell into place too easily. But, as I've noted, in my fervor to get the Division up and running, I wasn't as circumspect as I should've been. But even as the successes accumulated for us, I couldn't halt my second-guessing. It's said a liar won't believe anyone but themselves. Sadly, it's my job to not believe even myself and the people with whom I work. If it's too good to be true, then it probably is. Clay's work was more than good, and it was so true that it became unbelievable.

"Clay never divulged his process and means of digging up the information he found. I impressed upon him the need to codify what he was doing because I was certain he wouldn't be here forever, and whoever took his place would need a template to replicate our work. Joseph insisted that he was a jazz musician whose improvisation was all of his music. At first, he succeeded in getting me to believe he was being self-effacing, but there was too much standardization to his approach for him to make it up as he went along. Indeed, it was his regular tactics that evidenced his particular 'style' and not his improvisations. This paradoxical element showed up in all the cases he investigated.

"We were delighted at his early successes, but, sadly, all those cases were stymied by jurisdictional roadblocks imposed by other states, federal agencies, and other countries' law enforcement and extradition protocols. It became too consistently the result that any case he worked on ultimately had to be shut down because international, federal, or interstate laws and precedent forced judges to deny warrants, probable cause, and other means of bringing the perpetrators to justice.

"Clay was the first of four cyber investigators we hired and was our only one for the first six months, but, when Austin refused us any line-item in the state budget, it was two generous federal grants and one from a private foundation that have buoyed us in such a way that we haven't had to, for the last two-and-a-half years nor will have to, for the foreseeable future, waste time hounding politicians for money. Clay trained those three additional investigators, all of whom came to us with advanced Comp Sci and Cyber Security degrees, as well as years of experience. But he didn't teach them 'Clay's way.'"

"Wait," interrupted Selene. "Then what about all those days and weeks Clay told Diana you were out-of-town, in Austin, soliciting money from bureaucrats?"

"I have a concurrent chair at UT Austin, Dr. Grieve. For the last decade, I've split my teaching between Denton and Austin. That, and I necessarily have to do legwork to carry out our cyber investigations, coordinating with local law enforcement, the Texas Rangers, and the Highway Patrol across this huge state. It's a lot more interesting, I hope, than lobster-and-steak wining-and-dining of lobbyists and fiduciary committee chairs to secure funds."

Selene looked to Diana to see if this registered, Diana blurting out, "Professor Burt, are you Jewish?"

Burt paused. "Um, no. I originally hail from a fourth-generation dairy farm in Wisconsin. My father and grandfather were descendants of the hard-shell German Lutherans who emigrated there in the 1800s. It might be news to them that we were masquerading as gentiles all the while. Though I do like a good matzah-ball soup."

Diana said nothing in reply.

"Back to where I was. Because they didn't mimic Clay's way, they had variant results, which, initially, kept Joseph at the front of the pack. But it was the damnable consistency of Clay's results that finally led me to question him. He didn't take it well, though I never meant it as a reprimand. He rationalized it as tough luck and 'bloodsucking bureaucracy' that stonewalled his cases. He allowed no other interpretation. He thereafter became moody and suspicious of me, and, for a while, his work fell into line with those of his peers. No more was it lightning-quick and astounding, but it led to workable leads and actionable enforcement, if it wasn't headline-making material. And the headlines were no longer as important now that we were funded. I didn't hold any of it against Joseph because I was grateful for his early, attention-grabbing work that fueled our grant from the private foundation.

"But Joseph's toeing the line didn't last. I suppose he got bored or insecure about seeming merely mortal because soon we were reviewing his most stunning work yet—a child-trafficking ring that implicated members of the NSA, congressional representatives, and Dallas-Fort Worth local officials.

"I don't know if you can understand what a delicate thing it is to pursue high-office holders and members of the intelligence community, all the while operating from what is still a minor division of one state's Highway Patrol. The thing had referral-to-the-FBI written all over it, which would have completely removed it from our purview and flung it into the bureaucratic web of that federal agency that has no few ties to the NSA. Think of the end of *Raiders of the Lost Ark* to imagine how that might've ended up. Clay was eager to funnel it 'under-the-table' to a contact of his in the Bureau, but I kept him from doing that by saying that we needed to further comb it.

"If I hadn't been so aghast at what I found, I would've been astonished at the sheer scrupulosity and detail of his work. It wasn't an audacious fraud, nurturing belief via the bombast of its findings. No, it was subtle. Information enough to implicate high figures but not enough to confirm without much deeper undercover work. His knowledge of the inner workings of international governments, Congressional offices, local officialdom, and the NSA itself was something that alone would qualify him as a high-level analyst for the CIA. Still, it was too good. Clay relied on his perusers' tiring of having to sift the minutiae, and it was in the finest details I discovered the taint in the report. It wasn't large, mind you. But it was enough. Clay could have done without it, really. It was a fabricated personage who no longer worked for the NSA but whose career and whereabouts would be plausibly buried in classified records. This work of fiction had supposedly initiated the creation of the human-trafficking ring while at the NSA but which ring, hydra-like, grew out of his finite control till he became merely a hidden recipient of its services.

"You might ask how I could have known he was fictional if his identity was now covered up, his current whereabouts, if he were still alive, unknown. It might've been sheer luck or coincidence, but a creeping suspicion tells me it wasn't. Knowing Clay's electronic footprint, as insubstantial as it is, I think he couldn't keep himself from indulging in the chance to gloat over his deceiving us. For the fictional operative in question was one Hyram Silas Germane, who happened to bear the name of an acquaintance of mine from Wauwatosa High School. I couldn't contact Hyram to interrogate him on his NSA credentials. Hyram was dead, a casualty of U.S. military involvement in Somalia in the early 90s, something I'd had no clue about, having left behind Wisconsin and most details of local happenings 27 years ago. You'd be surprised to hear that there are/were 23 Hyram/Hiram S. Germanes of U.S citizenship across this country. Not a single one of them except my H. S. Germane bears the middle name "Silas." Clay thought himself beyond me, and, perhaps he is. He thought I would never suspect. Or, if he took my previous questioning of him seriously, he maybe was like the video-game writer who can't resist hiding the most subtle easter egg to demonstrate to one or two other rarified minds that he is capable of subterfuge they can only dream of.

"And what harm could it be, eh? He knew it was not enough for me to pursue disciplinary action. He could plead it was just one typographical error amidst thousands of lines of code. 'Silas' the middle name was listed only once, the rest of the report employing the middle initial, 'S.' Any human being could make such an error. But Joseph was not any such mortal, and he wanted me to know it, to punish me, to threaten that he could do a lot more if my further questioning of him demanded it.

"If this subterfuge seems pointless to you, imagine how it wore me out. Clay had gotten under my skin, letting me know he was a fraud of maniacal proportions and that there was nothing I could do about it but play along and perhaps go the easy route of advancing him out of our ranks to whatever next post would temporarily sate his never-ending ambition—or, better said, *insecurity*."

Selene shook her head. Diana's fingers were knotted together, her knuckles white.

"Only those manic about having control do such brazen deeds, to seize an unassailable throne, above the worries and cares of the rest of us. They act outside moral bounds because their endless hunger for security justifies it to them. The pursuit, vain or not, becomes its own beast, a monster that consumes them."

"The Golem," whispered Diana.

Burt paused. "Why, yes. Though I'm not Jewish, I had not a few Jewish friends growing up. When we shared ghost stories around our summer campfires, the Golem was always one to inspire shivers in all of us. Call it what monster you will, it's all-consuming. Yes, all of us strive for some form of control over our short lives. It's but a few who bond their souls to it. The pursuit is exhausting, teaching most of us another lesson entirely—that of letting go and embracing uncertainty."

Burt had realized he'd been droning on. Diana was sobbing into Selene's shoulder. "Dr. Burt, let me make some tea," suggested Selene, "Because I suspect you've more midnight oil to burn recounting this tragedy."

When they recommenced, Diana huddled over her cup, looking down, her mind testing possibility after possibility then alternating to damn her gullibility. Was her own need for security and control so encompassing that she could blind herself to Clay's deception, making a devil's trade—suspension of disbelief for the mirage of a happy life?

Burt had started again. "I was tempted to let it slide and find a bureaucratic opportunity to accede to Clay's implied desires and promote him to be someone else's problem. But just like Joseph's insatiable pursuit of security and certainty would only grow bigger, so would his power to harm others. What would happen if, instead of merely creating fictional trafficking rings, he sought to falsely implicate others in power, to extort them to his own ends? That, and I admit my ego—I felt trapped, damn it, and I couldn't abide being outgunned. If I'd let go of that ego, perhaps what we saw tonight wouldn't have happened and your life, Diana, wouldn't be so harrowed. I thought to myself, could this episode be enough for Clay? At the time, you two had just had Luna. Might his deceptions have been a flirting with power from which, in a return to sanity, he pulled back his hand? You've got to know, Diana, that I'm no angel. I admit my fault in this. But I swear to you that I never wanted things to come to this juncture, especially its ripping open your heart."

Diana gazed at him. "I know, Professor. I want all of this to be just a nightmare from which I'll soon wake. And maybe I will. But I've lived through some other nightmares in my life. If they're any indication, this one's only begun." She felt shame for her own part in this, her willfully always putting Clay in the least incriminating light, despite all the instances in which his actions screamed otherwise. At the same time, in the unexplored back vaults of her heart, she heard a huddled, desperate voice, her own, chastising her for collaborating with Burt.

Selene rubbed her shoulder. "Nightmares are of the night, dear, which does not last forever. I myself long ago left behind my childlike faith, but sacred writ still offers salient truths—namely, 'A light shines forth in the darkness, and the darkness will not overcome it.' Easy for me to quote, but, dear heart, I will stay with you through the darkest dark."

Dee nodded, the tears again welling in her eyes.

"Are you able to go on, Diana?" asked Burt.

She sipped her tea with both hands gripping the cup, the warmth stabilizing her, then nodded again. "Yeah. Let's get this out in the open."

"I told myself I had to know," sighed Burt. "So I did my own digging on Clay, keeping especially wary of leaving any electronic fingerprints on his digital records. That's what led me to the Forest County Courthouse, to paper and microfiche. They were only just recently converting their records libraries to digital, the massive scanning effort going in as plodding a fashion as only rural-county funding and organizational inertia allow. Thankfully, they hadn't gotten to the records from the late-1990s/early aughts. I was looking for everything and anything. I came up empty at first, as I'd expected. Also, Cyber is a demanding mistress, and I didn't exactly have leisure time to pursue my investigation. I was searching for the esoteric, the finest spider-web trails, until I realized I'd got it all wrong. Vital records. Driver's license. Car registrations. 'Start with the obvious, fool!' I said to myself.

"In one of my trips to Austin, I searched state vital records archives for the birth certificate of one Joseph Clay. There are literally hundreds of Joseph Clays in the Lone Star State. How to know which was the Joseph Clay I was looking for? Yes, I knew his age, but Joseph had told Highway Patrol at Academy that he actually had no idea of the exact place, day, or year he was born. His listed birthday was a date he'd chosen out of the blue. Highway Patrol doesn't require submission of a birth certificate for application and Academy acceptance. I could find no vaccination records, and the Station Creek Ranch was a dead end, as it, since Clay's tenure there, had suffered a fire and its board of trustees could not summon the funds to rebuild the place. No records there.

"It wasn't until I dared think like Joseph that I stumbled upon a realization—I was finding no records because Joseph didn't *want* anyone finding records on him. Aside from an SSN and DL (both of which he'd procured after leaving Station Creek) and the certificate of your marriage, there was nothing. Apparently, Joseph had found a means of doing away with his birth certificate."

Diana looked up. "Clay has no birth certificate. It's always been an ID issue for him, so he relies solely on his SSN card and DL. He told me he'd been home-birthed. No hospital to administrate his birth record. Though what home he could have had, I don't know. His mom abandoned him when he was four, so, no school records because he hadn't yet started kindergarten. And with that kind of mother, who'd expect vaccination records or even a visit to the pediatrician? He doesn't trust doctors, either. The two times he's been sick or injured enough were a doc-in-the-box visit, for which he paid cash and provided a false name—he was that paranoid of doctors—and an emergency room visit for a minor wound he'd received on duty, something he told me the Forrest County Hospital ER did for him totally gratis and under-the-table, 'cuz he was a cop."

"I should have guessed that," said Burt. "Again, I ran into a brick wall with medical records, which you just confirmed. He didn't own his own car, as yours was still in your name. So, no car registration. Then, it hit me that the answer I'd been looking for was right under my feet—I own a home. Joseph's domicile *had* to have some record. I'd no idea whether you two rented or owned, and I wasn't about to ask him out of the blue. But I knew the address and the plat. I could search the Forest County title deeds. If he had a landlord, okay, a dead end, as he was most likely paying cash or check, and had a simple credit-union checking account. Yet, I found the property and the title deed—in his name ... but it hadn't been previously. The original owner had been one Silas Ramczik. The title deed and records showed no sale—the double-wide and four acres had been signed over to Joseph Clay, free and clear.

"People don't just give houses and land away. Was Silas a rich, indulgent uncle? Digging up Silas' past was easy. Born in West, Texas, of Czech heritage, he'd remained in the Central Texas area until, in 1993, he earned a six-month sentence, two years' probation, and sex-offender registration for a charge of indecency with a minor. He now lives in Chillicothe, TX along the Red River, just east of the Northern Panhandle. Works in a convenience store and lives in what might as well be a shack. But his mother had apparently remained devoted to him, despite his proclivities for children, having given him the money for the double-wide and Forrest County land, as he wanted to get out of Central Texas, where his sex-offender status, as he later put it to me, 'gave him no privacy.' He's going on 61 now and was scared witless at the appearance of a law enforcement officer at his Chillicothe hovel. He was more than willing to answer my questions once he knew they had nothing to do with his sex-offender status.

"'One day, when I was living in Forrest County' as he related, 'I hear a knock at my door, and it's a young man selling magazines. I wasn't interested in no shit like that and told him leave, all the time wondering who the hell comes out here to sell magazines at one house in the middle of pasture? But he told me he'd left an orphanage and was determined to make it on his own. He was starting to do better than his peers on magazine sales because he just persisted and went where no one else would go. "People like magazines," he said to me, "no matter where they live." That actually impressed me,' Silas said, 'So I invited him in. I was living off my inheritance from my mom and didn't have the funds yet to install no satellite TV, just the rabbit ears that pulled in only two fuzzy stations. I was bored. Didn't have the money for no magazines, but I figured I'd let the punk rattle on till he got the hint and went away.

"'Oh, that little prick talked my ear off, but he was entertaining, just the same.' I think Mr. Ramczik's interests went beyond mere sociability, as you can imagine, given his history. 'That kid had a charm, I tell you. I gave him a beer, and we were laughing together when suddenly he stops, stares me straight in the eye, and says "As a registered sex-offender, Mr. Ramczik, how do you dare invite a minor into your home, supply him with alcohol, and molest him without thinking there will be consequences?" Swear to God I dropped my beer can so it made a puddle in the carpet. "Get the fuck outta here, you bastard!" I yelled and went to give him the bum's rush out of my home, when he punched me so hard, I crumpled to the floor. He stood over me and told me to sign over my title to the home and land or he'd report me to the law for assaulting him. He bragged about how easy it was to mimic bruising in the nether regions enough that'd convince a rural ER and police he wasn't lying. This was a goddamn nightmare, I tell you. I was panicking and trembling because I had nothing, just enough of my inheritance left over before I had to get some sort of job. I didn't know what to do. He was big and could have pummeled me to death. I didn't know if he was crazy enough to murder me, but I didn't wanna go back to prison either. With a trembling hand, I signed over the title to him, wondering how he'd pull off such a thing without a notary or title company. I could always contest it, but that sonofabitch made sure I knew he would report me right away if I so much as peeped anything to anyone. "Go to the police, you old fuck," he called me. "I've got your DNA in my knuckles and my testimony. Who's gonna believe a jailbird child molester over the testimony of a kid you tried to rape?"

"'What the hell is wrong with people these days?' Silas, the child molester had the gall to ask me. 'So, Officer, what're my options here to get my home back?' I didn't want to waste time trying to advise him, as he'd have a nearly impossible battle to return his property, and I wasn't totally sure of his veracity in relating the details. But when I got out of Chillicothe, I knew definitively that Clay had already engaged in extortion and therefore would have little or no compunction in doing so again to me or anyone else who got in his way."

Diana covered her face with her hands at the thought that the home where she'd made a marriage and family had been stolen by the man she loved.

"Joseph Clay may be a cyber prodigy, but his self-taught tendencies sometimes blind him to the obvious. Of course he'd realize that I wouldn't hesitate to install a key-logger on his devices and internet access. But it wasn't obvious to him that I knew that as well. So I used a key-logger but with an exploit that would trigger only when someone attempted to bypass it, all going unnoticed by the user.

"I then confronted him about his Hyram Silas Germane fictionalization. He never tried to explain it away. Just shrugged and said, 'You can't do anything about it. This is 100% solid work. I'll file a grievance with Internal Affairs and HR for your unjustifiable scrutinizing of me and falsely accusing me of nefarious activities when, after all, you and I both know it was a simple typo.' He tried to pass himself off as calm and collected, but I knew he was rattled enough to do something rash—namely, dig up and falsify information to incriminate me.

"After that, it was a matter of analyzing the keylogger results, which he made a lot easier with his bypassing of it only when he went to find information on me. I didn't have to sift through all his activities—the keylogger recorded his work only during the times when he was working on me. And that took him hours, Diana. The hours he wasn't home with you and your child.

"Amassing enough documentation of his activities in August, I consulted intensively with Captain Herschel and HR legal. In a closed-door meeting with Clay, we suspended him with half-pay for a probationary period of up to six months. Without revealing the keylogger or any of my suspicions, we made clear to him that we believed he was engaging in work directly detrimental to the reputation of the Division and to public safety. We also impressed upon him the punishable nature of his activities. Translation: we weren't eager to can him or to go so far as prosecute—unless he forced our hand. We wanted to rehabilitate him—well, at least HR did—but even if he'd come back from his suspension a new person, he knew he'd never work again in Cyber or anything beyond strict patrol duty. I surmise he thought he could call our bluff, that HR didn't want to get into the nettles of outright firing him or prosecuting him. And he was partially right about that—it wasn't an open-and-shut case on our end because, had it been so, HR would have pursued it to the nth degree. If he hadn't been blinded by his quest for control and security, he might've realized that he had no wiggle room. But this was the orphan who'd outwitted a man of his home and land, who'd created the Cyber Division with his bare know-how, who knew how to do things digitally of which he assumed we had no comprehension. He just needed time, he probably told himself. Six months to create an alternate reality in which he could bury me, the Captain, and a host of local politicos in a headline-stealing scandal that would forever secure him in the limelight. I realize now, Diana, that this wasn't a man who could come home to tell you even a smattering of the truth. For you and Luna were his only security. He'd worked tirelessly for that. He wouldn't give that up, even if it meant living a secret life separate from you."

Diana wanted to believe Burt. Wanted to receive Selene's comfort. But she knew that all of this was her doing. She could have stripped bare Clay's lies the first time he'd ever had rough sex with her back when they were dating. She could have left him, yanking away the dream he had so thoroughly lied to maintain. And because she'd not had the courage to do it at the first, second, third, or thousand other times he'd given her clear reason to doubt him, they now had a child whose life would be wrecked by what was next going to happen. And Diana had sworn her own child would never have to live the lies that she herself had, with her wreck of a family.

Burt finished by detailing Clay's exploits in the aftermath of the closed-door meeting. Clay took the suspension without a word and cleaned out his desk. They knew, despite his losing his login credentials and security clearances, that he'd already devised backdoor maneuvers to hack the systems he needed. They'd also trapdoor exploited those hacks to activate the keylogger again so that, no matter what device or ISP he used, they'd know his activities. At first, he'd been cautious, said Burt, trying to play it smart. Yet, all too soon, he began an obsessive pursuit of information he could twist into the downfall of his persecutors. He would make them pay. Too late had they realized the fervency of his efforts. They tried calling him in to deliver the news of his firing; they had no plans to prosecute him. But he stayed outside their orbit. Burt had had no idea Clay would come to the holiday party, let alone bring Diana. When Clay showed up with her, Burt and Herschel didn't know what to expect or what potential violence Clay might carry out. They had to act in the moment without disrupting the party.

"I think the depth of his fall and its having been rendered by people he assumed were beneath his abilities became too much," mused Burt. "He refused to grieve it and move on. Refused to see that his dream wasn't tenable. That's hard to do and will turn better men to gnawing themselves. His not telling you the truth, Diana, was not your fault. He didn't trust himself, didn't dare to believe you'd love him through this. Whether you still do love him, Diana, please know it's not your duty. You weren't made to save him. It was never you two against the world. It was always Joseph Clay trying to rise above himself and the world. The rest of us could comply or become his launch pad."

∞ ∞ ∞

Captain Herschel had seen to it that Golly was fed and let out that night, but Diana knew she had to go to the double-wide the next day. Selene had arranged for her brother and nephews to bring a trailer to clear out Diana's furniture and belongings. Clay was in muni lock up for the weekend. Burt didn't have to decide on pressing charges until Monday (he didn't plan to), which bought Diana time to fully get out of the double-wide. She felt nothing as they hauled her things to the trailer, hitched to Selene's pick-up to go to storage on Selene's brother's ranch.

"Forget the bed and the sofa. Just leave them." She would not put her body on anything he had shared with her. For she had *let* him share her things, *let* him call those things his. She had *let* him own her life, her time, her hopes and dreams, holding them hostage to his lies. She wanted to feel for him, but right now she couldn't. She'd understood and compensated for his shitty childhood, his unresolved anger, his rootlessness, his constant need for her to be the foundation of his ambition. She wondered how she'd gotten a PhD, tenure, and a child amidst his constant emptying of her like a busted dam. Now she would give nothing. He was gone from her. Maybe he'd always been.

As she viewed the moving procession, she transported back to watching the funeral home personnel move her father's body out of the old manse. Numb. She had known she was supposed to feel something, but she couldn't summon it then or now. Just watch others do things for her in her paralysis. Nothing was expected of her but passivity. They didn't want to approach her. What could they talk with her about? The weather? Pious platitudes? Her role was to play the mourner and thereby absolve them of contact and communication beyond the service they were providing. Afterward, they would go on with their lives and she would fade into a mist, like she'd done in leaving Penn State in the middle of her sophomore year of college, after the funeral. All was now mist curling about vine-crawling ruins. She could hear the condensation dripping off the stones and smell the loam under them, feel the small creatures crawling their pathways in the ground, taste the morning that buffeted the wings of the crows floating by. Then and now. They were one experience, for nothing had changed.

Luna, in Selene's arms, called out to one of the movers carrying the Sinclair Dino plushie Clay had brought home after he'd traveled to Amarillo for a Patrol continuing-ed event. She looked at her daughter for the first time. She didn't see herself, and that was good. Inherit nothing, Dee thought. Take nothing with you. Make a life of your own. Learn from my failure.

But Diana couldn't leave everything. Her heart was misplaced, out of the light. She had heard so much in the last 12 hours that she'd gladly put out her eyes to keep out anymore enlightenment. Just hole up here in the ruins.

∞ ∞ ∞

Burt didn't press charges, and Clay was released on Monday morning. Dee never saw the double-wide again. Clay made contact with neither her nor anyone from Highway Patrol. Every month, Burt sent a patrol officer to monitor the double-wide but it stood uninhabited, slowly giving way to the vicissitudes of the Texas elements. No action had been taken on the title. Clay had abandoned it entirely, it seemed. Similarly, Clay showed up nowhere electronically. His credit union account was closed the day of his release, its funds withdrawn. His SSN brought up no hits for employment, whereabouts, anything. He had disappeared, making his non-presence oppressive to Diana. She'd not grieved, hadn't dared to. She had a daughter to raise, a job to work, a home to keep. Dee and Luna had stayed at Selene's through a comfortless holiday season, despite Selene, her family, and Burt showering Luna with gifts. Diana was barren, with no change coming.

She found a house to rent in Selene's neighborhood that had been evacuated by four December graduates. The place needed a good deal of improvement and upkeep, which lowered the rent correspondingly. Diana welcomed the distracting opportunity to put her construction skills to it. With every nail driven, gypsum board replaced, tiling laid, the bitter taste of knowing she'd learned both her skills and unending pain from her father fueled her hammer strokes, each one driving home the lesson she hadn't learned with him and wasn't learning with Clay. If only she cared to know what that lesson was.

Luna was remembrance and incentive. She grew like a sweet-smelling wildflower and buzzed around Diana's life, stirring memories of skating on the ice of the creek-dam pond her father had built while Dee had been in the womb, her mother still a person with a laugh who didn't yet stare at the window, seeing nothing beyond it. Doppelgängers of past and present presaged nothing of her future—a cloud of unknowing Dee grew to welcome. No expectations. No dream of a house of their own and multiple children. No doing the things that normal people do. It wasn't so much a contemplative/Zen relinquishment of control as it was simple resignation at having fulfilled all the unwanted destiny she could stand. So, she hammered and painted and framed and tiled and celebrated Luna's dance recitals, tee-ball hits, and her entry to kindergarten, taking to school like Dee had done till the fateful years of Junior and Senior High.

Diana refused to promise herself that Luna's life would be different It would be what it would be. Diana would hold faithful to that, and no more. She spared Luna nothing except her own bitterness. Gradually, Luna stopped asking about her daddy. "Daddy is gone, and I don't know when he'll be back, baby."

"What happened to him, Mommy?"

"Daddy was scared of a lot of things, Luna, and he didn't know how to handle his fears except to lie and hide the truth."

"Doesn't he love us?"

"I don't know, sweetie, because he isn't here to tell us."

"What things was he scared of?"

"It's hard for me to say, baby, because I didn't understand what he was afraid of."

"Is he still afraid?"

"I don't know if he is. I hope not."

"If he stops being afraid, will he come back then?"

"I don't know, Luna."

"Do you want him to come back, Mommy?"

"I don't. Do you?"

"I don't think so, Mommy. I'm doing good with you."

∞ ∞ ∞

Indiscernibly, life filled the crater she was renovating, and the work was looking more and more to some sort of spec. She won the TWU Professor of the Year Award and, for a brief moment, forgot that her life had once been lived with another to whom she had given herself and felt given to, even while he'd taken so much. She dared to ponder that she had something yet to do. It wasn't hers to seize but would be revealed. In the meantime, she was living. She had her rituals and habits that reassured. Challenges at her work that delivered a quiet yet pulsing fulfillment when she met and exceeded them without grasping, panting, struggling. Blessedly missing was the stomach-pitting fear of all those nights when he would come home and of what mood he would bring. Back then, it had gotten so bad that she welcomed his working late, beyond when she had gone to bed. Sleep and oblivion from the demands of his raw nature, so vibrant in its promise, yet so caustic in its immediacy. Dee reflected on those times that she grew to dread even his coming home joyous and celebratory, for when would it turn? When would he smile one moment, only to lash out the next? How long would he haplessly feint at happiness dangling before him? How much longer would she take being dangled on the string?

∞ ∞ ∞

"Here's to the next step in your life," Selene toasted her IPA to Diana, who clinked the pint glass with hers and gave a wry twist of her mouth. "I don't know if my divorce being finalized calls for a luncheon toast," Dee said.

"It calls for something beyond a signature and registry at the courthouse. While I'm all for the ritual burning of relics like your marriage certificate, I've noticed that you haven't completely finished the repairs to the fireplace, the last of your Sistine-Chapel-drawn-out restorations of a place you don't even own. Breaking bread and bursting the dam of beer are a better lim-crossing ceremony than fire for something like this major step you've taken to reclaim your life. The pain is still there, I can see, Diana, but you're putting it more and more into perspective."

Dee looked down. "It'll always be there. I drugged it with Xanax and salved it with therapy, both of which helped me through the crisis. I've learned it's better not to fight it. I give it its own place, its due. Lately, it's been coming around less to collect dues."

"I was pleasantly surprised when you told me you'd filed the divorce papers."

"I'm not so stupid as to think that he's not still alive or that he won't come back, but I was tired of daily renewing that lease. I've amazed myself by not breaking down through the process. I've had more angst administering final grades. You don't think I'm doing the breaststroke in that river in Egypt?"

Selene laughed. "No, you're not in denial as far as I can tell. Rather, you're gradually reframing your life like you did that house. I wonder that you don't make an offer on it to your landlord. She doesn't need the income from the rent, and she adores you."

"I've toyed with it." Diana twisted her pasta on the fork. "Luna loves her school, and it's a quick drive to work *and* to the Lowe's on the bypass."

"It's also the home you've made—first in your need, and now in the image of your desire, the latter of which you've resolutely kept on the back burner. Time for desire to assert its status as the main course."

Dee looked at Selene suspiciously. "Are you talking about dating?"

"Oh, posh!" said Selene, waving her fork. "As if you need a man to complete you! Relationships do have their uses and fulfillments, but haven't you seen growing over the past two years a grace you denied yourself even when you were in a relationship? I'm not saying to forgo a partner or even casual dating. I'm just asking you to pull the curtain back to peek at Diana. Aren't you curious as to what life yet holds?"

Diana sipped her ale and paused. "The few times I've kindled that kind of curiosity, it's eventually burned down my house. I'm no longer curious at what I could be. I've got what I want right now—a life as a mother, professor, renovator, and *consigliere* for the Dean of the College of Nursing."

"And that last office is more than appreciated, especially the surrogate-grandparent benefits it brings. But I'm not referring to what you *could* be or what you *have* but who you *are*. As Socrates noted, the unexamined life is not worth living."

Selene had a knack for pushing this envelope and Diana returning it to sender. "All philosophers should, in turn, be forced to drink hemlock." Dee routinely rebuffed Selene's invitations to introspection but knew they'd germinate and sprout in her life at some point. She wasn't so sure that the idea of commencing divorce proceedings hadn't been planted by Selene. There was a reason she was an effective and longstanding Dean—she didn't manipulate, didn't even motivate. Just tended the garden.

"Yes, yes," offered Selene. "I realize that Socrates meant the stuffy old self-analytical bull-manure that philosophic doctors of his ilk prescribe, but you know I don't imply the same. I mean, simply, aren't you wanting to meet and be delighted by Diana Atestesso? I know her as well as anyone does, and I can vouch for her merits. Without her, my life would now be a spiteful hole of micromanaging people at the College past the end of their wits. She opens the door to a spring that I never thought would follow my always-winter/never-Christmas. She is a gift, you see."

A tear felt heavy on Diana's eyelid.

Selene looked at her. "You deserve to hear that, you strong, brave, fierce woman. Sometimes all we can do is show up and know that we are enough. You've done that admirably ever since I've known you, better and better every day. We *are* enough, it's true, and we don't need to—and indeed *can't*—be anything more. But there's the matter of showing up and meeting the one you showed up for. You need to do that as you take this next step."

∞ ∞ ∞

When Diana arrived in the school pick-up line later that afternoon, Luna wasn't there. Was Dee late for pickup? No, right on time, as the row of waiting cars attested. She checked her phone for any voicemails from the school. None. Had Luna been held after for some reason? They should have called her about that, dammit. She pulled out of the line and took a parking spot, trotting into the school office that was humming with parents and some of the older elementary students taking care of end-of-day business. She waited in line, checking her phone for messages. Could Selene have surprised her with afternoon babysitting so Dee could finish the fireplace? No texts, voicemails, or emails. Finally, she reached the desk. "Hi, I'm here to pick up my daughter, Luna Atestesso, from Ms Frazier's Kindergarten class. For some reason, she's not in the pick-up line."

"No problem," said the office aide, dialing the intercom to Luna's classroom. "Ms. Lawson, this is Carly. I've got Dr. Atestesso here to pick up her daughter. Were you holding her over?"

There was an uncomfortable pause as the aide listened to the reply. "Really? Okay, thank you."

"Dr. Atestesso, Ms. Lawson says that the office called in around 1pm for Luna and that she was picked up then."

"By her godmother?" Dee asked. "Dr. Selene Grieve? She's the only other person authorized and IDed to pick up Luna."

"Let me look, Ma'am," said the aide, checking her computer. "Uh-huh, I see Dr. Grieve on the list here. Let me see the check-out log." Clicks on the keyboard. "Hmm. Okay, let me peek back at the authorized pick-up list." More clicking. Peering. Pausing. Reading with her lips. "It says here in the log that Mr. Atestesso picked her up today … for a pediatrician appointment for the rest of the day. He's on the authorized list."

Something screamed in the caverns of Diana's mind. "No. That can't be! There is no 'Mr. Atestesso.' I … I'm a single mother. Dr. Grieve is the only other authorized pick-up person. 'Mr.' Atestesso must be a typo. I'm *Ms.* Atestesso."

The aide clicked her tongue. "Oh, I'm sure there's been some kind of mix up, though we don't have any other Lunas at the school. Very pretty name. Very distinctive."

"Thank you," mumbled Dee. "Can we please clear things up so I can retrieve my daughter?"

The aide called over Ms. Frazier, the Office Administrator, the two ladies cross checking the aide's terminal. Then Ms. Frazier went to her desk and paged through a notebook, bringing it back to the aide's side and referencing it against the computer. "I don't understand," said Ms. Frazier, "It shows Mr. Atestesso here on the computer as an authorized user—photo, notarized documents, fingerprints, the whole nine yards. But he's not in my printout backup. Dr. Atestesso, Monday morning each week, we do a complete printout of the pick-up database to either weed out those no longer registered as authorized or to have in hard-copy the documents of those authorized to pick-up who've been newly added. But Mr. "Don't you touch me, you sonofabitch!"

The Security Officer backed away and barked some code into his shoulder mic.

"Mrs. Atestesso," said Bowers, whose forehead glistened with perspiration, "The only sensible thing to do now is just stay put so that we can have you here to answer questions from the police. They can have an Amber Alert out in a jiffy."

Dee bore into him. "I'm not staying one more second in the place where *you* let my child be taken from me!"

She was through the office door, parents and school personnel moving aside. She tore her car out of the parking lot. She had to get to her home. That was what he'd hit next.

Burt had been flabbergasted. "Diana, calm down! I couldn't have Luna—I've been in Austin all week. I'm right now clearing Waco on I-35."

She'd hung up on him then, realizing that Clay had returned. On the day of their divorce. He would never leave.

She flew back to the house, running stop signs and hitting curbside plastic recycling bins. The pavement in the street in front of her place showed skid marks. Had those been there before today? The house exterior looked intact. She jammed her key into the front-porch door, slamming it open.

Her living room was in shards, her renovations blasted, torn, smashed, punched, wrecked. Crowbar marks ripped the original plaster all the way up the flight to the bedrooms. She scaled the steps three at a time, her heart beating madly. The upstairs rooms were a spray of glass and gypsum dust, lamps, nightstands, curios, mirrors, windows, and tiling shattered. Only Luna's room looked the same as it had that morning, all of her clothes and things gone but for her bed and furniture. She peered out Luna's window into the backyard. Something was hanging from the crepe myrtle tree.

She almost fell down the steps, twisting her ankle and cutting her hand on glass shards. Righting herself, she headed for the kitchen backdoor, and slipped on something wet, her head banging against a counter. The refrigerator had been upended, it's goods smashed and poured out on the floor amidst the fragments of the kitchen table and the contents of all her cupboards. Her vision reeled as she rose to her feet. "My God, no! Please, no!"

The kitchen spun around her as she crawled to the door through the muck and broken glass. Out the door, she got to her feet on the deck and stumbled to the crepe myrtle. On it, hung by the neck, was the still twitching form of Goliath, his eyes maced and weeping blood.

∞ ∞ ∞

The vet had to put Golly down, saying it was a testimony to the creature's spirit and tenacity that he'd survived, but that the nature of his injuries would cause him a remaining lifetime of blindness, toothlessness, and pain. Golly slid himself across the cold steel vet-clinic table and curled up against her. Her violent sobs wouldn't come till much later, when she was alone.

"It's as professional a job as can be imagined," Burt had said. "No fingerprints, no witnesses to his having been at your place, no reported sounds of destruction or your dog's distress."

She felt like Golly must have when it had happened. Stung by a dart, paralyzed, and helpless against the torture. Where had Luna been when it was happening? Had she seen it? Was she now forever scarred and raped in her mind, if not her body? Or had he been the ultimate professional? Sweet-talking her into believing they were going on an extended vacation, leaving her in the running vehicle that he'd ensured was unexitable, while he took away their home.

There were no leads. The police weren't definitively

confirming it had been Clay. But Diana and Burt knew it had been. Clay had to leave his mark so they would know. Diana wouldn't see that house again. Her renter's insurance took care of the damage but wasn't able to replace all her possessions, which were a total loss. So was her life.

Clay had cleaned out her savings, checking, and 401K accounts. She took FMLA leave for the rest of the Spring through the Summer, staying at Selene's small-ranch cabin, Selene summering with her there. Silent with Diana. Holding Diana. Listening to Diana. Singing to Diana. Rocking in the porch swing with Diana. Healing Diana, if the real Diana would ever be found again to be healed.

∞ ∞ ∞

Selene closed the hatch of Dee's CR-V. "That's it—all you need to generously sabbath."

The sun was rising. Dee wanted the early start to make it all the way to Bowling Green so that the second day of the trip wouldn't be as long, and she'd have time to settle into the old mountain manse before dusk. Despite knowing that this sabbatical was a plan well-made, she still felt like ashes—the ones she'd been sifting in Denton since the loss of Luna. Watching the dust rise from the ashes of her heart that stirred now. Traveling to the ashes of a past she'd thought she'd permanently left behind.

She sighed, shoulders slumped. At least she'd have 26 hours of drive time in which to resurrect some beloved old tunes. As a parting gift, Selene had bought her a ginormous iTunes gift card, Dee downloading titles she hadn't thought of since she'd high-school sequestered herself on the third floor of the old manse.

Selene put her hands on Dee's shoulders. "Diana," she said, taking her prophetess-mother tone, "You need release, dearheart. This place has too long claimed your grief."

Dee looked at her. "So has the place I'm going to."

"Ah, but the difference is that you have faced and stared down your grief here. You have unfinished business in your place of origin. All heroes must go the path of descent in order to ascend. You are no different."

"For Chrissakes, Selene, it's just a sabbatical."

"It will be only that if you close yourself off, Diana. I have a feeling, though, that even your stubbornness will not allow you to do that. After all, *you* were the one who came up with this idea."

Diana rolled her eyes. "That was when I was buzzed on beer, with you goading me on. My resolve was an idle threat."

Selene raised an eyebrow. "Who exactly was it threatening?"

Diana sighed. "I guess that's why I'm hesitating at cliff's edge."

"Yours are not Icarus wings. You needn't worry about the sun melting them. Indeed, remember when things get dark, as they will, that the fire that burns in your heart, Lady Atestesso, is much hotter than any nova. *And* that your wings are of tempered steel."

Dee paused, Selene staring fiercely into her eyes.

Finally, Dee said, "Wow. That's over the top, even for you."

Selene rubbed her eyes. "Yes, dear, I know. It was that second cup of tea."

Diana kissed her mentor on the cheek and got into the SUV. Before Dee started it, Selene gave a parting shot. "Regardless of my caffeinated purple prose, young lady, the gist of what I said still applies—you are a motherfucking bad-ass bitch mama warrior!"

Part II

The Manse

This house is full of m-m-my mess.
(Slamming.)
This house is full of m-m-mistakes.
(Slamming.)
This house is full of m-m-madness.
(Slamming.)
This house is full of, full of, full of fight!
(Slam it.)

With my keeper I
(clean up).
With my keeper I
(clean it all up).
With my keeper I
(clean up).
With my keeper I
(clean it all up).
—"Get Out of My House," Kate Bush

"Tiefer, tiefer.
Irgendwo in der Tiefe
Gibt es ein licht."
—"Hello, Earth," Kate Bush

"Hello, Miss Diana!"

She'd opened the door of the manse to someone she might've mistaken for a homeless person. Except that she'd grown up here. It was just old Rooster, the closest thing she'd ever known to a next-door neighbor, if you considered three miles and two left turns down a pothole-strewn mountain road "next-door."

She was surprised that Rooster had known she'd be here. "Rooster Cogbert, is that you?" Due, when he was a child, to the popularity of John-Wayne's *Rooster Cogburn,* he'd been forever tagged with that best-the-imagination-of-his-mountain-peers-could-supply sobriquet. He'd never minded but seemed proud of it, though he had yet to don an eyepatch.

"Yes, indeed, Miss Dee! I'd almost not've recognized you, but your beautiful smile is a dead giveaway. S'good to have you back on the mountain!"

It wasn't really a single mountain but an Appalachian fold of high elevation, creviced with hollows, saddle-passes (if they could be called that, the Appalachians were such geologically ancient, worn-down mountains), and streams, and divided from Chestnut Ridge by the eons-long inroads of the implacably beautiful and feisty—at least in it's upper reaches—Youghiogheny River (the "Yough," as in *"Yock,"* to locals). The Yough fed into the Monongahela in McKeesport before the Mon joined the Allegheny to form the Ohio and comprise the three mighty rivers that had given birth to Pittsburgh. As Dee's Dad had said, "Piss into the Yough or one of its streams like this one I built this dam on, Poplar Run, and you contribute to the Gulf of Mexico. With any luck, you might even drink the molecules from your original piss in next winter's glass of tap of water. You never know."

Brad had laughed, like he did at everything Dad said. "Gross, Dad!" protested Diana, noticing a leer from Dad to Brad. She grew to loathe that rhyming, unceasingly un-dynamic duo. She'd rather imagine putting a message in the bottle, or even a tear into their stream, if only to see whether it would come back to her, some echo that she existed and at least could touch a world outside the narrow one in which she felt confined. But she'd been young then. Coming back, she was now an older and wiser echo that bore no message but a stream of her own tears.

She shook her head to break such maudlin musings. "Sorry, Rooster," she apologized, "I've been on the road from Texas for two straight days, and I'm trying to get re-acclimated."

"Aw, Miss Dee, that's alright. 'Tad bit cooler here than Texas. And a lot fewer Mexicans."

"Well, they're Texans, actually, Rooster, and North Texas is half as far away from Mexico as Texas is from Laurel Ridge. But I do welcome the cool. A sight better than roasting in the devil's ass crack that sits down every Summer in the Lone Star State."

"Hee-hee, Miss Diana! You always had a rare way with jokes!" As he laughed, she noticed that Rooster hadn't grown any teeth in his gap-filled grin and didn't imagine the snuff wad she clearly spied was helping the condition any. Ah, it's good to be back home, she mentally shook her head.

"How's your family, Rooster?"

"Oh, well, mama died, lessee …" he scratched his head, "… oh nine years ago this November it'll be. Poor Bobby, my brother, shot hisself three winters ago. Guess he couldn't take not bein' able to find a job once't Anchor moved its plant complete outta Connisville." (He meant "Connellsville," but many mountain denizens pronounced it that way.) "Bobby had been on the last skeleton crew that kept the old factory runnin'. Least he had a job to that point."

"Work still hard to come by? What about tourism—Pittsburghers skiing in the winter and rafting in the summer?"

"Naw," he waved his hand and spit, "That's for younger 'uns who want the seasonal pay. Can you imagine an ol' cuss like me waiterin' at Seven Springs? They'd run me out the door before the tourist types could see the real rabble that lives up here."

Diana shook her head. "You do yourself a disservice, Mr. Cogbert. You were always right by me. If they can't abide a stand-up fellow like you, to hell with their tourist dollars."

"I thank you for the compliment, Miss Dee, but don't worry—I hear they tip for shit. Anyways, I get by. I hafta. See, I got a family now."

"Rooster Cogbert with a family? You told us kids you were never gonna get married, and we'd see you walking the mountains with a long white beard like Rip Van Winkle!"

"Now, I ain't sayin' Shelly an' I ever got *married*. But she does right by me and me by her and our two kids. I may be a bit old to be a daddy, but I still keep up with my kids. Bobby, now, he's got some promise at baseball. Never took to ball much myself, but I haul him every spring all the way to Mill Run, the only Little League team left in the mountains these days, since Normalville shut down its one. Helluva good team, Mill Run has. District Champions last year, and I think they could be state-bound this year. Who knows? Maybe even Williamsport. A fella can dream."

"That *is* news, Rooster! You should be proud!"

"You know I am," he smiled, and rubbed his nose on the back of his sleeve. "You oughta be proud of *yourself,* Diana! A professor an' all. Then again, you were smarter than anybody I ever knowed."

She blushed. "I'm not so smart as lucky. I had some breaks fall my way, and others that didn't."

"Yeah, well, all o' us can say *that.* So, you takin' a break from professorin' here in your gorgeous old home?"

Wow. Word travels fast, she thought. "As a matter of fact I am, and it comforts me that my nearest neighbor is you. I was thinking I might not recognize anyone here."

"We don't fergit much around here, 'cuz nuthin' changes.

Snows in the winter and is beautiful in the summer, but for too short a time. You sure yer gonna be able to hack it here through the winter? I know yer tough and remember how bad the cold gets, but least you had family with ya back then. Three miles from me ain't exactly ideal when the roads get blocked and power goes out, though you got a good generator for the place. But unless you gotta a ton o' gasoline, it won't run long. The heatin' oil man won't make it up the driveway from November through February if we get the snow this winter like we did two years ago. You could stock up on some coal just in case. That ol' coal furnace might work if I give it a kick or two. I could fit you up with some coal. Still got it here, though folks don't burn it like they used to. The richie-riches got their gas lines, which're sight better than power lines that a heavy snowfall'll take down. But this old place," he said, looking about him, "sure ain't fitted with no gas."

How did he know about the generator, not to mention the heating oil and the furnace? "Thanks for the heads up, Rooster. As a matter of fact, I was expecting a call from the property management company that takes care of this old musty house. They're supposed to apprise me of all the things I need to know that I might've forgotten, but you've beaten them to the punch."

Rooster scratched his head. "I don't know 'bout no ma'gement company, but I do have all the keys to the place. I didn't wanna put all of them under the porch swing cushion—just the front door key, y'know, jes to be safe an' 'at."

Dee paused, a glint of understanding breaching her thoughts. "Are you being nicer to me than I deserve and not telling me outright that *you're* the property management company, Rooster?"

He shuffled his feet and spit. "Well, I didn't wanna assume, Miss Dee. After the home health couldn't take care of your mama in-home a few years ago, you n' Bradley got her inta that home. Brad tol' me to look after the place till he could get some outfit to do it. You know how *that* worked out. What prop'ty ma'gement company is gonna make a buck haulin' to the sticks to oversee an ol' place that needs tender lovin' care like this gem does? After 'while, Brad kinda asked if me and Shel' could do it. I bargained him into makin' it worth my while, an' … well, Rooster Cogbert, prop'ty ma'gement company, is here to greet you!"

Dee laughed. "Rooster, you are a piece of cake and always have been! I should've known you'd be the faithful one to see to it that the place is pristine—and I'm not just saying that! It *is,* much better than a management company would keep it."

Rooster actually blushed, then spit again. "A lot of the inside stuff is Shelly's doin'. She'd of bin out here with me to greet ya, but Michelle's got her end-o'-school awards, an' I ain't much for that sort o' thing 'cuz I'm grubby from work n' such. But she rode me hard to make sure the place was fit for a woman to occupy … which meant she came over t'inspect it herself … *three times,* till I got it right in her mind."

"You two sound so sweet! I can't wait to meet her!"

"Now I ain't tryin' to win yer compliments, Miss Dee. I get paid fer this. But … you could do me a favor, if ya don't mind."

Dee grimaced. "I can only imagine what skimpy amount Brad is paying you!"

"Now that ain't what I'm sayin', Diana, though yer not far off the mark," he winked. "But me and Shel're doin' fine. It's just that Mr. Bradley asked me to find out if you were gonna need our services once you took up here for the year. He seems to think that, what with all yer daddy taught you, you'll Man-Mountain-Dean the place yerself. Right now, I maintain the phys'cal plant, so to speak, an' Shelly does all the cleanin'. We figure that, even though yer capable, you might 'preciate us keepin' on doin' that for ya, so you kin do yer professor things.

Truth is, though we're doin' okay, it'll be a tough year for us if we lose yinz's income …"

Now she understood the full import of Rooster's welcome visit. Dee knew she could hold down the place on her own, but Bradley need be none the wiser about that. Besides, he already discounted her in so many other ways, *and* having Rooster and his wife to take care of things would leave her more time to research and write. "Actually, Rooster, it's perfect you stopped by! I'd no idea that you two were holding down the fort, and I'm grateful. Also, I can't do without your help, no matter how much Dad taught me. If some machinery is beyond my repair skills, I'd have no clue who to call to come out here who'd be honest, let alone competent. Who would know this place by now better than you?"

This, of course, was the keenly hoped-for response. "Oh, Miss Diana, Shelly an' me'll see you through the winter an' then some. You can count on us!" He shook her hand, then spit.

He spied the roof and said, "Oh, yeah, I was also gonna tell ya that some satellite guy was out here the other day, snoopin'. I didn't 'xactly turn the thirty-aught-six on 'im, but he did tell me he'd come out here again next week. You gettin' Dish or D'rect TV? Couldn't tell from his truck, 'cuz he's one o' them open contractors from Uniontown. They're hit-n-miss, lemme tell ya. I could get a more honest one for ya."

By which he might mean a relative or friend who needed the work. No harm, she guessed. "Thanks, Rooster. It's not for TV—it's for satellite internet. I know the phone company is finally running cable lines out as far as we are here, but they were never very reliable on phone service, and the cable brought only 10 channels. Besides, I checked them out while I was still in Texas, and they don't have the internet speed I'll need. Sooooo, it was actually Hughes that was going to install satellite for me."

Rooster shook his head. "You know best, but I think them

Hughes morons'll fuck you over. Now my cousin, Nedry, he's the main man 'round here for D'rect TV—they was bought by ATT or the other way 'round—an' he'll square you in a jiffy with slicker-'n-snot intrawebs. No worries—I'll get you set up, an' he'll be out here next week, mebbe quicker if I light a fire under 'im. All you hafta do is call Hughes an' tell 'em to fuck off. Sound good? Ned an' I'll get you the rest of the way. Hell, he rigged me up with all the Pirates, Pens, 'n Stiller games I kin handle, fer dirt cheap. An' Shel' loves to watch them *Queer Eyes*. So many different people it takes to make the world go 'round, huh?"

Not much had changed up here, and she was falling right back into the spirit of things. If only she'd wanted to in the first place. "Are you sure this Ned is on the up-and-up, Rooster? I don't want to start my sabbatical in the mountains with internet police coming down on me because my satellite isn't legit."

Rooster laughed. "Hell, the revenuers stopped coming before I was even born. Granpappy said their not comin' no more took the fun outta makin' white lightnin'. Naw, you ain't got nuthin' to worry 'bout. If you wanna pay full price, Ned kin 'range that, but for family, friends, and friends of friends, he sorta cuts out the middle-man, 'cuz he knows all them codes 'n shit to type inta his little pad thingy he uses. He'll charge you an up-front, then it's dirt cheap each month like I toldja. Speakin' o' cables 'n wiring 'n such, lemme give ya a quick tour o' the old house, to show you any changes you mighta missed since you wuz last up here."

The tour was anything but quick and all but unnecessary, as she knew the place inside and out, having remodeled almost all of it with Dad. Rooster stopped at the stairway to the third floor. "Tell ya the truth, I rarely bin up there," he said, pointing to the top of the stairs. "An' it's been shut up since afore your mama went to the home. Brad tol' me to never mind it, so I just lay the rat bait-traps for the third floor and attic an' leave it at that. Looks like dusty old bedrooms and old furniture. Ooo-wee, I bet there're some antiques up there that'd fetch a pretty penny. I don't heat up there in the winter but wouldn't be needed anyway, 'cuz the heat from the floors below keeps anythin' from freezin' that ought notta.

"I gotta say though, that when yer daddy hired me to help him with that dam at the crick pool, I used to look up the hill from down there by the crick, and I swear one time at dusk as he 'n I wuz finishin' up, I saw someone in the window o' the big third-floor bedroom. This was before you wuz born, so I don't know if you heard tell of it. She was a pretty thing starin' out that window. Not at me, mind ya, but at somethin' far away it looked like. I rubbed m'eyes and looked agin, an' she was still there, but when I tole yer dad, I turned back 'n she wuz gone. He said I wuz seein' things 'cuz I was late gettin' mah after-work beer-drinkin' on, an' he may of bin right about that. My gawd, your daddy could build anythin', Diana. Hell, both elementary schools on the mountain wuz his buildings. An' that dam? It's still the most maint'nance-free thing 'bout this whole property. In late fall, I just clean out the leaves, and in the spring, the up-mountain-thaw debris from the sluices, and it still runs like a charm. Too bad the acid run-off from the strip mines that closed up in the 90s killed the fish in it. But there'll still be a few suckers in there. Hope you don't mind, but I let Bobby and Michele fish in it when they wuz smaller an' could still be thrilled with that kinda thing. Now it's video games an' sports 'n such."

Dee nodded. "Rooster, if they ever get the notion to fish again or want to ice skate in the winter on it, provided it's solid, they're welcome without having to ask. In fact, this winter, if it hard freezes, I may break out my old skates and give it a go. But I never was into sucker fishing."

Rooster shook his head and smiled. "Miss Dee, you ain't changed a bit, and as you get older, you favor your daddy—in both your eyes and personality. Graciousness is what it is. Your daddy gave me a job," Rooster mumbled, putting a hand to his eye, "—oh, 'scuse me, got sumthin' in m'eye. Anyway, he gave me a job when nobody woulda. I hadn't a lick of construction know-how, but, hell, he took me on, sayin' he thought I was honest and had a strong back, his only two requirements. What I'm able to do today to help keep my family goin' is owed to your daddy."

They were back at the front door, standing on the porch, eyeing their view from the manse's hilltop perch. "Okay, Rooster. You're my go-to. I'd give you my cell number, but the reception out here is for shit."

"No worries! I seen to it that the land line in the old house works fine, and I know that number. Lemme give ya mine." He pulled a gum wrapper from his pocket and a pencil from behind his ear and scribbled his number. "Shelly 'n me don't have a computer, an' we don't get to the libary in Connisville much t' use the ones there, though Bobby is sharp on 'em at school, so I'm givin' ya his email, too, just in case."

As he stepped off the porch to his rusted-out pick up, he turned back. "Oh, and Miss Diana, if you wouldn't mind doin' us one more favor ..."

"It's no trouble, Rooster. What do you need?"

He took off his CAT hat and ran his fingers over his mostly bald pate. "It's Shelly. She's kinda weird 'bout how she does her cleanin'. Till school's out, which'll be another week or so, she cleans on Saturday mornin' 'round nine. In the summers, then, she comes here on Tuesdays, 'cuz she doesn't hafta work her lunch-lady job at the el'ment'ry school durin' vacation. Then she brings the kids, 'n they help. Anyways, like I said, she's weird about it. Wants it to be perfect afore you see it. So, if it's not much trouble, wouldja mind not bein' here when she cleans?"

"Of course not, Rooster. She has her pride, I'm sure! While the weather's still good through the autumn into early winter, I'll routinely have to go to the library in Greensburg, Penn State

Fayette Campus, or sometimes Pittsburgh. I'll just make those days be when she cleans."

"We're thankful to have you here," he tipped his hat to her as he got into the truck. "Sure you don't wanna stay permanent?"

No. No thank you, she thought.

∞ ∞ ∞

Dee knocked at the locked glass door on which Finn's hours were posted. Yes, she knew it was 10am Saturday and the place didn't open till 11am. An enormous bearded figure appeared on the other side of the glass and broke into an enormous smile, opening the door.

"What are you doing here, Diana? When'd you get into town?"

Finn wrapped her in a wooly bear hug, lifting her off her feet. She could smell his cologne and felt the press of the thick silver chain around his neck. When she could breathe again, she answered. "Of all the Finn joints in all the world, I'd have to walk into yours! I mean, I'd *have* to, or you'd never forgive me if I was in Connellsville and didn't."

"Damn right," he said. "Hop up to the bar and explain your sudden appearance."

She'd kept up with Finn on Facebook, but his presence was an always larger-than-life welcome. "Just got Edmund Fitzgerald Porter back on tap. It's like I had a premonition of your arrival."

"It's early, but how could I refuse?"

He poured them two pints, then led her to a table in the back, out of sight of the windows. "Allan is always here at least a half-hour early. "

"Alcoholism'll do that to ya," said Diana. "Let's join his club."

"No thank you. Though I can't resist a porter with my best lady. Anyway, I try not to let him in before 11am, just to keep him honest. If he sees anyone in here he mistakes for a patron, he'll rattle down the front door. One time I had a distributor's rep here at 9am in plain clothes, no uniform shirt. Allan was screaming and banging down the front door. The rep looked kinda nervous. I said, 'Relax. He only does that when you don't have any Cuervo. You *did* bring the Cuervo this time, right?' Never a missed tequila delivery after that. Alcoholics can be of some help, am I right?"

Dee laughed. "Does it ever pang your conscience that you're aiding and abetting someone's habit?"

"Actually, yes … till the next bill comes in. I'm an adult who chooses his bills. Allan's an adult who chooses his poison. I always see to it that he and no one else are stumbling drunk outta here or attempting to drive. You should see my Lyft account."

"You always have been a softie, Finn. Speaking of which, I'm not keeping you from your prep, am I?"

"No. Saturday days I've got a new cook, Todd, who seems to have mastered arriving on time. He's back there prepping. I'll jump in for the 4pm shift, and he and I'll overlap through 7pm, if I get a crowd that merits his staying that late."

"Business bad?"

"It's not been good, but when has it ever? It's like heaven gives me a reprieve—every quarter we'll have a night or two when everyone in Fayette County decides they're hungry for a Delmonico, fine beer, and better whisky. Just enough to keep me out of default, but not enough to make me dream of opening a chain of anything but serial loans to keep this place running."

"I'm sorry, old friend," she said, patting his hand.

"I'm the one who chooses to stay. I'm a big boy, and, like Allan, I choose my addiction."

"You should pull up stakes and come to Texas. Everything in Denton is booming. An Irish Pub would pace the boredom of the humdrum chains we've got. See one TGI Fridays, seen 'em all."

Finn sighed. "Even if I could settle my debts here, I can't imagine myself in Texas. Yewww thank Ah kihn dew one o' them thar Lone Star drawwwls?"

"Stop! You don't know how true-to-life your exaggeration is!"

"Exactly my point. Everything's bigger in Texas, including the egos, and I'm not sure I could put up with 'em. Though their blue laws are only slightly less reprehensible than Pennsylvania's."

"It's not exactly Berkeley, but Denton is getting more open-minded as both UNT and TWU grow. I bet we could find you a comfortable niche there."

Finn raised his eyebrow. "You saying that you're a prospective investor?"

She rolled her eyes. "As if. When he took Luna, Clay hacked all my bank accounts, cleaning me out of my savings."

They both looked at each other, knowing they'd hit a tender spot. After a pause, a couple glances around the interior, and several gulps of porter by each of them, Finn asked, "Any progress in finding Luna?"

Dee traced the condensation circles on the table. "None."

"Damn," grunted Finn, looking away.

"I can't escape it," Dee said. "Guess that's why I'm here."

"You sound like Allan. But seriously, what brings you back to Fayette County?"

She sighed. "I'm supposed to be on sabbatical, in a quiet place where I can write. For a year. In the old manse."

"Wow. Sounds like your heart is 1/927th into the proposition."

"More like 1/927,000th."

"Why here? Why the mountain?" Finn asked. "Why not, um, Barcelona?"

"See above," she pointed her finger in the air. "The money thing. I can live in the manse rent-free and, unlike Barcelona, nothing about Fayette County invites me to spend frivolously, unless it's antidepressants."

"Speaking of which," mused Finn, "I have a theory on that."

"On what? The need for antidepressants in these environs?"

"Hey, these are *my* environs, thank you."

"Oh yeah, sorry, Finn. At least *I* can go back to Texas when my sabbatical's done. You're stuck in the environs."

"Your sympathy-for-losers is duly noted and posted on the aforementioned environs' public bulletin board. Anyway, I have a theory on why Fayette County and environs have been depressed since before the Great Depression itself, and Pittsburgh, Morgantown, even Steubenville have had multiple renaissances."

"Go on. I'm depressively intrigued."

"Nice. Think about it—what spurred the economic collapse in the first place? Hint: it's something you're right at home with, sore to speak."

"The manse?"

"Yup. Who originally owned it?"

"Everyone knows that—Cesaré Fricci, better known as Chester Frick, the coal and coke baron who built the place as a summer residence when coke—the bituminous-based variety and not the drug-king kind—was king. He also died there. What does he have to do with a continually overcast economic outlook?"

"You said it—coal and coke were king. You know how many hospitals, libraries, schools, foundations—you name it—bear the Frick family name, even if the current residents have forgotten their history and think it a common surname? Hell, Connellsville's football team back in the day was called the 'Cokers.'"

"Then the bottom dropped out when the steel plants converted to electricity to hit the high temps needed to forge steel," Dee continued. "Who needed dirty coke then? Turbines could be generated by the ample waterpower in the area, especially when the dam-builders got going. Frick refused to see it coming, in a wish fulfillment that led to his demise."

Finn shook his head. "Now even Pittsburgh's steel mills are gone, replaced by your trade—the ballooning medical industry. All that time though, the beehive coke-oven holes in the mountains have been covered up by enough trees that the tourists coming in for mountain fun have no idea the beehives still lurk there. Hell, strip mining has come and gone in all that time. Remember how, along 119, before you hit the old Fruehauf plant, you could turn down the old Dunbar road and, in the winter, see those ovens carved in the sides of the mountains?"

"Gave me chills," she snugged her hands around her shoulders.

"If Percy Bysshe Shelley had been around, he'd've written 'Ozymandias' as 'Oven-a-mandias.' And that's my point—there was no Shelley around. Still isn't. Ever wonder why?"

Dee just looked at him. "Ooookaaay, you've got me stumped. What do the lack of Brit Romantic poets have to do with Fayette County's continual depression since the 1920s?"

"Nothing," grunted Finn. "And that's just it. Not Marie Curie, Albert Einstein, Stephen Hawking, Heddy Lamar, Allan Turing, nor anybody else with a quick mind has anything to do with this area. Don't you think it curious, Dee, that no truly notable minds have broken out of here since the collapse of coke? General Marshall had his birthplace in Uniontown, I know. But he was born before the collapse. One of the disciples opined, 'Can anything good come out of Nazareth?' Geesh. At least that one-and-done backwater produced Jesus. What've Connellsville, Dunbar, and Uniontown generated in terms of great ones since Fayettenam's collapse—other than Wild Cherry's 'Play That Funky Music, White Boy'? (Uh, present company excluded from that dismal assessment.)"

Diana searched her mind, recalling the afternoons in early Junior High, when she was on the bus, rolling back up the mountain after school, passing a normally abandoned shack on the side of Three-Mile Hill Road. But on alternate Tuesdays, there'd always be a handful of celebrants with cheap beers, sitting on the hoods or beds of their beat-up trucks, raising a toast to the bus passengers. She one day worked up the gumption to ask her seat mate, Jody Dahl, who those guys were. Jody, with a straight face, even solemnity, had said, "Those guys? Hell, they got their assistance checks today. That's what m' old man's doin' right now, in our trailer. Prolly what I'll be doin' when I'm his age."

But no place in this world is unadulteratedly bad, depressed, hopeless, right? Places have their cycles. Yes, this cycle is a long one, but not in the annals of history. Even the United States is a mere blip in time compared to, say, the history of India or China, both of which knew times when they were conquerors and when they were conquered. Sure, she had a lot to hold against her place of origin. But it wasn't evil.

"Aren't you painting with a broad brush, Finn?" she asked. "Just because some persons' achievements aren't as famous as Einstein's were, doesn't mean they weren't of great heart or mind."

"True," agreed Finn. "And, yes, you and I would like to think ourselves exceptions, but ..." He held up his hands and looked around him, a pounding sound coming from the front door. "... then again, here you and I—and Allan—are."

"Gee, thanks. Now I feel as depressed as Fayette County after the coke collapse."

"Exactly, Dee!" said Finn. "And when the mines and coke processing facilities collapsed, what did their tenders do?"

"Um, abandoned them, 'cuz even the banks weren't interested in that gutted, rutted landscape."

"Right. And what happens to an untended fire?"

She searched herself. "If you're lucky, it goes out. If not, it catches the whole joint in flames."

"Bravissima!" he exclaimed. "Or, in the case of Fayette County, 'Cativissima'—very bad flames ... that no one proceeded to notice. And they're still burning."

Dee squinted her eyes. "I don't see any flames."

"But, like Roger Daltrey says, 'After the fire, the fire still burns.' Dee, have you ever driven past a Texas oil well that had caught fire?"

"Yeah, they're alarmingly common, but eerily pretty at night, if you happen to drive by one in the countryside."

Finn kept going. "What if you'd drive past that same well two weeks later?"

"Um," muttered Diana, sipping her porter. "Still on fire?"

"A year later?"

"Well, now that you mention it, there was one in Forrest County that kept burning for a year-and-a-half. But I guess they have to burn out eventually, right?"

"Only," said Finn, his finger held in a vertical point, "when its fuel runs out. Dee, the coal and coke mines didn't fail because they ran out. No, they were economic dinosaurs blitzkrieged by the meteor of technological advancement. (And thank God they were, or our currently clear skies would be smudged with coal smoke.) There's metric shit-tons of coal still down there, miles below. And it's burning, Dee. The coal mine fires still burn."

She looked at him, her jaw dropping. "And they can't be put out. And no one knows about them."

"Oh, some know. Your Penn State and WVU geologists for sure know about them. They're probably still reckoned in some filing cabinet by the conglomerates that bought the remains of the old coke concerns. The EPA probably knows. But because no one sees the fire, it's not a priority. Fayette County has been played like a fiddle while it's basement burned for nearly a century."

Now Dee's finger was poking the table, splashing condensation. "And where does the residue go? Fuck me—into the water table!"

Finn nodded vigorously. Repetition seemed to have inured him to Allan's continued pounding of the front door. "I'm not saying we don't have clean water according to PA and federal standards. But those standards haven't been tweaked, I imagine, to discern the potential effects of hydrocarbon burn-off on the water supply and human ingestion of it. It goes into everything, Dee—crops, yards, swimming pools, your backyard garden, evaporation, the clouds. Ah, the circle of life."

"So you're saying," Diana gripped her chin, pondering this, "That coal and coke runoff has been a self-cycling toxin in this area for decades? That it's like a mass lead or arsenic poisoning, and that explains the perpetual depression?"

Finn nodded. "Correlation does not equal causation, I know. But you remember when we were kids, and the Ad Council had those creepy commercials about kids eating lead paint? And, voilá! No more lead paint leads to no more lead paint eaters … but it didn't happen that way here. Sure, we once ingested lead paint, but what else are we still ingesting that might explain the decade-after-decade futility, even when *all* surrounding areas have had multiple cycles of crest and trough? Albeit, a helluva lotta West Virginia bears a resemblance to its Fayette cousin across the Mason-Dixon Line. Though the Mountaineers weren't coke barons and hung on as long as coal did in this country, their fires still burn. Look at the petrochemical plants in Ashland, KY. The narrative goes that this is Appalachia and will always be that way. Funny how the original white men who stole these mountains from the original Native Americans didn't seem addlepated, nor did those original Natives Americans who'd thrived here. And it was the invading white Appalachian residents—hard Scotts-Irish types—who'd had the grit and ingenuity to build a coal, coke, and hydrocarbon empire in the first place. Hell, where did oil get its foothold in the modern West? *Oil City, PA*, in the Allegheny Mountains north of here. I'm not saying this is some vast conspiracy or that it's anyone's fault. Maybe it is, but that's not the point—from a mental acuity and cognitive-behavioral development standpoint, Diana, we've been trying to fend off Muhammad Ali with both gloves tied behind our backs."

"Son of a bitch," she gasped.

"More like, 'son of a cousin,'" Finn snorted. "It's dismal as shit, and I may be wrong, but I've done more research on this than you'd think is countenanced. It's a narrative that helps me soldier on, despite the odds I face. It's shit, Dee, but I need it. I need some origin story to put it into perspective."

As Allan's pounding became more plaintive, Dee thought to herself, "And maybe now I know what it is I'm here to find out."

$$\infty \ \infty \ \infty$$

Two weeks later, on a Tuesday, Diana, left the house at 9:10am. "Hmm," she thought. "Either Shelly's staying on the Saturday schedule, despite school's letting out last Friday, or she's not the most punctual. Then again, she probably has kids in tow. No need to be a bitch about this."

Her irritation surprised her. After all, she'd agreed to the arrangement, but didn't Shelly have the ovaries to ask it herself? And, really, why would Shelly be so pent up about cleaning in front of her? Dee wasn't royalty, hadn't been around here for years, and wasn't staying here permanently. "I'm overthinking myself—again," she muttered aloud, as she turned onto Poplar Run Road, which, eventually would lead to 711, which, in turn, would become, 11 miles down the mountain, Crawford Avenue in Connellsville, which at last would lead to the Carnegie Public Library on the aforementioned Crawford Avenue, christened after Jeremiah Crawford, one of the founding fathers of Connellsville, along with Zachariah Connell, C'ville's namesake. She didn't have to do any research today, and even if she had, the Carnegie in C'ville would hardly have been up to snuff for the task. At least it would provide Wi-Fi, something that Rooster still hadn't seemed to arrange with cousin Nedry. "Miss Dee, I am so sorry," he'd sounded genuinely mortified over the landline phone. "It just slipped my mind. What with the kiddos gettin' out of school and Bobby's Little League, me and Shel' have been run ragged."

A week later, Rooster reported, "Don'tcha know it, Diana, but Ned hadn't told me he wuz takin' his kiddos to Myrtle Beach for a week to celebrate school bein' out. Ned and his wife are divorced, an' he gets 'em only so often, so I guess he's takin' 'vantage of it. Won't be back for a week, I guess. But callin' him to arrange it when he gets back it is at the top of my honey-do list—er, not that I'm sayin' yer my honey, Miss Dee! It's just a way of saying things, I guess. But I promise it'll get done. By the way, did you check out the coal bin? I can set you up real cheap with some coal as a winter back up. Just drive my pick-up right to the ol' coal hatch 'n shovel'er in."

Sigh. She was beginning to feel like Oliver Wendell Douglas of *Green Acres* fame to Rooster's Mr. Haney.

Actually, she didn't mind the delay. The weather had been gorgeous, Dee only now remembering that it wasn't always grey and dismal on the mountain, the endless winters still looming large in her memory. The Mountain Laurels had blossomed, as well as the red azaleas Mom had planted in the front yard, long ago, when she was all there. Their petals were wafted by the early-June breeze down to the surface of the creek pool, making it look like something out of Monet. Who could concentrate on neonatal research in such idyllic climes? Her return had had a bigger impact on her than she'd anticipated. She hadn't expected to *like* the old place, but she was finding, despite her memories and misgivings, that she genuinely did. Maybe the old homestead was putting its best foot forward for her homecoming. Maybe she was doing the same, letting her guard down to win a new relation to the place, one not colored by the compromises and violence that had carved jags in her heart. She was making her first tentative advances to encounter the place on new terms, in a way she hadn't been allowed as a child and teen. "You are claiming agency, Diana," Selene would say.

Damn it! She'd left fallow for two days a response to Selene's last email. She'd do it first thing at the library. Then Dee noticed that her laptop bag wasn't on the front seat. She braked the CR-V to stop at the intersection of Poplar Run and 711. It had always been a horrible intersection, with strip-mine trucks barreling down the slope from the north, to make a blind turn right at the intersection. Then she remembered there were no more coal trucks. As the car slid to a stop, she glanced into the back seat. No computer bag. Damn it! Had she put it in the trunk? She yanked the emergency brake and stepped out. The hatch window told her what she'd already suspected—she'd left the bag on the kitchen table. Shit. Back in the car. Turn around. "Oh well," she sighed. "It's not like I'm going anywhere in a hurry to do anything significant. Story of my life."

She gently braked the CR-V as she approached the steep driveway of the manse. Like riding a bike, she could never forget how to do this. Brake ever so slightly and feather the wheel so you hit the dip between the road berm and the start of the drive diagonally, saving your back-tooth fillings. Don't brake too long, because you have to hit the drive with a full head of steam. Even flooring the pedal won't be enough to get you up the drive if you don't have that head start. Dee grinned to herself. She'd forgotten the minute joy she used to take in doing this just right. Too many times she'd seen the UPS driver or a meter-reader putter out mid-driveway, only to drift back, to regroup in the gravel landing where, by necessity of the Everest-grade of the driveway, all had to park their cars in the winter, taking a long stair Daddy had built up the hillside, that she'd dubbed 'The 39,000 Steps' in homage to Hitchcock, a reference Dad and Brad had never gotten, though Mom, even in her catatonia, cracked a smile at one time.

Her front right tire hit a gravel patch that nearly yanked the wheel from her grasp, but she turned into it, not panicking, letting the momentum of the CR-V fill in what the fuel injection hadn't yet supplied. Either they now made Hondas better or she hadn't lost her touch because she felt no pause in the transition from momentum to asphalt grip, the roar of the motor shooting her up the grade effortlessly. It had been a blast bringing home her one-and-only college boyfriend for Thanksgiving during her Freshman year and watching his eyes get big as saucers as he saw her speeding toward the grade. "Aren't you gonna slow—"

At the top, prying his fingernails out of the dash, he gasped, " down?" and stared at her like she'd cut off his balls. She always knew that relationship wasn't bound to last. Daddy hadn't approved of Mr. Tight-Butt. Then again, the only thing Dad had approved of, including his own prodigious construction feats, was Brad's linebacker career at Penn State.

When she got to the top of the slope, she saw a paint-bare 90s Tacoma, cleaning equipment in the bed. "Shit," she thought. "Shelly's pride be damned, I have to get my computer." Perhaps she could sneak in. Maybe Shelly had heard the gravel flings of Dee's coming up the driveway and hid in a closet. But when Dee had gotten inside, the vacuum was running, a woman in a long ponytail, her back to Dee, pushing it. Dee beat on the wall, stomped her foot, but Shelly didn't hear. Not until she'd turned off the vac did she glimpse Diana and scream, falling to her seat in the couch behind her.

"I am so sorry!" Diana pled, her hands to her mouth. "I tried banging around to get your attention. I didn't mean to scare you."

The woman stared in panic, her face falling. Dee recognized her. "Mish? Mishie Ritenour? What're you doing here?"

Shelley looked down at the vac. "Hi, Dee. It's me. Go by 'Shelly' now."

∞ ∞ ∞

The pair spent an hour reminiscing. "I haven't seen you since ... since ..." Dee gasped.

"... Since after you left for Penn State and me for IUP."

Mishie seemed mortified, not happy at the reunion.

"You're—you're Rooster's ...?"

"Wife, Dee. Common-law. Never saw the point in officially

tying the knot. He's good to me and the kids, even if he isn't exactly Liam Neeson. Don't look so horrified."

Diana looked down at her hands as if they could help her monitor whatever her face was saying. "I'm not … horrified … just, well, *surprised*. I didn't know you even knew him that well."

"I didn't when you and I were in high school. But Indiana University of Pennsylvania didn't exactly work out. Guess I was never cut out for college, despite what Hickey the erstwhile guidance counselor tried to push on me. Came back and did some waitressing. Gawd, Red Lobster smells like hell on a body. Mom had a heart attack. She never took care of herself. Her assistance check and my waitress income didn't cover her prescriptions, and Medicaid is for shit. When she died, there was just too much debt. And I started fuckin' around. Guess I had to relieve the boredom. Roost came along. Knew Bobby wasn't his. Paid off my debt with his savings. My version of a sugar daddy. He adores me, Dee, though I can't say why. We ain't exactly *Modern Bride* cover material, but we manage."

Diana paused. "Don't say it like you're apologizing to me, Mish. You don't owe me a thing."

"Goddamn right I don't!" snapped Mishie. "Er, sorry. Guess I've a chip on my shoulder. I really am happy most days. Except when I come here."

Dee felt awful.

"Don't get me wrong, Dee. I treasure our past. But it's past. And even when we were besties, I never had a fraction of what you had, despite your generosity. I'm not blaming you, and I wouldn't have made it through high school if it hadn't been for you. But when I come here, I remember what I dreamed, and … well, even though reality is happily tolerable for me, it ain't what I dreamed, y'know?"

Dee chewed on this. "Is that why you had Rooster tell me to keep away when you come to clean? You're ashamed?"

Mishie's eyes smoldered. "Like hell I am! I just don't wanna hafta look to you like I am. Failed at that, I guess."

"Damn it, Mish, you know I'm not that way."

"Do I, Dee?" Michelle asked, staring at her. "Tell me what I'm to expect after 20 years. You left here. I don't blame you. I'm fuckin' proud of you. But I *didn't.* And I gotta say, without any shame, I'm glad I didn't. Leaving here was never gonna be me, no matter how hard you and I tried to convince ourselves. We kept each other going, Dee, through the hell that was high school. But it couldn't last. I ain't playin' the class card on you, old bestie. Things just pan out the way they pan out. You're a professor now, your head in books, like you always loved to be, till I brought you outta your shell. Students look up to you. I've got kids and a husband who, in their own way, depend on me. I'm okay with that. Really."

Diana looked around the room, finally alighting her eyes on Mish. "I'm okay with that, too, Mish. Really. I just didn't … know. I've been gone so long, it's like, coming back here, I'm meeting myself again, like I'd walled up that old me on the third floor."

"People change, sweetie," said Mishie.

"I know," whispered Dee, "but we'll always have plaster-of-Paris."

Shelly snorted. "I thought McPhee was gonna fuckin' stroke out!" she laughed. "She came back to the art room, and it was like *The Witches of Eastwick* crossed with *Beetlejuice!* We were covered in that shit, and so was her desk. Who thought the pottery wheel could fling with such force!"

Diana was squeezing her side, "We just wanted to mix it quicker! We didn't know!"

"Bullshit!" Michelle guffawed. "With all your construction background, you knew *exactly* what you were up to. You *wanted*

McPhee's jugular to pop out. She went totally apeshit. You were always the master planner, and no one, including Principal "asleep-at-the-wheel" Dorfey, ever had a clue. Butter wouldn't melt in the mouth of that sweet little Atestesso girl."

"I know, I know. But I swear I didn't premeditate stuff like that. It just came to me, like I was someone else, on autopilot."

"And you *knew* they'd blame me! Fuck, I didn't care. Self-fulfilling prophecy. Bring it. They were gonna come after me anyway. Why not make 'em feel smug about their judgment?"

"I never counted on that, Mish, I swear. I always stepped in and told them *I* was the one behind it."

"Which only led them to peg you as the virtuous one I'd corrupted into always taking the fall. My God, though, McPhee woulda taken a huge fall if she'd done with that boxcutter what I think she was planning. Thank our stars, Finn looked in and broke up the party. She wanted to slit our throats!"

Diana calmed down. "I talked with Finn the other day."

"Why the hell didn't you hook up with him, Dee? Everyone thought you two were, at the minimum, friends with benefits."

"Finn, despite his gruff exterior, never fostered that mindset, despite the banter I know he heard in the locker room. That time he beat the shit out of Kress? Finn told me it was 'cuz that little snake asked Finn if I was available snatch. And you know me—I was *not* about sex with high school pricks. Ugh. It's a wonder they bathed."

"'Least you got some clearance for having Brad as a brother. Sister of the football god gets some privileges. That, and they thought if they fucked around with his sis, he'd bring back the Nittany Lion defensive line to lay waste to 'em."

Dee shook her head. "Like Brad ever cared about me like that."

Mishie nodded. "Oh, he cared enough about you to make sure you didn't dent his legacy. I get the idea that the large fish in Connellsville's small pond quickly learned he was a guppy in the State College ocean of sharks. That is, until Sandusky, the pervert, put him in that nickelback alignment, small linebacker he was, and he made that incredible interception that commenced the 61-7 slaughter of Michigan State and won the team the $4.5-million-bounty of the Capital One Bowl on New Year's Day instead of the Toilet Bowl in Flushing on a mid-December weekday. The bucks and media exposure mean everything in college ball. JoePa had his pride, but getting the $$ for the program and the rest of PSU's athletic endeavors was his triumph. He didn't care, when Cameron Wake went down with injury, that pipsqueak Brad Atestesso took Wake's place. Keepin' it on the down-low in the Paisan'-child-molester brotherhood, y'know."

"Geesh," Dee gulped, "I knew you were always into football, Mish, but I had no clue how Brad had started in that bowl game. All I knew was that he couldn't—or, more likely, *didn't* want to come home when our father died on New Year's Eve. Said he'd already said his goodbyes and that 'Dad would want me to be here, Di', not sitting by his dead carcass in Petrucci's Funeral Home. It's my chance to enlighten the opinions of the pro scouts.' Pfft. Like there was any chance of that unless, the National Ego League scouts were in Orlando that day."

Mish smiled. "I'd like to think my football knowledge is the one skill set from high school I still use today. Comes in handy in engaging conversation with Roost and Bobby. They know they gotta keep on their toes with me. It's the little things, Dee, that keep ya goin', y'know?"

"Speaking of little things, are your kids here? I'd love to meet them."

Michelle looked down at the floor and played with a ring on her finger. "They're with Rooster today. He didn't have anything goin'—rarely has anything goin', to tell the truth. Employment for a 56-year-old hick ain't exactly growin' on trees in Fayettenam. He brings in the small potatoes you and Brad give us for babysitting this joint."

"Okay," said Dee. "But some other time, alright? I'm here for a year. I could babysit so you and Rooster could actually go out and enjoy yourselves for a change."

Mishie squirmed. "Actually, Dee, I left my wild days back in high school, not that those were terribly wild. Takin' care of Mom and now Bobby, Michelle, and Roost kinda roots me. We aren't the goin'-out types, anyway. And, honestly, 'cuz you and I could always talk straight, Dee, you and I don't have anything in common anymore, 'cept your being back here for the next 12 months. You may have the time, but my life is the way it is. I'm set in my ways, y'know? Don't wanna upset the applecart to carve out a place in my life for you, only to have you leave again. I ain't blamin' you, Dee. It's just the way it is."

Diana's heart ached.

"And, if you don't mind, Dee, not to twist the knife in any deeper, call me 'Shelly' from now on. Rooster never knew me … before. All he knows me as is Shelly. And I'm used to that. Plus, it wasn't bullshit what Rooster told you about me not wantin' anyone watch my cleaning. I know you wouldn't ever stand over me, nitpicking my work. But I like workin' alone, 'cept when I bring the kids, to teach 'em the value of a job well done. So, if you wouldn't mind …"

"No, no! Of course not, Mish—er, Shelly. I completely understand. Lots of water under the bridge and all … but Shel'?"

"Yeah, Dee?"

"It was all good water, right? Clean, cool, and good."

Shelly smiled. "Yeah, Dee. Yeah. Ain't got no regrets."

∞ ∞ ∞

Two days later, a week-long rain killed any chances of satellite-dish Ned arriving and Dee's fulfilling her wish to dangle her toes in the creek pool. The weather hadn't heated up enough to merit a swim in its cold water, and something told her that, even if it was Texas-hot, she wouldn't swim there again. Mish was right. Water under the bridge. Keep it on the down-low.

On the first day of the rains, she felt like the Pevensies in *The Lion, the Witch, and the Wardrobe*—here it was Summer holidays and she was trapped inside. A good book! Yes! Something she hadn't indulged in for years. She went to download *The Chronicles of Narnia* to her phone only to realize that, on the mountain, she had no signal and therein no access to the digital world. Never mind. Reading hadn't been the same since Luna …

… Hold on! Were all those old books still on the third floor? Ugh. They'd be musty as fuck after all these years and no HVAC.

The third floor. She paused. She'd already scripted her remodeling plans and had even hauled all the supplies she could fit in the CR-V. Let the 84-Lumber delivery personnel take on either the Denali Driveway or The 39,000 Steps. Until such a juncture, she hadn't the lumber to rough out anything, but she could do the prep work. Yet, the third floor was the last renovation on her list, *if* she had the time to get to it during the year. But to sell it to a prospective bed-and-breakfast or ski-lodge buyer with deep pockets, she'd need the bait of extra Victorian-charm bedrooms and bathroom to haul in the biggest return. Her stomach dropped when she thought of the vintage clawfoot bathtub up there. Why the dread? If anything, that item alone, even if she never remodeled the upper story, would fetch a hefty price at auction, or even on eBay. Was she intimidated at the prospect of moving it? Even if she couldn't find a buyer willing to foot the bill of retrieving it, she knew her way around a pulley and winch. Blue-Line Rentals might even have a mini-lift that their truck could navigate up the driveway. Still, the image of the tub settled with an unnerving thud in the back of her mind. She shook her head and rubbed her eyes.

"Where were we?" she said out loud. "Christ, I'd better get used to talking to myself—I'm here solo for the year, and it's not like Toastmasters International is gonna haul ass up my driveway in the dead of winter."

Her driveway. She liked the sound of that, even though the whole point of being here was to speedily and profitably make this place *not* hers. But she couldn't sell it for the price she pondered if she didn't renovate it. And she couldn't renovate it without getting off her ass. A back-of-her-thoughts impulse said to never do the third floor, asking-price-be-damned, but she at that moment made the resolution to halt the second-guessing and to stop listening to that whining, cringing Diana. This was *her* place, goddammit. Nothing was off limits.

"To the third floor we go!" she announced to walls surrounding her. "Lead in, MacDuff!"

∞ ∞ ∞

Her old bedroom remained exactly like she'd left it the last time she'd been here—Dad's death and funeral, the lost semester. She'd come home from State College as soon as she had gotten the ambulance-service message that Daddy'd had his first stroke. After a week in the hospital, then the Greensburg rehab center, it was either put Dad in a home or take him to the manse and have home health come to do PT. He'd looked at her with mournful, even terrified eyes. Putting him in a nursing home was out of the question. That's where he'd sent Mom—he knew too well what awaited him there. He still couldn't talk, but he responded to PT, though the stroke meant that he most likely would never walk on his own again. Even before the stroke, Dad had never really been the same since his accident with the saber saw when she was 16 and had to rush him down the mountain to the hospital, heart in her mouth, as she'd only just gotten her driver's permit.

The eyes of terror, she came to call them, never left Dad's face, even after she and Brad had brought him home.

"Why do I have to stay with him at all?" Brad had demanded. "It's my senior year, and I have a football career to think of!"

She had no idea where *that* had come from, considering that he'd never started a game his entire Penn-State tenure. The only games he'd been in were, in his words, "Fourth-quarter mop-ups versus the Iowa School for Blind Girls. How can any scout see my true abilities *that* way?"

"And I *don't* have a college career?" she'd rejoined.

"Jesus, Di', you just started your sophomore year! You can defer a semester or two. I'm on the brink of my future!"

"Brad, I'm not holing up for the autumn and winter with Dad, like I have no life. You've seen the look on his face—it's like he's petrified of us. You can as easily haul your ass down here mid-week, and I'll do weekends. Your profs already make your studies a piece of cake 'cuz you're on the football team. Surely they can let some shit slide, knowing your dad just had a stroke. As it is, I already could flunk two of my classes because of absences, and I've given my profs notes from Dad's doctor vouching for why I've been gone."

"Then tell them you need to take family medical leave or some shit like that. I can't do that, and I can't stay here another day, 'cuz I got practice throughout the week and games on the weekend. The choice here is clear, Di'."

"It's a choice for *you,* Brad. *You're* the one all but saying you don't give a shit about Dad!"

"Then put him in the fucking old-ass people's home, Di', but that'll be *your* choice, 'cuz my future is non-negotiable!"

So, she'd weathered a long, rainy autumn with her Dad, watching him die.

In the closet of the third-floor master bedroom, the box of CDs she opened flooded that time back to mind. Kate Bush's *The Dreaming* and *Hounds of Love*, two old favorites from Junior and Senior High, as well as Genesis' *Nursery Chryme, Foxtrot,* and *Selling England by the Pound,* steeled her to face Dad's haunting eyes. The weary weeks made her feel like Cathy in *Wuthering Heights*, her Dad some misbegotten, stroke-ravaged Heathcliff, the Freudian associations of which she'd forced to the back of her thoughts.

Bathing Dad in that loathsome clawfoot bathtub. Wiping the dribble from his lips as she helped him feed himself. Watching him agonizingly try to do his PT homework—picking up marbles with his toes, to deposit them into a metal bowl. Cleaning him up after his going to the bathroom. She'd been pursuing a Bachelor's in Biomedical Sciences, to prep her for an eventual nursing career. Dad that autumn had made her the nurse she now was.

The worst were the nights, listening to his uneven breathing, worrying that he'd die while she slept. If he could talk, he chose not to. Maybe he was taking Mom's way out, via the silent treatment. But that was ridiculous. He was recovering from a stroke, not punishing Dee. Besides, what had she done to merit punishment? Was it just being herself? Being a daughter instead of another football star? She'd hear his breath catch, jolting her out of bed to check on him, only to see his eyes locked on her in stark fear. Was he contemplating death? But what had he to mourn? Guilt about putting Mom into a nursing home where she was living out her days? But no, no. If anything, Mom seemed happier at the home, though she still never talked to anyone. Maybe her comparative cheer there had to do with their therapies. Dad had sold the construction company and spared no expense for Mom's care, though, while she'd been in the house, he'd hardly shown Mom a commensurate devotion. Always the fortunes of company drove him. Back then, Mom had been totally functional. Just woke up one day when Dee had been on the verge of age 13 and stopped talking to anyone. If Dad or Brad asked her for a sandwich, she'd dutifully get up and make it. She still did all the shopping, cleaning, and school or sports transport back in those days. Just said nothing. To anyone. It was like she'd made the career decision to stop talking, as if words were a waste. Diana could see how words were definitely a lost cause with Dad and Brad. In her earliest awareness, Dee had taken it as a given of life that Mom and Dad didn't have the best of marriages. She thought every kid's home life was that way. It seemed to work for them. Dad had a growing construction company to run. He came from a long line of Italian-immigrant workaholics, always striving, always seeing the most recent conquest as a prelude to a greater challenge, with no time for the preening of laurels. Mom had resigned herself to that reality. Age six, Diana remembered a day when Daddy had brought home roses to Mom, and a glow spread over her face like Dee had never seen. It hadn't been the roses, though. It was the attention, the acknowledgement that Dad had given her. That evening, Dad and Mom got a babysitter to stay the night with Dee and Brad and went into Pittsburgh for what Dee surmised had been planned as a night on the town. But when they'd returned, they weren't speaking to each other. Dad paid the babysitter and drove her home. Later that day, when Dee and Dad were fitting in the new furnace he'd brought home the week before (yes, as a six-year-old she'd grooved on such things and was hella good at them), he'd cussed a fit because he couldn't turn a rusted bolt that clamped down the old furnace. Dee had stared at him in wonder, for he was normally up to any challenge, using work-smarter strategies where brawn didn't suffice. When he threw the wrench to the ground, Diana reached up to stroke the stubble on his chin and kiss him on the cheek. He fell to his knees, sobbing and hugging her, in shudders and tears Dee never saw from him again.

At no time after that could she remember Dad and Mom so much as exchange a peck on the cheek, Mom saving her love for Dee and Brad, sparing no hug for them … till the day she stopped talking. Was it because Mom knew that her daughter had started her period, having detected blood on her sheets in the morning? Was Mom not up to dealing with anyone no longer a child? She'd laid the mini-pads on Dee's bed and walked out the door in a silence that she never thereafter broke.

To cope during the nights with stricken Dad, Diana donned her Walkman headphones, setting the disc to eternal repeat. If she woke in the morning and he was dead, then, she would deal with it. Living or dead, she was certain that his eyes wouldn't change, like he was terrified of her, like she had the power of life and death, like he was dependent on her to stay alive but feared unto the grave that she would keep him in never-ending pain.

The third-floor bath still showed its original narrow-board hardwood floors. She and Dad had retro-fitted the first- and second-floor baths with new plumbing that had necessitated taking up the floor. As careful as they were, they could preserve only a third of the original flooring. So, she and Dad had replaced the floors with salvaged vintage tiles from his various residential demolitions/guttings. Not so the third floor, like every other room on that story, Dad had sealed it off from his ambitions. Not long after his saber-saw catastrophe that had shredded his thighs and genitalia, she'd worked herself up to asking him if she could occupy the third floor, renovating it as she went. He hadn't batted an eyelash, immediately acquiescing, which, come to think of it now, was extraordinary. The haranguing he gave her about her driver's permit, mandating that she could not get it till she was 16 (and not the state-allowed 15-and-a-half) had been rivaled only by his perfectionism on every work project they'd done together since she'd first started tagging along with him.

Dee had been born in the manse, her parents having bought it when Brad had been only three. Back then, it was a tremendously risky proposition for them to sink debt into that money pit even when Dad's aggressive expansion of the modest-by-comparison home-renovation service he inherited from his father, a first-generation immigrant, pushed him into obligations, both financial and vocational, that made any attempt to remodel the mansion impossible till Dee had reached age five. By then, his company had taken off as a large contracting concern, delivering everything from major concrete foundations and steel-frame construction, to repair and renovation, to turn-key school and hospital projects. Till that point, the old mansion had sucked money in the form of a principal-light/interest-heavy early term, squinching their means of paying for big-ticket remodeling items. Mom did what she could in the way of small projects, as it was the money she'd inherited from her parents, killed untimely in an auto accident, that had made the original purchase possible.

Dee's earliest memories alternated between Mom and Dad incessantly arguing about the house and their out-of-the-blue working harmoniously together in the rare instances Mom could get Dad to help her. Diana's fondest Christmas memory came from the holidays when she was four and the whole family sat around the glowing fireplace that Mom and Dad, adhering strictly to Mom's freehand design, together built out of hearthstones and tiles that Dad had rescued from the dismantling of the old coke counting house and headquarters originally owned by Chester Frick, the man who had built an empire on coal and died to himself and that empire in this very manse, which the old baron had had built in 1909 by the finest architects and construction engineers from Pittsburgh, sparing no expense. After work, from which Daddy uncharacteristically came home early, night after night that November, the two whispered to each other and laughed, stealing kisses, her father never showing his usual terseness and obsession with completing the job beyond spec and perfection. It was the sad truth that that time had been the highpoint of their relationship in Dee's lifetime. Shared projects and harmony after that were non-existent. So five-year-old Diana filled the gap.

At first, Daddy had rebuffed her attempts to help him. "Go on, Dormouse! Vai! Play with your dolls. Mama buys lots of them for you. This is no place for a bambina."

Young Dee had found his reaction puzzling. "But Daddy, if building is for boys, how come Brad's not here?"

Crouching over the sawhorses with a circular saw poised to cut, Daddy had pulled off his goggles, blinking the sweat out of his eyes. "Bradley is playing football with his friends."

"He's always playing football, Daddy. Even when he's not, he doesn't help you. He watches TV or plays video games."

Her father had sighed. "He's a boy, and he works hard at football. Gonna be a big star, which is better than having to work for a living."

"What if I wanna be a star at 'struction, Daddy? I could be your star helper!"

Daddy had paused, eyeing her up and down. "Bah, you're just like Mama. Go help her in the kitchen!"

"Mama's good in the kitchen *and* with 'struction. Why can't I be, too?"

"'Cuz you're being a pain-in-the-ass. I have to cut this, to frame-out the downstairs bathroom. It's dangerous, see?" He revved the saw, which, instead of scaring Dee, intrigued her. "Go on! Go! Get outta here!" He bellowed.

Dee retreated to the shadows at the bottom of the basement staircase, peering from the stairwell as the saw churned out sawdust and sheared length after length of 2x4s. Dad had then trudged back upstairs to fit the pieces. Dee followed, mesmerized by the way he measured and sized, calculated and scribbled on a small notepad he pulled from his work-shirt breast pocket, stitched with the Atestesso & Son Construction logo Mom had designed. Diana stealthily trailed after him upstairs, then back to the dark basement, which was no longer scary because she was here with Daddy, the saws and drills and angle cutters and lathe all roaring a victory to her ears that chased away any monsters in the shadows.

As he lifted the saw to cut more lengths, she dared whisper, "Daddy!"

He hadn't heard her and started cutting, but the saw unexpectedly bucked, making him drop it and jump back.

"Daddy!" she now raised her voice.

"WHAT!!??" he roared.

Unperturbed, she pranced over to the splintered chunk of wood that had collapsed from the buck notch and held it up to him. She hardly minded the hotness of the piece's cut edge. "This piece is too small," she said.

"What?"

"It's too small, Daddy! You measured 16 inches, but da centers are 16, so you hafta cut it longer for dat one space, or it won't fit da corner."

If you've ever seen a cat follow a flashlight beam back and forth, you'd approximate how her father's gaping-mouth and eyes switched repeatedly from Dee's visage to the plank in her hands.

After a long pause, he retrieved the notepad from his breast pocket, reading it over three times, then snatched the tape measure from his belt, slapping it onto the piece she held and measuring that three times.

"You're right, Dormouse," he whispered, like he noticed her presence for the very first time. "How … how could you tell?"

"I watched you."

"B-but … how could you tell? Do you know numbers already?"

"Most of them," she explained solemnly.

"To this precision?" he asked aghast.

"I don't know what p'cision means," she replied.

"How could you tell just by looking, Dormouse?"

She shrugged. "I don't know. I just watch, and the numbers come into my head."

He collapsed into his work chair and pondered this for what felt like an eternity.

"Daddy?" she asked. He looked up again like she'd just entered the space. "Can I put down dis piece of wood?"

He opened his hand, and she deposited the cut into it. When he put it onto the work bench, she hoisted herself into his lap.

"Okay, Dormouse Di'," he said. "Listen to me." He grabbed the saw. "You know what kind of saw this is?"

"It's da circle one!"

"Right! You see the gloves and goggles Daddy wears?"

"Yeah! You look like Iron Man!"

He laughed! "I wish I was Tony Stark, Dormouse! Or at least made his armor! Like his outfit, these things are for safety." He yanked the saw's plug out of the wall and turned it blade-up. "Touch," he commanded. "Gentle, Dormouse, gentle."

Like a holy-land pilgrim gazing at a relic of the true cross, Dee looked in awe at the saw teeth smiling up at her and touched her finger to a tooth. She looked up at him.

"It's sharp, Dormouse, eh?"

"Of course it's sharp, Daddy. Hasta cut da wood!"

He'd belly laughed, Dee feeling the rumbles against her back, all the way to her toes.

She didn't make her first cuts until she was seven. By then, he'd put her through every safety drill and gopher duty imaginable. Only when she was older did she appreciate that hers was an apprenticeship more thorough than any professional got.

The two of them transformed that house, except the third floor.

∞ ∞ ∞

She toed the extremely dusty narrow-board flooring under the equally dusty clawfoot tub. Something dark was under the dust. Several large blots. Dee bent down, brushing the dust with her fingers. Dark-brown blotches that wouldn't scrape off stained the wood. Blood. She never remembered blood spots there. Dee had taken countless baths in that tub. Had she cut herself in her earliest attempts at shaving her legs? With that much blood she ought to have remembered. But that begged the question of, if so much blood, why hadn't she cleaned it? Her father had handed down to her his perfectionist ways—she wouldn't have missed a mess of this size.

Dee didn't want to alter these floors in any way—they were a huge selling point. But if she couldn't remove the blood, she'd have to strip, finish, stain, and varnish them across the third floor. She hadn't calculated *that* tiresome task into her plans.

The first order was to clean the entire third story. Despite the years of no habitation, the third floor, Diana decided after the clean up, actually needed little renovation—except for the

157

goddamn mirror/medicine-cabinet some idiot in the 1950s thought was the single necessary amenity to the bathroom. That simply had to come out, but it wouldn't be hard. She wasn't a master plasterer, but she could always find a vintage mirror at a thrift shop that would cover any plaster sins she might craft to mend the hole left by the vacant monstrosity. Before cleaning, she'd pondered redoing the plumbing to afford a walk-in shower but concluded there was simply no way to incorporate that particular amenity in a way consistent with the vintage aesthetic. People could walk into a shower at any number of homes or hotels. How many of those boasted an era-genuine Victorian bath with now completely unfindable wormy chestnut narrow-board floors? In fact, the more she stayed up here, the more she felt back at home. It had been her only refuge in her high school years—from both the outside world and her dysfunctional family. She stared out the window of the master bedroom which was comprised of the 270-degree turreted tower that was the singular aesthetic of the manse's architecture. Up here, she'd felt warm when all the world and the floors below had frozen her out. From up here, she could see the creek pool, dotted with flower petals in the spring, shimmers in the summer, leaves in the autumn, and snow drifts in the winter. She'd never tired of skating on the frozen pool, even when its solidity was questionable, but she'd stopped swimming in it after her first year of Junior High. It wasn't a beach, and the thought of water snakes had crept up on her in puberty. Serpents were supposed to symbolize goddess power and mystique, but puberty and adolescence were the single most powerless era of her life … until Clay had stolen Luna.

Luna. If Diana had her here, she'd rock her on summer nights in the porch swing, holding her close just like she'd hugged herself through countless tear-filled summer nights in the window seat of her tower prison. Diana would nestle Luna in new window-seat cushions and sing to her while the winter frost curled wisps on the panes, just like she'd fallen asleep during the winters of her freshman and sophomore years to the

music she'd never stopped playing. The music that blotted out
the silence of her mother, the departure of Brad to college, and
the wounded brooding of her father after the saber-saw
accident. At first, Dad wouldn't hear of her having Mish over,
mortified at an outsider's seeing his wife catatonic. After the
accident, though, Dee just stared him down when Mish walked
in the door. The pair then laughed all the way up to the third
floor to smoke their pot. Even if Dad smelled it, which was
unlikely, as the third floor drafted exceptionally well, the saber
saw had carved something essential out of him. Either that, or
Diana had gotten old enough to see through him in a way he
couldn't deny. When Dee told him she was installing a power
dumbwaiter to the hallway outside her third-floor bedroom, he
didn't hesitate to give her his credit card. As an adolescent, she
never felt she'd demanded much, especially since Mom had
checked out of Dee's life starting at puberty and Dad was
zombie-like around her after the saber saw. But she'd been
implacable in her resolution that she had to have it. Dad had
done no construction since the accident, which was a relief to
Dee in that she wanted to do the dumbwaiter totally herself.
Audacious in its conception and execution, it pushed her to the
limit of her abilities, demanding she pore the manse blueprints
and specs. Further, it had required all sorts of remodeling of
walls in the second, first, and basement stories. Why she'd been
so adamant about doing it had remained a mystery to her until
now. She turned 360 degrees around the third-floor master
bedroom, taking it all in. "I somehow knew I'd be back here,"
she said aloud in a quiet but equally determined voice as when
she'd announced she was installing the dumbwaiter. "To finish
the job."

The dumbwaiter not only made her life in the castle of hell
more bearable during her adolescence and, later, her nursing
Dad through his death, it also taught her the bones, joints,
marrow, and every nook and cranny of this her former prison.
Now, she returned to transform the place in more than just
appearance, but elementally. It would no more imprison. Its

liquidation would free her to take up Finn on the prospects of a restaurant in a place more welcoming to Finn's unique talents than the endless coal-mine fire of Fayette County. Plus, it meant she wouldn't have to haul tools and hardware up the steps. But all that depended on whether the motor was still operable after its long layoff.

Ever since Daddy apprenticed her all those years ago, the basement had ceased to be to her what it had been to Kevin McAllister in the first *Home Alone*—a den of demons. The smells of must, dampness, grease, sawdust, and electric-motor ozone triggered safety, belonging, and purpose to her. But this time an even more pleasant surprise awaited her in the cellar—the dumbwaiter motor was in tip-top shape, cleaned, greased, and equipped with pristine belts. This mint condition matched the pulleys in the top of the shaft, as well as the integrity of the cables. "Well, Mr. Rooster Cogbert, apparently your management of this place is more than worth your delays in getting cousin Ned out here to install the internet."

∞ ∞ ∞

She had the chance to thank him in-person the next week, with the sun again shining and Ned in tow. From their post at the creek pool, she and Rooster watched the satellite-dish champion of the mountains scale several ladders while Diana dangled her feet in the chill but refreshing water.

"You ain't worried 'bout no water snakes, Miss Diana?" Rooster teased her.

She smiled back. "I think my toes will hypnotize them. See?" She lifted out her feet, evidencing the pedicure she went into Greensburg to procure two days before.

"Woo-wee!" he exclaimed. "Shel's feet would look amazing with one o' them pedis, but it ain't something we can afford on the regular."

"I don't know, Rooster," winked Dee. "Her birthday's coming up, and your not-completely-independently-wealthy boss/manse occupant might slip you a bonus for just that purpose."

"What I done to earn a bonus, other'n delay your satellite gettin' here?"

"For one," Diana counted on her toes, "You long-distance put up with my brother and his cheap ways for years. Two, I was happily surprised to find the dumbwaiter and motor in as good of shape as when I'd installed that apparatus 20-plus years ago. And third, all my Daddy's tools are clean, oiled, and accounted for. I'm not saying you ever would have been tempted to steal, Rooster Cogbert, but I can imagine that you borrowed them as needed. Good for you, returning them better than you found them."

"You installed that dumbwaiter? The whole thing, Miss Diana? I thought it had come original with the place and that your papa had upgraded it with the motor. Oh, and, yeah, I mighta borried some tools here 'n there."

"The dumbwaiter was entirely my brain- and labor-child. I framed and carpentered the shaft and its fitting throughout the house."

Rooster pulled off his cap. "Diana Atestesso, why the hell you a perfessor? You could be makin' bank as a carpenter or a buildin' engineer. Hell, restart your Daddy's company! I'd be one o' yer foremen in a heartbeat!"

"I prefer 'superintendent,' Rooster. Gender-neutral."

"Oh yeah, whatever. I'd be yours no matter whatchacallit."

She lifted an envelope to him. "What you are right now for me, Rooster, is a friend, and you deserve this."

He stepped back like she was handing him a water snake. "Miss Dee, all kidding aside, there ain't never been water snakes in here since I helped your papa build the dam, and cleanin' the dumbwaiter and the tools was just part of my job. After all, it helped me haul stuff up floors 'n such. My back ain't what it usta be. I don't deserve nuthin' extra."

"Then take it because I want you to have it. I'm here to make something new of this place. And that should start and end with the people here. Besides, if you don't take it, I'm going to let the envelope and its contents float over the dam."

He let her put it in his hand.

"It's not much, Rooster—just what I calculated I would have had to spend on power tools and refurbishing the dumbwaiter. Better going to you than Lowe's."

He folded it, tucking it into his back pocket. "Now that you put it that way, I can live with that on my conscience."

"Good. That makes me happier than twiddling my toes in a mountain stream."

"There's something else that'd be on my conscience if I didn't tell you right now, 'cuz I fergot the other day. But it's more convenient now that we're down here." He pointed to the dam head. "Lemme show you sumthin you need to see."

She replaced her sandals and followed him. "Now, you cain't see it so good right now with the water higher in the spring, but notice that little fault line there?"

There was a crack in the river-rock mortar comprising the dam. It hadn't reached the top of the dam but nonetheless proceeded down underneath the water deeper than she could see.

"Now I know yer a wizard with dumbwaiters, but I'm thinking you don't know as much 'bout dams. I didn't either, till your pappy hired me to help him build this. Since then, through the years, I've built a few for rich folks with fancy backyards who contracted with Atestesso. Normally, this wouldn't pose no worry, 'cuz this is solid concrete 'n cement, with rock and rebar foundation. Jes a crack on one side, an' no more, sumthin you'd 'spect to have with mortar 'n such. But come over here, t'other side o' the dam."

They traipsed to the other side. The crack on the pool-side had been about a third of the way to the middle, the entire dam being about 10 feet wide. "I need ya to step inta the spillway with me, if ya don't mind." They slopped into the splashing water that descended about eight feet from the damn crest. He pointed to a matching fissure on the spillway-side.

"Now, see, agin, this normally wouldn't be no concern, as you'd 'spect that crack to kinda just horseshoe right over the top of the dam, with no depth of any kind. But here," he hoisted himself up on a foothold so he could reach his finger to a spot on the crack. "See here, where the water ain't spillin' an' you kin see the crack dry-like?"

"Yes, right there," she pointed. "But what's that stain trailing down with it?"

"That's what I'm sayin', Miss Diana. "That kinda triangle stain around the crack is where water's comin' through, ever so slightly. An' see that droplet?"

"Yes, but isn't that just a splash from the spillway?"

"I wish," Rooster said, dabbing it away with his finger. "Now wait."

The pair watched as, inexorably, another drop had formed in place of the one he'd blotted away, eventually welling into a tear that trickled down the dam side. "Translation, Miss Dee—water's gettin' through."

"Is the dam in danger of failing any time soon?"

"Wouldn't the insurance company like to know that, 'specially if some kids are playin' here and it busts. I ain't no engineer, but I can tell you that there's another crack in the middle that we cain't see it, 'cuz it's under water. See, last year, when it was a milder winter'n most, me figurin' this dam was nearly 40 years old, I waited till the water was at its lowest in February, durin' a hard freeze. Came out here in m' insulated boots and dug in to check the silt level, which I then cleaned out the rest o' that day."

"Then you definitely deserve what's in that envelope, Rooster!"

"Yeah, it wasn't an easy time, but you might wanna hear this afore you thank me too quick. See, if a dam is built right, in sorta harmony with its surroundings, it'll last forever, just like a nat'ral canyon wall—that is, till the dam silts over, 'n the dam becomes a glorified waterfall. So, thinkin' I wuz doin' you a favor 'n cleaning out the silt, I actually exposed them fault lines to the punishment o' the water. The water wa'n't comin' through thanks to the silt, but then I came along. I'm sorry, ma'am."

"How could you have known?" protested Diana. "You were doing your job. Is it simply a matter of my Dad not having built the dam right?"

Rooster scratched his stubble. "Like I said, I ain't no engineer, and when I was helpin' him build it, I was a green-behind-the-ears 18-year-old. But having nearly 40 years o' construction under m' belt, I've noticed sumthin 'bout everythin' a body builds—no matter how hard ya try to make it perfect, it's that tryin' to make it perfect that works in flaws you cain't see. It's like yer workin' so hard to make it right over here that you don't see the domino flaws yer creatin' over there. It ain't imperfect so much as just bein' human. Some of the best work I ever done had spots and stains in it only I could see. Takes a while but you git over thinkin' it's flawed when no one else don't. It's like leavin' your mark—ya learn to live with it. Or not."

Dee's brow furrowed. "As you've noted, neither of us is an

engineer, Rooster, but if you were to follow your gut, what do you think of the reliability of this dam? I don't have the money, time, or expertise to rebuild it. And rather than just waiting for it to break, I'd rather bust it myself and release Poplar Run back to Mother Nature. I know I sound like a patient with a terminal diagnosis, but how long do we have?"

"Lessee, it wuz last year I found them cracks, an' I checked 'em through the spring. This one here grew 'bout an inch, 'n the one just past the middle there grew three inches. On one hand, this damn could last as long as the Grand Canyon. On the other, well, water ain't no more predictable than the next heavy-rain. I don't know what kinda nat'ral strains would pop it at one or t'other fissure, but if a body would wanna bust this dam theirself, just aim a good 10-pound sledgehammer punch to one o' them fault lines, and the water'll do the rest. Ooo, but I wouldn't wanna be in this spillway way when the hammerin' happens. Water's more dangerous 'an fire, for sure."

∞ ∞ ∞

"So, how's your summer going?" Finn asked two months later. Monday's were dark at Finn's, and namesake Finn elected to take the rare day off, delaying any distributor deliveries till Tuesday. He'd brought a picnic basket overflowing with craft beer, meats, cheeses, nuts, and dried fruit. They dined by the creek pool, something Dee had convinced Finn was feasible, considering his justifiable fear of poison ivy, which had, in childhood, put him into anaphylaxis so bad his throat closed over. "Why not your wrap-around porch?" he'd asked a week earlier over the phone. "You said you'd repainted it and stocked it with furniture."

"'Stocked' and 'furniture' are slight exaggerations," answered Diana. "We can set up the ancient card table and chairs, ooh-la-la! But I'm telling you, there's no poison ivy by the stream or anywhere up here."

"You mean," Finn countered, "There's no poison ivy that you've ever *noticed.*"

"Finn! I shit you not. The altitude precludes poison ivy. It's never been here. What *is* here is August, which'll be humid as fuck on the porch. The shade of the trees and cool of the stream make the pool the perfect place."

"So you're okay soaking your feet in a puddle full of water snakes?"

"For Christ's sake, Umble J. Finn! Crawling out of that hole of a bar and into the sunlight won't turn you into ashes. I *also* have told you that there haven't been water snakes *ever* in the pool."

"Is the altitude too high for 'em?" His voice buzzed back over the land line. Dee was at the ancient wind-up phone in the front parlor. She literally had to wind it up to get the operator to patch through her call. She should've gotten a cheap-ass touch-tone phone at Best Buy in Uniontown the other day. And she still had to run land-line wiring and jacks up to the third floor.

"I'm beginning to think *you're* the one who can't take the altitude," she quipped back. "We've been trying to plan this all summer. Before you know it, the leaves will be falling, then the snow will make it harder for you to come up the mountain."

"Ah," Finn had noted, "At least the snow'll keep the poison ivy down."

She had, in the end, prevailed, and Finn seemed to be enjoying the picnic, despite himself.

"So, how's your summer going," he asked, "I mean, project-wise—both construction and writing?"

Dee grimaced. "About that writing … yeah, not so much. I figure when winter sets in, if it's not a mild one, I'll have incentive to hole up on the third floor and publish my little nursie heart out."

"Ah, procrastination!" laughed Finn, quaffing his saison. "The world's number-one participant sport."

"I'm a world champion, at least when it comes to fulfilling the terms of my tenure. But as for the renovation, I've been gangbusters on the third floor. It's done! Paint, trim, bathroom, bedrooms, new window-seat cushions, new screens, ugly wallpaper gone, windows resealed, you name it! The only thing I haven't replaced is that fucking medicine cabinet. I haven't been able to find the right mirror to replace it. Otherwise, I could open the third story as a bed-and-breakfast—Ma Atestesso's Mountain Arms Boardinghouse—if I wasn't already entrenched up there. Believe it or not, it's high enough to catch updrafts when the windows on all four sides are open and is darned pleasant. I'm glad I tried it before attempting to install AC. I should've accounted for it's having been architected and built before the revolution of residential HVAC. They were a lot more resourceful in 1909 when it came to building with natural ventilation as a must. My next stop is the attic and roof inspection, though, for the latter, cousin Ned tells me that the metal roof Dad and I put up there just before Dad's accident has another 20 years on it."

"Well done, Bob the Builder! When do you hit the second, first, and basement floors?"

"All in good time, Finn. I've got another 10 months. If it takes longer to sell it than I planned, Selene'll let me stretch my sabbatical into next Summer."

Finn looked hard at her. "Really? You're going to gut it out in Fayettenam for 15 months? Dollars to donuts you go all *Shining* and burn the place down before February."

"I think Selene was right. I needed to reclaim this place. I actually enjoy it here. I've been sending a steady stream of completed-work pics to Brad. 'Here, eat this crow, dumbass!' is how I'd say it if I wasn't such a prim and proper lass."

"You enjoy it here for the time being. After the fanfare of fall foliage, winter cometh. Do you really wanna relive that frozen fresh hell?"

Dee shivered a little, despite the humidity. "Don't be such a Debbie Downer! Yes, I've grown acclimated to the mild-by-comparison North-Texas winter, which might as well just be a rainy season with the triannual ice storm tossed in. But I'm making this place my own—something I'd had little leeway to do when I was a child or a home-healthcare amateur, trapped here. I've spread my proverbial wings, and they're not those of an old crow come home to roost, mind you."

"Don't underestimate the resourcefulness of ravens, Dee," noted Finn. "They're an ancient harbinger of feminine power and intuitive intelligence. Definitely not Edgar Allan Poe's idea of a good time, but, then again, he was a dude."

"Okay, then," agreed Diana, her chin held up in an Artemis pose. "I'm the Raven Queen returned to reclaim her rook, and I'll bring the vengeance of the Furies down on any Tom, Dick, Harry, or Brad who dares gainsay it."

"Maybe that Eumenide will stoke enough fire to melt winter up here. Oh, by the way, if you're looking for a mirror, come to Finn's storage room. I have one in there I rescued from the old White Horse Tavern on the Pike when they closed down. Vintage 1840s. I've no use for it. At the time I snatched it, I hadn't a tape measure and overestimated the space I needed it to cover. So, I've been saving it for my own renovation of Finn's in the faraway someday fairy land that my prospective future funds live in."

∞ ∞ ∞

A week later, she packed the mirror into the SUV. It was a glorious old antique that Finn could have sold to generate prospective fairy-land funds, but he wouldn't hear of her giving him cash for it. Thus, she resolved to go down weekly to Finn's for steak and beer while the weather held out, and to promote Finn's on social media, whether the old bear noticed or not.

The mirror couldn't fit in the dumbwaiter, but Rooster said he'd come over in a jiffy to help her haul it up the stairs. In mountain parlance, "jiffy" translates into sometime between now and sundown next. So, she dumbwaitered tools up to the third floor and prepared for the long-awaited glee of releasing that fucking medicine cabinet from the surly bonds of the bathroom wall.

Using her Makita to unscrew the support bolts was easy enough, and the medicine cabinet came out with a little prying at the tops and bottoms and corners. Instead of studs and carved-out plaster, she found *another* medicine cabinet—or at least the shell of one, definitely of a much older make. Apparently, whoever'd installed the 1950s piece of shit had bothered removing only the mirror, hinges, and shelves of this previous one, slipping the 1950s one right into the denuded cavity of the old one. Covered it up nicely. "Why so lazy, 1950s home-improver? How hard could it be to remove the older cabinet entirely, then nicely smooth out the old hole and seal it right?"

Then Dee discovered why. The ancient shell was fixed in the wall like a Fort-Knox vault. No amount of yanking, prying, or hammering was loosening it, and, after a solid half-hour of sweat and not a little cussing, she'd gotten over her reluctance to damage collateral plaster around it. No worries. Finn's mirror was huge and would cover a much larger area than the medicine cabinet did. This thing needed to come out, dammit!

After another 15 minutes in which she'd dusted the pedestal sink and floor below it with several layers of plaster and chicken wire, she stepped back, her sweat mixing with the plaster residue to make her look like a Sundstrom-masked Pillsbury Dough Boy in the mirror of the discarded 1950s cabinet.

"What the fuck? Is it goddamn welded into the studs?"

The interior of the cabinet shell was a smooth ivory white, showing no indentations or marks other than the scratches she'd made by her vain efforts. Dee picked up her hammer, claw facing the cabinet interior, adjusted her goggles, and let fly the hardest blow she could make. She'd thought to punch a hole, into which she could saber saw out the old metal cabinet, invisible stud moorings be damned.

It was her hammer blow that was damned, not making a dent, with only some flake-cracking at the blow. She took off her work gloves and scratched at the crack, trying to pry it off with her fingernail. Nothing doing. She tried scraping it with her painter's tool. It was like trying to make a divot in older porcelain plumbing, though she managed to get a sliver off. Hard, shear, impenetrable. She paused, then turned to the clawfoot tub that still hadn't seen her bathe in it, even though she'd replaced the pipes and ensured the water could summon the needed pressure to fill it in a reasonable amount of time. Not a chip or discoloration on the old tub. She ran her fingers under the outside rim and finally felt roughness. Sliding to her back, she shone her LED work light on the underside and saw a place where the tub's surfacing had been clipped. It looked like the chip she'd made in the back of the cabinet. Was the cabinet porcelain-coated with some previous era's version of a spray-on truck-bed liner before its time?

Equipping her impact drill with the staunchest chisel fitting she could summon from her toolbox, she took it to the cabinet interior. The resonance of the pounding told her that the cabinet was flush against two 16-inch centers on either side. Dee pounded along those like a frenzied Rosy the Riveter, feeling as if she was rattling out her one dental filling. Whatever this shit was, it was thick, but she was making headway. Finally, the largest chunk she'd yet seen fell from the top-right corner, into the sink. The spot from which it fell exposed a hex bolt, partially covered with the substance. She chipped away at that until the bolt was fully revealed, then back with the chisel to the other three corners of the cabinet interior where she unveiled three more hex bolts. Diana attached a point tool to the Makita and tucked away at the hell-porcelain, as she'd dubbed it, till it was completely free of the bolts. But the bolts wouldn't budge, even at the Makita's highest settings. Determined, she retrieved from the basement the portable compressor and its accompanying drill. "Let's see if you can rattle this fucker!"

Goggled, Sundstrom-masked and slick with sweat, she looked like the original *Terminator's* Sarah Connor as she fixed the bolt bit to the drill and rammed it onto the bolt head. The drill screamed and whined before she heard a screech of metal against wood, and it finally bit, slowly, then furiously spinning out the threads, the bolt clattering into the sink. In ten minutes, the other three were out. Gripping the lip of the cabinet with a huge pair of Channel-Locks, she yanked the cabinet a half-inch out, then an inch on the right side, plaster dust falling from it. Then the Channel-Locks to the left side. An inch-and-a-half there. Back to the right, until she'd winkled it out, catching the heavy bastard before it could bust the shit out of the faucet. She nearly fell over but somehow kept her balance, resting the behemoth, next to the 1950's cabinet on the drip cloth she'd spread out for what she'd thought would be a 15-minute dismantling.

Standing back, she stared at the thing. It's wall-inset rear exterior showed no coating, just a coke tempered steel shell. Dee turned to the massive hole in the wall to inspect the studs that had held this monster in place, the bolt openings in them smelling of burnt wood. But the studs were not what drew her eyes. Between the studs were hundreds of age-stained, folded sheets of paper—so many, so tightly packed after nearly a century of settling, that they didn't move out of place. She picked one off the top like she were removing the peak from a house of cards.

It was a two-inch, tri-fold strip, ragged at one end like it had been torn from a book. Opening it, Dee read in a spidery but flowing, flowery, antique script,

25 December 1929, Christmas Day

I am lost unto this world.

"Miss Diana?"

Dee jumped out of her skin. "Oh, Jesus Christ!"

Rooster mumbled, "I'm so sorry. I rang the doorbell and pounded the door, but I guess you didn't hear me 'cuz you was runnin' them tools."

"The mirror!" she said, closing the bathroom door behind her. "Don't mind that mess. You wouldn't believe how difficult it was taking out that old medicine cabinet!"

"Naw," said Rooster, following her down the steps. "I've worked many an old home salvage. They built things to last in them days. Was it moored to the studs like nobody's business?"

"With 3/8-inch bolts!" she said, pulling the key fob from her pocket and hitting the hatch button.

"Sounds about right. Don't be afraid t'ask me to come hep you with something like that. Ain't sayin' you cain't do it yerself, mind ya, but double the brawn can make the job go quicker."

"Thanks, Rooster, but your coming to help me haul this mirror up the steps is more than above-and-beyond the call of duty. You're not my gopher."

"Miss Diana, you know Shelly 'n me'd do anything for you."

She looked at him. "Tell me that *after* we get this mirror up the steps!"

∞ ∞ ∞

After they'd leaned the mirror against the bathroom wall and Dee had assured Rooster that she would certainly call him when it came time to hang the mirror and that she wouldn't dare try that job by herself, she escorted him out of the house, neglecting to offer him a lemonade this time because she desperately wanted to sprint up the stairs to understand what all the slips of paper meant. She wondered if Rooster had noticed them. "I'm sure he did—he doesn't miss much. It'll leave him scratching his head at the least."

The summer-evening light was fading by the time she made it to the third floor, so she flicked on all the hallway and bathroom lights. The papers were still there, the one she had begun to read now laying in the sink. Diana plucked another from the heap, only to hear the landline ring on the second floor. She would've let it ring out, but damned if anybody made answering machines anymore, and Laurel Highlands Telephone's voice-messaging service was still in beta. She tore back down the steps, leaving plaster-dust footprints behind her. Picking up the phone on the seventh ring, she said, panting, "Hello?"

"Diana, it's Selene. They found Luna."

Part III

Luna

Unhappy girl
Tear your web away
Saw thru all your bars
Melt your cell today
You are caught in a prison
Of your own device

Unhappy girl
Fly fast away
Don't miss your chance
To swim in mystery
You are dying in a prison
Of your own device
—"Unhappy Girl," The Doors

"Where is she?" Diana demanded through the open front-passenger window when Selene pulled to the gate at Love Field in Dallas.

"Get in the car, Diana. I'll explain. The first thing is to navigate out of this hellhole airport traffic."

Diana was beside herself, having gotten little or no sleep since Selene's phone call. At first, Dee was going to drive straight to Denton, but Selene suggested that perhaps a 26-hour-long car trip would put Diana further on edge. "Your best course of action is to fly, dearheart. I can pick you up at either airport, DFW or Love Field, whichever affords you a sooner flight."

"Where is she?" Diana had said over the manse phone what seemed an eternity ago.

"She's with us, dear—Burt and I."

"How is she?"

"We're still taking that in, Diana. The State Police literally brought her to us a half-hour ago."

"Can I talk to her?"

"Dear, she's under physical and mental evaluation right now. It's best that you get here as quickly and safely as possible so you can see her in person. If you can, imagine your shock right now, then treble that for what she must be feeling."

"Did they put the sonofabitch behind bars?"

There was a pause. "Clay is still missing, Diana. The State Police have no idea how Luna got to where she was found. Burt and I will explain *when you get here."* Selene had then refused to answer anymore of Dee's questions, insisting that the speediest way to see Luna was to get on a plane.

Diana had frantically called Finn, who dropped everything at the bar, drove up the mountain, and took her to the airport, all the time trying to ease her mind about what she would find when she finally saw her daughter after a three-and-a-half-year absence.

"Do you have a flight?" Finn asked.

"No, I didn't have time to get online or call. Just take me to the airport. I'll get on standby with someone, anyone!"

"Dee, you know I'm the last dude who would mansplain to you—"

"Then don't!" she snapped.

Finn persisted. "Diana, hear me out! I can turn us around. You can sleep at my place after you book the earliest flight to

Dallas. That way, you'll get some shuteye *and* be with someone who can help you settle down. Chances are, at this hour on a Sunday evening, there are no more departing flights from Pittsburgh International to anywhere in Texas, and you'd at best book a red-eye that won't take off for another six hours, leaving you stranded at the airport."

"Yes!" she exclaimed, holding up her phone. "Here's a Southwest flight departing Greater Pitt at 4:05am for Love Field in Dallas! Keep going to the airport!"

Finn sighed. "Is it non-stop?"

"I don't care! It's the earliest flight! That's what Selene said to do!" She madly tapped her phone. "It has connections in Chicago."

"But, Dee! We could book you on a later non-stop flight that probably will get you there sooner, without the connections and *with* a night's sleep!"

"Keep driving, damn it!"

She hated it when Finn was right. Her Chicago connection was delayed seven hours, eventually landing her in Dallas at 4:40pm, enabling her and Selene to get stuck in I-35 rush-hour traffic.

When they finally pulled up to Selene's door at 7:30pm, Selene gripped Dee by the wrist before she could jump out the passenger door. "Diana!" Selene said in a resolute tone. "You must steel yourself!"

Dee stared at her. "For fuck's sake, I'm her mother!"

"Yes," said Selene. "A mother Luna hasn't seen for more than three years, after who knows what she's been through."

"All the more reason I need to get in there now!"

"Diana!" commanded Selene. "She may not recognize you!!"

Dee halted. "What?"

Selene stared into her eyes. "Diana, dear, your little girl is eight years old now. Burt and I aren't sure that she knows who *we* are."

Diana looked frantically about, the Texas heat now weighing her to the seat. "What did she say to you?"

Selene shook her head. "Diana, Luna hasn't spoken a word since she was found … to anybody. I don't know what will happen when she sees you, if anything."

Out of the car, running up the porch steps, Selene behind her, Dee burst into a living room with several Troopers, a plain-clothes detective, Burt, and a wafer-thin raven-haired girl with saucer eyes sitting on the couch, staring at the TV.

∞ ∞ ∞

Diana had desperately wanted to take her daughter into her arms, to soak up her tears, to kiss her head. But she halted. She could not, *would not* intrude. She had waited this long. She could wait longer for the sake of her daughter.

Luna didn't look up. It wasn't even clear whether she was watching the television. She was eating a Pop-Tart, chewing it like the task demanded all her focus. Not ravenously, not hurriedly. Just chewing as if it was the thing to do that, at present, mattered.

Taking Dee by the arm, Selene led her, with Burt, into the kitchen, the plain-clothes detective following them. As Diana sat down and Selene prepared tea, the plain-clothes man extended his hand to Dee. "Dr. Atestesso, I'm Dr. Terry Moffatt, head of Pediatric Psychiatry at Fort Worth Methodist Hospital."

Dee looked up at him like Luna had been staring at the Pop-Tart.

"May I talk to you about your daughter?"

As he sat down, Selene put the tea with milk in front of her. "It's still hot, dear," she whispered.

"Is my daughter in shock?" Dee asked. "I can't imagine why, given the retinue of law enforcement offices milling about."

Burt broke in. "Diana, Luna's been like this since we found her."

"Yes," said Dr. Moffatt. "Her vitals are completely normal. Her pupils aren't dilated. As you could see, she's able to eat, as well as respond to sensory stimuli. Dr. Grieve helped her take a bath where, per Dr. Grieve, your daughter seemed to play and bathe like any child her age would. She's just not talking."

Diana looked over at Selene. "Does she respond when you say her name? Did she act like she knew you enough to trust you?"

"She seems to know her name," said Selene. "And she's readily let me her hold her hand, one time even offering it to me."

"I've definitely concluded," said Moffatt, "that her hearing is fine. She let me do an examination of her—Dr. Grieve was present and can confirm—your daughter's vocal cords seem to be in proper working order, as she had no problems saying the requisite 'Ahh' when I applied a tongue depressor. She'll follow our requests, but she simply will not respond with her voice beyond sneezes, yawns, or clearing her throat. She even reads, and at an advanced level for her age. She evidences no signs of physical abuse or neglect. But without vocal interaction, we can't be sure of her mental state."

Diana stared at each one of them, moving her gaze from face to face, searching for a reassurance beyond the clinical, some sense that what was happening was real. That it had happened in the first place. That she could be here right now, in a kitchen in Denton, Texas, not knowing if she still had a daughter in the way that other mothers had daughters. Life unhinged, and she bowed her head and cried.

When she looked up again, it was because a hush had fallen over the house, someone having clicked off the TV and everybody having halted their conversations. When she looked up, a wafer-thin, raven-haired ghost child was standing before her, looking into her eyes. The girl took in Diana's entire face, pausing at the tears on her cheeks. She raised her small finger, touching it to a trickling tear, then draped her arms around Diana, clutching her for the next two hours without saying a word, until she and Diana, together embracing, fell asleep on the couch.

∞ ∞ ∞

Selene insisted on accompanying Diana and Luna to Pennsylvania, paying their first-class airfare herself, never having given Diana a say in the matter.

"But—" protested Dee.

"You simply cannot go back there alone and attempt to settle back into that house with her. Luna needs some familiarity, especially seeing that it's likely that, whatever that brute did to her, she's enjoyed nothing approaching a stable existence. You don't, at present, have a home here in Denton, and you've pending responsibilities in the Keystone State that demand your attention. Further, you simply must carry out your sabbatical if you want to persist in the College—really, your profession has been your only constant through traumas that make Helen of Troy's look like a boat party across the Aegean. Yes, we're heading into a semester, but it's not like the College hasn't done that before. I'm hardly a capable administrator if the place crumbles the first instant I've taken time off since I assumed the Deanship. Together, you and I can heal whatever ails her. You're her mother, and I'm a psychiatric nurse with years of clinical pediatric experience. You can further renovate the domicile and continue your writing while I take care of Luna's needs. Fresh-air walks in the mountains will be just the tonic we need to recuperate from this madness. Last, I wonder if you've calculated that, just because you'll be in Pennsylvania doesn't mean that Clay can't follow you there? Though we've our own certainties that it was him all along who abducted her and returned her, we've no idea why. You shouldn't be alone, Diana. It's too much, and I won't hear of it. If you get tired of me, I suppose you can throw me down the flights of stairs you've bitched about having to climb so much. However, nothing short of omnipotent force will hinder my resolve in this matter."

Actually, Dee had been relieved that Selene was accompanying them. Her mentor's take-charge demeanor was invaluable at the airport. On the flight back, eight days after Dee had arrived in Denton, Selene set up Luna's first-class seat and meal, as well as the Pixar movie, *Inside Out,* on Luna's back-of-seat display. Luna's diminutive giggles and solemnities at the touchy-feely parts warmed Dee's heart. Though Dee couldn't fathom the calamities that might've transpired in Luna's life with Clay, those paled in comparison to the graces imparted by Selene.

Dee closed her eyes and thought through all that had transpired during her brief sojourn back in Denton. Moffatt and the experts he called in were stumped by Luna's silence. Gradually, Diana ceased to see it as something to fret over, as she had her daughter back, healthy and whole in seemingly every other way. In the end, Moffatt advised against taking Luna to Pennsylvania, as he wanted to run more tests and put Luna in play therapy to get to the root of her voicelessness. "Diana," Selene had said to her out of Moffatt's earshot. "The man is an exceptional psychiatric professional. We're lucky to have his attentions. However, he's just that—a physician, and a male one at that. Perhaps I'm jaundiced, but every enigmatic case for them is an incentive to dig deeper, to 'solve' the patient as if *that* is providing the needed care. Luna needs to heal in the arms of her mother. If she remains silent, then we'll be none the worse for wear if, after your sabbatical, we then pursue the root cause. In the meantime, let us administer our own special arts of healing, versus playing Dr. Holmes in the Case of the Quiet Child."

As it was, Luna had been CAT-scanned, x-rayed, MRI-ed, and examined head-to-toe by three separate specialists, all tests returning nothing out of the ordinary other than the fact that Luna was in the 25th percentile of her age category for weight and height. They implemented a battery of booster immunizations, as well as a thorough dental check-up. Although Dee was an RN, she could go a lifetime without ever again seeing the inside of the Fort Worth Methodist Hospital complex. Through it all, Luna was patient and exceptional in her acceptance of the whisking from appointment to appointment, blood-draw and inoculation, therapist interviews and encounters with panels of psychiatrists. In between, Selene made sure Luna had moments she could call her own, insisting that a visit to Chuck E. Cheese was every bit as imperative as her getting a clean bill of health. "For God's sake!" Selene put her foot down. "She is a child and should get the chance to *be* one! There'll be time enough for us to homeschool her while I'm there with you. She's already reading at what appears to be an eighth-grade level, and she'll have the guidance of two PhDs in the house. Thus, we must also advocate for the simple blessings of *play*, which I will readily see to!"

Finn had picked them up at Pittsburgh International, hitting it off with Selene once Dr. Grieve had detailed the boundaries he must respect in his interviewing them on the trip back to the manse. "We certainly are indebted to your graciousness in providing transport and for your stalwart friendship with Diana both now and in the past. However, I want to make abundantly clear that such intimacies do not give you *carte blanche* to interrogate Diana about recent events. That is sacred ground, Sir, upon which I will not let you tread with threadbare sandaled feet!"

Looking up from the sleeping form of Luna whose head was cradled in her lap in the back seat, Dee whispered, "Selene! Are you nuts? This is my best friend of all time! He already knows about virtually everything that's happened, except what we learned in Denton. He'd have my permission to know even if he wasn't playing Lyft Driver for me!"

"That's alright, Dee" said Finn into the rearview mirror. "I thought Selene was gonna be totally uptight and as protective as a rabid junkyard dog. It's so disappointing to see how blasé she is about the whole thing."

For once, something shut up Dr. Grieve, until she started belly laughing. "Oh, Diana, I can see why you keep him as a friend—he can take shit and bazooka it back in concentrated pellets! Well done, Sir!"

To Finn's questions, the two provided a recounting of what Burt and the Highway Patrol had found in their continuing investigation. Law enforcement had had almost no leads or sightings over the three-plus years after her abduction. Despite Amber Alerts and the obligatory Wal-Mart and post-office bulletin board photos of Luna, the Patrol had only one reported sighting, last January, of a child matching Luna's description, and that had been in a Walgreen's pharmacy in Laredo, though a thorough review of the store's closed-circuit video yielded no positive identification beyond a grainy image of a man of Clay's height and build and a child with black hair.

Luna had been found on a coin-operated rocking horse outside the Rayzor Ranch Marketplace Walmart Supercenter after an unknown number posted a text message to Burt's phone:

She's at https://goo.gl/maps/aLuYJ1viKk6RXDqE6. You always did need coordinates to find your own ass.

Burt didn't hesitate, and Walmart was then rife with plain-wrapper vehicles till they'd reconnoitered the area, finding it bereft of any sign of Clay. Burt himself had remained parked close to the rocking horse, keeping his eyes locked on Luna till Patrol had given the all-clear sign that there were no booby traps. The Explosives team had been called in, just in case any incendiary devices had been planted.

Afterwards, Burt shook his head. "It was definitely Clay, though we can't officially declare that. He always has to let us know it's him, but he'll do so only when he's rigged the game in his favor. Absolutely no electronic trail to follow via the text message or the Google-maps link, despite our combing the cell-network and potential ISP data. No fingerprints on the scene or on Luna. No sightings of a vehicle or someone leaving her on the horse—right underneath a bulletin board of missing children with her very photo on it—despite a frame-by-frame review of Walmart's surveillance systems. Luna's silence seals the deal."

So Diana returned home with her daughter and her guiding mentor, bewildered at the mystery that was her life but grateful to no longer be alone in the manse.

∞ ∞ ∞

"Luna, dear," coaxed Selene. "Draw another one for Auntie Selene."

Passing the kitchen table, Diana almost dropped her MacBook Pro when she saw the table littered with fiery orange, red, and yellow drawings. Selene looked up at her with a knowing eye.

"Sweetie," Dee asked. "Can you tell us what it is you're drawing?"

Luna kept a look of concentration on her face as she

methodically applied a spectrum of lemon-to-crimson color-markers to her work. Her reply was, when she judged the picture finished, to show the rendering to her viewers and point her finger to it.

Diana took the works in her hands, slowly turning and angling each one to understand what her daughter was communicating to them. Some of the drawings were conflagrations, exploding over the entire page. Others showed vertical or horizontal flows of fire coming from earth, sky, or carried on a wind invisible to the viewer. On another, this one replete with vivid blues and silvers, a river under a star-strewn night sky battled a ball of flame. Her most minimalist drawing showed a dime-sized ball of red-yellow-and-orange fire poised to explode from the center of an otherwise blank canvas. The most disturbing was one of a castle-like house engulfed in flames, a Rapunzel-esque maiden, hair made of fire, stranded in the topmost tower—this last one being a repeated motif any time she drew, some renderings surrealistic, others impressionistic, still others abstract, and this one, the most unsettling, as realistic as an eight-year-old proto-prodigy could render.

"Baby," Dee had asked her the first time Luna had drawn the Fire Maiden, as Selene had coined it, "Is that you?"

Luna paused for a full minute, eyes fixed on a faraway vision. She then slowly, imperceptibly shook her head and pointed her finger at Diana.

The Fire Maiden didn't look as if she were in distress or being consumed. And that result, however less disturbing, didn't seem to be the by-product of Luna's autodidact inexperience with artistic convention and symbolism, for the drawings consistently showed the Fire Maiden summoning the fire, spouting it, raising it with her hands, and in one poignant vision, raising a sword of fire over a hauntingly blue river, as if she rode the waves.

"I don't mean to go all Lifetime Network," whispered Dee to Selene after Luna had run out to Dee's backyard garden to pick peppers and other bounty. "But these don't look like the cries of a helpless person seeking in vain to arm herself. If anything, it's Luna's take on Carol Danvers and *Captain Marvel.* She's not asking for powers she doesn't possess. She's using ones she already has."

Selene bowed her head in thought. "Far be it from me, a psychiatric professional, to *not* overanalyze, but I think it's simpler than that, Diana. Luna is trying to tell us something."

"And what is that message?"

Selene eyed her. "I thought you might know."

∞ ∞ ∞

Dee had cleaned the mess in the third-floor bathroom soon after they'd arrived at the manse, mounting the mirror, via deft rope-and-pulley work, over the crater in the wall above the sink. There was no time to do the plastering—indeed, no time for any renovations now that Luna was here. Dee hadn't been eager to hide from Selene the fact that her publication work was nil to this point, so she plunged into that, putting all remodeling plans on hold. She gathered the "thousand wisps of paper," as she'd labeled them to herself, into a blue Lowe's bucket that she lidded and deposited in the basement. Time enough later for that mystery, of which she'd solved at least a small part—how the papers got into the stud space behind the old medicine chest. The steel backing of that monster piece showed a slit in the middle of it, through which some of the porcelain/enamel wonder-coating had run and solidified. Someone, in the intervening years, she assumed, had coated the interior of the cabinet with that substance, covering the slit, which itself was a prosaically utilitarian historical artifact—an opening into which to dispose safety-razor blades out of harm's way. Below the slips of paper, she'd found a clutter of used rusted blades when

she'd shone a flashlight beam into the hole behind the plaster.
Someone had used the slit to secret a time-capsule version of
messages in a bottle, these missives washing up from their
1920s origin onto today's beach. She was about to read one of
them when Selene had called up to her that dinner would be
ready in five minutes. It was all Dee could do to store the slip-
laden bucket in the basement and wash her hands. Selene did *not*
tolerate mealtime tardiness, as Dee and Luna had previously
discovered.

Diana had to admit that Selene's presence was the needed
tonic, and her work took off. With Selene's babysitting and
homeschooling of Luna, Diana was free to venture to libraries
in Greensburg, St. Vincent College, Penn State's Fayette
Campus, and even Carnegie-Mellon and Pitt. On two of her
Pittsburgh jaunts, Selene and Luna joined her, Selene touring
Luna through Pittsburgh's Kids Science Museum, the
installation-art mecca of the Mattress Factory, the Carnegie-
Mellon Museum of Natural History, and others. On the second
trip, Diana, at Selene's behest, cut short her research that day so
that the trio could attend Buhl Planetarium's latest star show.
Through it all, Luna's eyes took in everything she saw. They
bore no wonder or astonishment but rather the ken of ancient
Artemis returned to take in what new things under the moon
humanity had wrought.

None of those experiences changed Luna's drawings or
acrylic paintings (in the 'Burgh, Selene had bought Luna a
brushes-canvases-paints set, the colors in which would've made
Van Gogh sever another ear to have)—all of Luna's resulting
work told tales of fire that burned but, instead of consuming,
revealed. What that revelation was escaped Diana, and Luna
would not or could not further illuminate.

Diana was breathless when, after a day of research/writing
and renovation shopping, she came home to discover that Luna
had painted a fireball mural along the vintage bead-board
wainscoting of the third-floor master bedroom that she and

Diana slept in. Selene, of course, had not only *not* discouraged Luna mid-paint but had helped her, Luna's hand-motion directions bearing the artistic command of Michelangelo instructing apprentices in the prepping of the Last Judgment in the Sistine Chapel—except that Luna's mural showed only one demon, who did not dominate the scene but, in the background, seemed to catalyze it. Not the creator of the fire nor its fuel, but the flint to its spark. That demon was a nondescript, almost inert, lump with eyes. Eyes that knew. It wasn't until long after that Diana realized that the eyes of that Fire Lump bore an uncanny resemblance to those of Luna taking in the stars at the planetarium.

At the center of the mural, amid the ignited fire, was a maiden of extraordinary beauty, like something out of Tennyson or *Le Morte D'Arthur,* who stood astride the fire without dominating it, though it was clear that she was the master of everything in the scene. An amazon, without harshness or rippling muscle, faerie queen without the gossamer and wisps, huntress fair but not chaste, specter without the horror of un-life, rosy-cheeked as if daring the viewer and the demon to invite her to wrath. From this towering figure poured a joy that superseded any jest or merriment but burned like the certainty of crystal morning promising a never-ending day. Behind her, though, the sun was setting, the moon already dominating the sky.

Luna had taken her mother by the hand after Diana had stood in the doorway for almost a full minute, slack-jawed at what she was seeing. When Luna had become aware of Dee's presence, she guided her to the center of the mural, in front of the maiden. Inexorably, she pulled Diana down to her knees until her mother was eye-to-eye with the maiden. Then Luna pointed to the figure until she was touching its nose, the paint still wet, now moving that pointer finger till she touched Diana's nose. A smile like Selene and Diana had not before seen blossomed on Luna's face, and Luna said simply, "You."

Diana wept because she could not believe that utterance, then fell into Luna's arms, Selene crouching down to the two, till all three were a weepy mess.

∞ ∞ ∞

"But where is Luna in all these paintings and drawings?" asked Diana over tea with Selene the next morning. Luna was still asleep, her artistic exertions and Dee's taking the three of them down the mountain to Bud Murphy's for pizza had spent her.

"I've already told you, Diana, they're not autobiographical. They're neither story nor fantasy, nor an expression of her inner self. Ockham's Razor, dearheart—the simplest answer is usually the best. They are a message."

"To me?" asked Dee incredulously.

"Luna's made that abundantly clear with her dexterous index finger. *Yes,* you!"

"But—" Diana's eyes searched the ceiling, the cabinets, and her tea, till they rested on Selene. "I'm no maiden of fire. Look at me! I'm a frumpy academic—not a Valkyrie. And why fire? Should we worry that my daughter's a budding pyromaniac?"

"She's certainly a budding artist," noted Selene, "and she's ratcheted up her skill to be commensurate with the clarity of her message, seeing as how we, or shall I say, *you,* haven't been getting it. She's telling you something, Diana. If that something isn't how you see yourself now, perhaps it's Luna's vision of your future."

"Why would she, an eight-year-old, with prodigious art skills, but an eight-year-old nonetheless, want to paint me as Éowyn on fire steroids?"

"Diana," Selene said, pouring a refresher into her tea cup and stirring it, "We've no idea what Clay put her through, except perhaps art lessons with the Georgia O'Keefe of pyrotechnics. We don't know what she's seen. However, she might be telling you that what she sees right now is more urgent than anything that she—or *you*—have witnessed in the past."

"What's that supposed to mean? Don't tell me you're gonna start talking in riddles."

"I'll not play Sybil to your Augustus, nor am I trying to be cryptic. As you note, Luna is eight years old. Her artistic skills are exceptional for one so young, but sometimes genetics and subsequent experience put all the eggs into one basket rather than doling them out evenly. Luna's experience basket has been filled to overflowing with rotten eggs, but it seems, too, that her artistic-flare basket is replete with fiery dragon eggs, and ne'er the twain shall meet."

Dee rolled her eyes. "Now you're not talking in riddles but mixing up trite aphorisms with classical and fantasy references. You drop a tab of acid in your tea?"

Selene smiled. "Let me remind you that, if anyone's life experiences were a movie version of an acid trip, the casting director would definitely have picked *you* for the lead and me for a supporting role. And it is just that misshapen circumstance that makes what I'm saying all the more likely—Luna has experienced realities we can't imagine. So much so that she hasn't been able to articulate them in speech. But her brush is eloquent, and I don't think that's because of practice so much as it's of *urgency*. She's telling you something vital you need to know."

"Okay, Delphic Oracle, how am I supposed to figure it out? It's not like a Rosetta Stone is hidden in this house that enables me to translate Luna's fire-art-speak."

"Isn't there, Diana?"

Dee stared at her. "What are you trying to say?"

Selene scanned her eyes about, staring through the walls and ceiling. "This is an old house that's seen its share of occupants. Lived-in places draw energies and people."

"Are you, the Grand-Dame nurse scientist, going to utter some ectoplasmic occult divinations?"

"I'm certainly *not* talking such rubbish. But I am talking about *people* and how they leave a mark, something we've borne all too much of in the case of your ex-husband. People leave smudges or graces. You can see it in both the fateful and resurrectional repetitions of history. 'Like calls unto like,' as the Psalmist says, to note an aphorism. To this point, your life has borne the smudges of your father, your silent mother, your heedless brother, and the malice of Joseph. I'd like to think that I and Luna have brought you some grace, but, as far as basket-doling goes, sadly, more rotten-egg baskets have amassed in your life than grace-filled ones. Mind you, grace eggs weigh significantly more than those of malice and misfortune. But, perhaps, akin to what Malcolm Gladwell notes, your life is at a tipping point, a moment of truth. It's no accident, then, that your daughter, who bears such gifts and such calamity, much like Cassandra or, more hopefully, Cinderella, and I, your mentor/wisdom-figure would converge at this place, at this time. Something in this house called you, and you called us."

"For what?" asked Dee, who'd found she'd been holding her breath.

"Perhaps for us to witness something to you … and that may be what Luna's pointing you to."

∞ ∞ ∞

Three nights later, Diana had fallen asleep with Luna in the king-sized bed of the third-floor master. Since reuniting with Dee, Luna had slept no other place but next to her mother. Diana's heart was warmed that she could provide a sheltering presence for Luna, who, as Selene had said, "has experienced realities we can't imagine." Yet, on those nights when Dee awoke with Luna still slumbering, instead of a vulnerable child, Dee saw her daughter in a guardian pose, as if she'd fall asleep while still on watch, poised to jump to attention at a moment's notice. "Who's sheltering whom?" Diana wondered.

Tonight, Diana didn't rouse … that is, until she felt a presence standing beside the bed. Dee jolted awake. "Mommy, there's a ghost."

Luna stood over her, pointer finger curling, summoning Dee to follow. Wrapped in a gauzy dream, Diana rose and glided behind Luna's lead, across the room, to the mural. At its center, the Fire Maiden glowed with a preternatural light. Dee rubbed her eyes, for she saw movement, then fell back onto her seat, bewildered. The Maiden was alive, her eyes moving, her lips voicelessly beseeching Diana.

The figure was the Fire Maiden but wasn't. A specter, faintly aglow, arms stretched to Diana, implored her. Yet the painted Fire Maiden was still ablaze, a power emanating from her limbs, eyes, and gesture of command. The Fire Maiden was goddess where the specter was a fading daughter, clinging to her last frays of substantiality. The two were nonetheless one, each speaking a message the other could not hear but both of which clung to Diana, not as separate visions of Luna's art and Diana's dream. No, they proceeded *from* Diana, taking all their life from her breath, heat from her heart, pain and joy from her passion.

Diana awoke on the floor with Luna, both curled in a sheet beside the mural. For the first time, Dee noticed that the Fire Maiden in the mural was pointing, but to what?

∞ ∞ ∞

Summer trundled into autumn, and, except for the two single utterances Diana had heard from her daughter, Luna spoke no further word. She drew and painted no more after the night of Diana's dream. The leaves on the trees replaced Luna's fiery art with their own, the ridges clustered with endless conflagrations of scarlet, orange, and yellow. As autumn waxed, so had Diana's publishing work. Selene's edits were minor, so complete had been Diana's research and analysis. She submitted her studies and articles to academic journals and began the long wait of coming winter for the replies while she renovated the second-floor.

One day, in mid-October, the garden having already frosted and turned to stubble, Selene awoke from a nap and could not find Luna. "She is so quiet that one misses her presence, as it feels like a guardian spirit you take for granted," Selene had mused the other day to Diana.

Dee and Selene walked about the property, calling her name, for Luna loved the outdoors, no matter the weather, and would have delighted in sitting by the stream in a cold autumn downpour or walking endlessly on the trails in the forest. Indeed, Diana and Selene had done so much walking with Luna that they both had lost weight, despite Selene's generous cooking.

"Before we take to the trails, Diana," said Selene, somewhat out of breath, "Let's give the house one last run through. Where could that child have gone?"

Selene started on the third floor and Diana the first, the two meeting each other as they combed the second floor. "Could she be hiding?" wondered Diana aloud.

"I've never seen her go off without our invitation," Selene shook her head. "It's like she was swallowed by the earth." They looked at each other, the two saying, "The basement!"

Down the steps to the first floor, they hastened to the kitchen where the cellar door stood ajar, Diana's heart in her mouth at the chance that opening the portal all the way would reveal Luna broken at the bottom of the steps. The basement lights were on and the staircase empty. "Luna!" Dee shouted as she rattled down the flight. Turning from the stair, she saw a light from the other side of Dad's worktable, and she ran there to find Luna hunched in a corner, holding the LED work light and scanning a piece of paper in her hand. Beside her, the blue Lowe's bucket had been opened and emptied, its paper-slip contents now laid out in orderly fashion, Luna's hand poised with the last page, ready to lay it in place. As she looked up, she said, "I finished it for you, Mommy." Diana would not hear her speak again until everything had started closing in on them.

∞ ∞ ∞

The first snow in mid-November was the morning that Selene fell down the second-floor steps and broke her clavicle. It was also the day that Diana received the first of several acceptances of her studies, essays, and reports submitted to *The Journal of Pediatric Nursing*.

The snow accumulated a mere two-inches, soon melting as the temperature rose to 55° by sundown, which, given the time of year, came earlier and earlier, today's sunset at 4:45pm. Diana felt in a battle with encroaching darkness.

Driving back from the hospital with Luna, Selene being kept overnight for observation, especially for potential blood clots, Diana parsed through her mind how that one step could've come loose. A month ago, she'd started the second-floor renovation by shoring the staircase. As Rooster had said, "They built things sturdier in them days." All but three steps were solid, properly load-bearing, and sure to last for years to come. The three spotty ones were matters of decades-old nailing having come loose. Playing it safe, Diana bought new lumber for them, finishing the step boards to fit the existing staircase aesthetic, all but the stain and lacquer, which she'd do when the carpentry repairs were finished for all floors. She glued the new stair boards into place, in addition to tacking them down, not with nails but with stainless-steel, recessed-head screws for a more secure attachment. Yet, the stair that had flipped up behind Selene's heel was one of the three Dee had repaired, the broken step smiling a toothless grin down on where Selene lay in a moaning heap on the first-floor landing. Along with the broken collarbone, Selene had suffered a hematoma to her forehead and deep contusions to her hip, shin and shoulder. She was lucky to not have broken her hip or experienced a spiral fracture of her leg. "She's got very strong bones for an older lady," observed the Frick Hospital Orthopedist.

"What bullshit!" Selene had muttered, sluggish from the pain meds. "To hear him talk, you'd think I was already taking a swan dive into the grave. And I'm *not* staying on these opioids when I'm out of here. I'm already constipated like an old Scottish MP!"

Three days after she'd gotten out of the hospital, Selene broke the news to Diana that she was going home to Denton. "My brother will hear no protest from me. He doesn't want me flying, and he doesn't want my injuries to have a holdover effect into my 'senior years,' as he calls them. He's bringing up his battleship-proportions RV to take me back to Texas where, as he terms it, I can see a 'real doctor and not one of those Yankee quack sawbones.'"

"Selene, you never had to come up in the first place," Diana said, her heart nonetheless sinking at the thought of Selene being gone. "But I'm so grateful for the care, meals, and companionship you've given us. Look how I repay it—my shitty carpentry throws you into an invalid state. I am so mortified and sorry. All I seem to bring you is grief."

"If anything could get me to tell my brother to ram his USS-Missouri-sized RV into his lower colon, it would be your chastising yourself. Have you not seen a one of the paintings Luna made? *You* are the Fire Maiden, as well as the naiad of

Poplar Run. I couldn't stay here beyond Christmas anyway, and, whether I'd damaged a few bones or not, the arrival of the cold weather is not treating well the joints of this Texas-born-and-raised spitfire. Luna has become whole, dear, even if she doesn't yet talk much. *You* have given that to her. Let her enjoy the coming of snow, and the two of you nest. You've already accomplished the needed publishing work. Now you can finish this mansion and sell it. Dearheart," she cooed, taking Dee's head to her breast and hugging her, "I don't blame you in any way. 'Accidents will happen,' as Mr. Costello once sang. For you to claim this place as your own, I have to be gone. I can mend in Bo's ridiculously outfitted RV-cum-AC/DC-tour bus. Chomping to use it properly since his Sally died, methinks. He's never been able to feature trying to camp in it solo, as her loss still weighs on his heart. Thus, even as I recuperate, I will continue my healing vocation. Also, you don't want me around, as nurses make the worst patients."

"I thought that was doctors," Diana said.

"No, no, dear. Doctors are pricks *all* the time. We nurses know how it should be done and, in a recuperative state, we put no governor on our criticism engine. Aren't I illustrating that this very moment?"

Dee shook her head as she raised it from Selene's chest. "You illustrate only courage, heart, generosity, and graciousness, all leavened with that spitfire wit of yours. I'll miss the fuck out of you."

∞ ∞ ∞

Two days later, Brother Bo drove off, Dee, Luna, and Rooster waving Selene goodbye. "Rooster, I need your second opinion," Dee said to him as they walked back to the manse.

Inside, Diana watched as Rooster closely inspected the broken step. Diana had not yet fixed it, as she wanted an objective third-party take on whether she'd truly fucked up and nearly killed her best friend. Rooster felt around the moorings of the step box, trying to shake it, pry it, rattle it. He peered into it with flashlight and thoroughly examined the screw holes. Running his hand along the inside of the step box, he paused, summoning out three decapitated screw heads. "Here're the culprits, Miss Diana," he grunted, rolling them into her palm. "Shoddy hardware."

Diana examined them closely. "I don't understand. I bought high-grade, Rooster. For a place like this, you can't go cheap, and I take pride in building things to last."

Rooster retrieved one of the screws and put on his cheaters. "Yup," he said, after a pause. "316 stainless steel. Damn, sister, unless you weren't buildin' no staircase but a seafarin' vessel, you overbought. These things'll stand up to years on the ocean and a helluva tensile strength at that!"

"Even then, Rooster, I can fathom one screw catastrophically failing. But *three?*"

Rooster pulled a magnifying glass from his inner jacket. "Ooo! Ya see *that?*" he asked. Diana bent closer. The screw head hadn't cracked. The head had been halfway sheared off, leaving a month's worth of stair traffic do the rest of the work. "These other two're the same way," affirmed Rooster.

"Wait here," she said. She came back to Rooster with her tool belt in-hand, fishing into the front pocket. "I packed a new box of screws into this when I was re-doing these steps." She pulled out several screws, handing some to Rooster. They held them to the light and noticed that, just below the head of each one, the screw had a notch pushing past halfway of the screw diameter.

"You got yerself an entire bad box. Take it back to the Lowe's to see if there's been a recall. Hell, you n' Selene might even wanna do a lawsuit."

Diana kept examining the screw. "I don't think so," she said, eye squinting. "Here, rub your finger against that notch," which Rooster dutifully did. "That's no manufacturing defect in the die or plating," she continued. "Someone's taken a hacksaw to these."

She grabbed her crowbar and went to pry off one of the other repaired steps, nearly collapsing down the stairs when, mid-pry, they heard a snap and the stair flipped in the air, Rooster catching Dee before she could fall.

"Sonofabitch," she snapped, more irritated than scared, and picked up the flipped board, holding it up to Rooster. "See? These ones, too, are cut through, just past halfway, so that, whenever you drive them in, you either break off the head or weaken the tensile strength so much that a sneeze'll pop off the screw head. It's a testimony to these screws that not one head popped off when I was driving them into the steps. Then again, maybe that was the intent—for the head to pop off later, when the thing you built was being used."

"Are you sayin' that someone bought screws from Lowe's, went home, hacked 'em, then slid 'em back on the shelf at the store, jes to cause some havoc?"

Dee looked at him, but she wasn't seeing him. "I'm not sure what I'm saying, Rooster. But I don't have a great feeling about this. Would you mind helping me examine the other materials I bought the last two months?"

The rest of that morning, they pored over all the hardware and other load-bearing and fastening goods she'd purchased, not refraining from opening sealed packets in order to make sure that the blame wasn't indeed a manufacturing defect. The sealed boxes of the same Everbilt brand in the same and different sizes showed only pristine wood screws, not even one in a box evidencing a defect. The kitchen table was strewn with screws, Luna coming in from her reading in the third-story bedroom, to pick up a damaged screw. She looked at it hard, then walked to the trash can and deposited it there, looking at Diana and shaking her head once in a "No" that precluded ever using those ones again. Then she was out of the room with a box of cereal and the iPad Selene had bought her, to read in her chair in the parlor.

"Could yer daughter've monkeyed with 'em?"

Dee paused. "No. There's no way. She stays away when I'm working. The power tools spook her, and, with our not knowing what happened to her during her abduction, I haven't wanted to push the issue with her. I do a lot of my work after she goes to bed. I can't imagine her having the sudden fortitude to wake in the wee hours, grab a hacksaw, and shear off screw heads. But let's check my Dad's old workspace, just to be sure."

In the basement, Dee pushed the blue Lowe's bucket under the table. Inside were the slips of paper now neatly ordered and paperclipped by Luna. As she nudged it under, Dee noticed some glints down there. Tiny metal shavings were accumulated under the vise clamped to the side of the tool bench. Hanging just above on the pegboard was an angle grinder with a diamond-saw-edge blade dusted with silver. "Okay. There's the angle grinder, 'n there're the shavins'," attested Rooster.

"What the hell?" whispered Diana. "There's no way! Luna has no idea where I pack the extension cords, and the plugs are too far away to operate this grinder here at the vise. Besides, why didn't I ever hear the sound of this when Luna was awake?"

Hauling the angle grinder upstairs, Dee walked to the parlor. When Luna looked up from her reading perch and saw it, her eyes flickered, seeming to assume Mommy was taking it to use somewhere in the house with Mr. Rooster. But as Diana got closer, laying the thing on the coffee table before Luna in her chair, Luna dropped the iPad and backed up as far as she could into the cushions.

"Luna, do you know what this is?" whispered Dee.

Luna shook her head, then put her hands to her ears and squeezed shut her eyes as Diana picked it up and brought it closer to her. Tears squeezed out of her daughter's eyes.

"Miss Diana, I think she don't like it one bit."

Diana halted. "Yeah, I'm seeing that." She flung the grinder to the far edge of the parlor, and Luna immediately jumped from the chair, into her arms, burying her face in Dee's breasts and sobbing. "Shhh, shhh," whispered Diana. "It's okay, baby. I'm so sorry. I'll never do that again."

Rooster excused himself.

∞ ∞ ∞

The third step snapped off as readily as had the one she'd crowbarred earlier. "What the hell is going on?" Dee wondered.

She went downstairs to examine the work bench area. Everything was in order the way she'd remembered it being every time she went there, multiple times a day. She wasn't a neatness freak, but she did like to have a place for everything so she could readily grab what she needed. The only things out of order had been the uncleaned grinder blade and the minuscule metal flecks under the work table … almost as if someone had wanted her to find them. To know.

A chill passed over her, and she planned no more renovating till after Thanksgiving.

∞ ∞ ∞

Mother and daughter passed an eventless week leading up to Thanksgiving and through the holiday to the Monday after. Cold rains precluded outdoor activities, and, after having so disturbed Luna with the angle grinder, Dee kept an especially tender heart for Luna. So she spent the time reading *The Chronicles of Narnia* aloud to Luna, or playing board games with her, delighting at her daughter's squeals of laughter or contemplative, homey contentment over the turkey breast, stuffing, and mashed potatoes they feasted on Thanksgiving day, the other days making cold sandwiches from leftover turkey and cranberry sauce. Luna cried when Reepicheep sailed past the Lily Sea over the wave at the end of the world and cheered when Puddleglum broke the spell of the Green Witch. Sunday afternoon, the snow started and became, as the moon rose, blizzard-heavy, just as Diana's Dark Sky iPhone weather app had predicted. Having finished *Narnia*, Dee gave Luna choice of the next book. From the library, after a 15-minute perusal, Luna came bouncing back with Neil Gaiman's *Neverwhere* in tow.

Dee looked at her. "Are you sure, baby? I know you're almost nine, but this one can be scary, even though it has a good ending."

Luna emphatically nodded and curled up kitten-like beside Diana in the window seat, her freshly shampooed hair wafting a pleasant scent of home and contentment. Somewhere past the first chapter, Diana heard a creak in the attic that made her pause her reading. She looked out the window. There was no wind, the snow coming down straight in heavy flakes. Luna hadn't seemed to notice the ominous sound as she was starting to nod off. Diana kept reading till Luna had fallen asleep. Despite the fact that Luna hadn't brushed her teeth yet, Dee put a blanket over her and let her slumber on the window sill. She could go a night without worrying about cavities.

The next morning, Luna awoke before Diana and was raring to play in the snow. Over the weekend, knowing winter was to arrive, Diana had found the snow boots and eiderdown jacket she'd worn in her childhood play dates with the snow. They were a wee-bit large for Luna but would still serve well. Having seen them laid out, Luna was more than eager to put them on.

Diana was not yet fully awake, knowing she herself needed a trip to the bathroom, a wash of the face, and coffee before she could face clearing the front stoop, the walkway, and the 39,000 Steps. Going to pee, she was irked to find the toilet seat up, nearly sitting on the exposed bowl. Why would Luna have left the seat up?

After washing her face in a water flow from which it took forever to coax warmth via the distant water heater, she reached for her toothbrush and noticed the cap was off to Luna's Captain Marvel Kids Crest. That was weird. Luna always had to be reminded to brush her teeth and certainly never did it after waking up. "Whatever," she mumbled through her own toothbrushing. "Maybe the prospect of snow has put her on full alert and lit her up like a Christmas Tree, thinking she has to have her teeth clean to play in the snow."

Oh, bother! They'd not pulled the Christmas Tree from the attic and set it up over the weekend, so engrossing had been the reading. Luna hadn't missed it yet, so, no news on that front was good news. Putting up and tearing down a tree would hopefully not be added to Dee's to-do list. As she blotted the towel on her mouth after rinsing and turning off the water, she again heard the creaking noise she'd noted last night. Was the house shifting with the weight of snow on the roof? But no—the pitch was so steep, and the metal roof did a sure-fire job of not letting heavy amounts of snow accumulate, which was a major relief. Having the place come down around her ears after remodeling it would not be her idea of tying a bow on this sabbatical.

Despite Selene's injuries and departure, Dee felt healed by this sojourn in the mountains. She'd gotten Luna back, filling a hole in her heart. She'd renewed a friendship with Finn. She'd reclaimed a homestead that had once hung over her psyche in nightmare memories. And she would turn a profit from it to convert into savings for a future for her and Luna.

In the kitchen, she stirred the Irish Oats, the cinnamon and apples she'd put in making the first floor smell like something out of Dickens. Luna was already in the boots and eiderdown, sitting at the table, spoon at the ready. Their Ezekiel Bread popped from the toaster and Luna plopped her spoon onto the table and rushed to smear peanut butter on what she apparently felt was the perfect complement to oatmeal. Diana made Luna a cup of decaf in the Keurig because she knew that her daughter's beverage of choice to accompany PB toast and Irish Oats was nips of her mother's fully caffeinated java. "Nope. Not goin' there," Dee mused. "My little girl doesn't need the stimulant, thank you very much. Just the warmth the unleaded java'll impart."

After breakfast, they tramped to the basement to retrieve a broom, the snow shovel, and a toboggan. While there, Luna had tapped on the Lowe's bucket and stared at Diana.

"I know, honey, I know. I've had other things to do. It can wait till after I get the snow cleared from the walk, the steps, and the car."

Luna gave her a look of "Well, I'll let it go this time, but …" then was out in the snow seconds after Diana pulled open the front door and started clearing the porch of the six inches plus that had accumulated there. Emerging from the porch, Diana smiled at her daughter's frenzied attempt to snow-angel the entire front yard. "Could you do some of that on the walk?" she yelled, but Luna's head gear and waving arms muted her mom's suggestion.

It took the balance of the morning to clear the snow. A quarter way through the job, Diana paused at the top of the 39,000 Steps. Proceeding from the bottom were footprints that weren't filled in where the stairs extended under trees, the branches above having taken a good deal of the snow that otherwise would have covered the footfalls. Near the top of the steps, the prints were totally filled. But on the first few stones of the walkway, when Dee cleared the snow, imprinted in what had been the slush before the snow were the frozen prints of a large, heavy boot, so big it had to be that of a man. The snow had started late afternoon and hadn't come down heavy until after dusk. Had someone been up here? If so, why didn't they knock or ring the bell? Dee gazed around the hilltop yard to detect any other footprints, but the snowfall had done its job of leveling any features of the landscape under a layer of white. She made a mental note to examine the walk and the yard once the snow began to melt, which would be in the next few days, the high today hitting only 30° but predicted to steadily rise by Thursday back into the 50s. "Enjoy the snow while you can, kiddo," she thought and resolved to ask Rooster whether he'd tried to visit them yesterday afternoon.

After three chapters of *Neverwhere* and dinner, Dee solemnly promised Luna that, if Luna went to bed when Mommy told her, Mommy would start reading the notes from the blue bucket. This was an easy deal for Luna, as her eyes were drooping over dinner from her expenditure of energy in the snow-angeling of one-third of the yard, a prodigious effort by one so diminutive.

It took one chapter of *Neverwhere* for Luna to halt her mother so she could brush her teeth and go to bed. While Luna brushed, Dee retrieved the bucket from the basement, showing it to Luna to reassure her daughter that she indeed would keep her promise. In response, the Great Negotiator was in her pajamas and bed in record time. As Dee reached into the bucket, she looked over her shoulder to see Luna peeping an eye to watch. "Baby, I'm just getting them out to organize them for my reading. I'll read them after you're asleep. So, get to it, kiddo," she winked.

Luna winked back and curled up contentedly.

28 October 1928

Who will save my soul?

Father will not relent and blames me for Mama's passing. He will not hear reason on the matter, so I languish here because he does not let me back into the world, for I am a monster, an "abomination," as he calls it.

e.

31 October 1928

Father is on the porch with a gun, while I watch from my third-story prison. He vows to never let me out so long as I continue this "absurd charade," as he calls it. I lament that I will not partake of Halloween, but father says that I am guised already in a ridiculous costume. His shotgun is filled with rock salt to ward off the Halloween vandals.

"'trick or treat,' indeed!" he scoffs. "I'll treat any tricks they try with a little trick of my own, the hoodlums!"

I pled with him that we have the means for him to hire guards to keep our home safe from vandals, that he and I could spend the night inside, that I miss him, that I miss his being my father. For the first time in my life, he is here at home and not always away on business, and he shuns me.

"Fool and disgrace!" he said. "A man does not hire others to protect his home. If you were not a pernicious weed, you would be down on the front steps with me, holding a gun yourself. So stay in your tower and let a man defend the castle."

e.

1 November 1928

Father hurled me into the confessional. "Bleed your sin from your lips to the priest, though you won't find absolution."

Father has no new-found faith, but he will dare enter the Church if only to shame me. I confessed no sin, for I've no soul to save.

And no amount of Father's money will ever buy atonement for his evil or mine. I did not kill mama. He did.

e.

∞ ∞ ∞

Dee awoke on the window seat in the wee hours, slip of paper clutched in her hand, bedroom light still on, bucket beside her. For a moment, she thought she was back in the double-wide, waiting for Clay to come home after his having run out on her.

But she was in the manse, and something had awakened her. She heard the creaking again, this time insistent. It was coming from the attic. Though she didn't believe in ghosts, she wasn't eager to hazard the attic in the dark, as there was no light up there. Installing electric there, at least for lighting, had, in fact, been one of the renovations she had on her still lengthy list. Nonetheless, Dee went into the hall, to look at the ceiling hatch that led to the attic. For a moment, in the darkness, she thought she saw a flash of light pass through the crack between the attic hatch and its lintel. She reached up for the hanging cord to pull down the door and its folding steps, when she heard a ghostly groan from the bedroom.

She found Luna sleepwalking, something she'd never done. Moaning, Luna walked to the window seat and knelt before it, clutching her fingers at its lip, trying to open it, but Diana knew that it offered no lid or storage. Diana was beside her and saw that her cheeks were flushed. "What are you doing, sweetie?" she asked, wondering if *Neverwhere* had indeed caused a nightmare.

"I must leave," Luna almost chanted, in a distant-echo voice. "You must redeem. I seek only release. To be who I am."

Luna's eyes looked like they were peering into the source of the echo, her fingers still clutching in vain to open the window seat. With a strength that belied her tiny frame, she budged it with a searing screech, pulling it up from the nails by a half inch. The effort took its toll as sweat trickled down her temple. Diana touched her hand to Luna's forehead, pulling it back at its heat. Luna fell, sick and feverish, into Dee's arms.

"You must release me," echoed the spectral voice. "You have been here many moons with me. You know me."

"Luna!" Dee whispered desperately. "Wake up!"

But Luna would not or could not, falling limp. Diana carried her to the bed, and not for the last time noticed that the Fire Maiden in the wainscoting mural was pointing at something.

Laying Luna on the bed, she rushed to the bathroom for a washcloth that she soaked in the coldest water the tap could afford, then sopped Luna's forehead with it. "Baby, sweet Luna, what's the matter?"

Her daughter's lips were chapped, and a fine patina of perspiration covered her face, the shirt of her Captain-Marvel pajamas blotted with a crescent-moon sweat stain. Diana took her pulse and found it racing and fluttery. Dee's stomach plunged. She had to break the fever. Even more urgent, she knew that dehydration could make Luna's situation dire. There was no time to attempt to take her to the hospital, and she wasn't eager to trust the Laurel Ridge volunteer EMT service. Taking a corner of the washrag, she stuck it between Luna's lips and squeezed a trickle onto Luna's flecked tongue. Measles? Mumps? Chicken pox? Unbuttoning Luna's PJ top and pulling up her bottoms up from her calves, she found no pox. She felt the glands under her jaw. No swelling signs of mumps, and no visual indication of measles. Putting her ear to Luna's chest, she found her breathing shallow and panting but no sounds of congestion in her lungs. Dee palpated her abdomen and pressed her ear to Luna's tummy. All the normal digestive sounds and palpation responses, with no sign of swelling in the appendix. Trickling more drops into Luna's mouth, Diana stroked her throat and got a swallowing response.

For the next two hours, Dee kept up the water trickles after she'd coaxed children's liquid Tylenol down Luna's throat. She tried the ear thermometer again—104.1°, another degree higher. Then Luna spasmed, Dee thinking she'd gone into seizure, but she was throwing up. Diana bent her over the bathroom garbage can that she'd had the presence of mind to bring in. Luna vomited until she had dry heaves. She looked at Diana. "Mommy, I don't feel good," then collapsed back into the bed.

Dee wasn't sure if Luna had expelled the Tylenol, so she gave her another dose. The night felt endless, punctuated by Luna's tossing and groans and spelled on the half hour by Dee's monitoring Luna's pulse, respiration, and temperature. In between those vitals, she continued to squeeze water into her daughter's still parched mouth and to change the cold compresses on her forehead, throat, and chest. As she bent her head to listen to Luna's heart, Dee heard the creaking again coming from overhead. She looked to the Fire Maiden, remembering the strange dream she'd had, but the fiery one's visage didn't change, keeping constant vigil on Luna while implacably pointing to the window seat. The creaking stopped as soon as it had started. Was this place scheming against her? Had she dared to claim it back from the shards of the past and make it her own, only to have it rise up and throw down Selene, strike down Luna, and weep out visions of ghosts, footprints of phantom visitors, and the hauntings of a demon in the attic?

When, through the frost flowers on the turret window, she saw dawn, Diana put her hand to Luna's forehead. Luna felt cooler, Dee taking her temperature. 99.2°. The fever had broken, thank God. She used the wash rags to dab Luna, then peeled off her PJs, replacing them with a cotton nightie. Dee rolled into the bed to cradle her daughter and enjoy the oblivion of sleep.

She startled awake to the doorbell ringing and an incessant pounding on the door. The time on her iPhone read 10:23am. Luna was curled in a fetal position, her mouth halfway open, emitting an even breathing. Dee stumbled out of the bed, throwing on her robe and slippers. When she finally got to the door, she peered through the peephole she'd installed. Mish. She opened the door.

"Hey, Mish," she offered, her eyes still bleary. "Come in."

Cold air poured from the open doorway, but Shelly stood there, chest heaving. "You goddamn bitch!"

Diana froze. "Mish, are you al—"

"No, I'm *not* fucking alright!" Shelly screamed, steam harrowing from her mouth. "You made sure of that, didn't you?"

"What?" Dee's stomach roiled. Something had gone horribly wrong, and she was to blame.

"Don't act like you don't know, you fucking cunt! You've ruined us!"

Diana rubbed her eyes and clutched her robe to her chest. "Mish, it's cold. Come in. There's been some misunderstanding."

"No!" retorted Michelle. "I'm beginning to understand a whole lot better than I used to! How long was Rooster your little darling project, Miss Butter-Wouldn't-Melt-In-Your-Mouth?"

"Mishie! You're worked up, I can see, but I've no clue—"

"It ain't *my* job to clue you into to the bullshit you've dragged us through. You know goddamn well that asshole from the property management company came to our door and reamed Rooster a new one!"

"What property management company?"

Michelle stood aghast. "Are you really gonna try to fake this one, Dee? Do you have the fucking gall to lie to me all over again? The mother-fucking property management company *you* fucking hired 'cuz 'Ms. Atestesso has determined that Mr. Cogbert's services are no longer satisfactory'! How long have you been planning this, Dee? Was it since I told you I didn't wanna renew our friendship 'cuz we're not kids anymore? Did it sting you so much that impoverished redneck Mishie who married an old rub-a-dub rejected you? What did you think? That you and your rich-ass could just traipse up here and party with me like old times? Then, when I talked like the adult I am, you got your pretty little self all bent out of shape and decided to teach me a lesson for failing to adore you this time around!"

Tears rolled down Diana's eyes as she gaped in wonder at the Fury who'd arrived at her doorstep.

"And you fucking stand there just having got out of bed when other people whose goddamn shoes you don't have the right to lick *work* for a fucking living! Rooster's broken, damn it. Are you satisfied? He fucking worshipped you! You could do no wrong by him, slipping him a few bills like a treat to a whipped dog. His head's so far up your ass that even now—" Here she started sobbing. "Even now he's sitting at home not blaming you for one goddamn thing. He thinks he's too old, and that you decided you needed someone younger and more professional … and he doesn't hold it against you!!!" She screamed, the veins bulging from her throat. "You never fucking deserved him, and you sure as hell never deserved me!!" Michelle hollered and threw something into the yard.

"There! There are the goddamn keys to this fucking horseshit hellhole that my husband has looked after for years for a spoiled bitch who repays him by dumping his ass on the curb like so much trash. If this is how you treat people, your husband had every right to fuck you up and to steal your daughter. Maybe he knew something the rest of us are only now getting wise to!"

Diana stood in the doorway long after Michelle had reached the bottom of the hillside staircase, started her truck, and left.

∞ ∞ ∞

"Brad, I'm telling you that a property management company representative was at Rooster's door, informing him he was dismissed. *I* didn't contact a property management company."

"Di', what the hell are you talking about?"

"You know damn well, Brad! You've been trying to undermine my plans for this place since the get-go. You hadn't ever told me in the first place that *Rooster* was the 'property management company'! I had to find that out from Rooster himself, which was embarrassing enough. Then, when I'd put my trust in him, you pull a stunt like this, and my high-school best friend is on my front stoop accusing me of bloody murder!"

"Whoa, whoa, whoa, Di'! When I hadn't heard any word from you about Rooster, I assumed no news was good news. *I* didn't hire any property management company. Why the hell would I when you're up there?"

"Because," seethed Dee, "You've never taken me seriously."

Brad actually laughed. "The fact that I haven't started legal proceedings against your hare-brained plans for the house shows I more than take you seriously. But a phone call like this makes me wonder if you *do* have drug-dependency issues, though I'd thought getting Luna back might settle you down."

Diana was nearly apoplectic, but she forced down her rage. "Brad, in the end, I don't give a fuck what you think, and all your threats are idle. What I *do* care about are the lives of two people and their kids—people I care about, who've been ripped apart by this stunt of yours. I'm not sure I can salvage the relationship even if you came up here and apologized to

212

Rooster yourself."

There was a pause on the other end of the call. "Princess Diana, there's no way in hell I'm apologizing for anything because, like I've been trying to tell you, *I didn't DO anything!* I don't know what you're talking about. Rooster was always my go to, especially at the price. And think about *this*, Di'—why the hell would a management company break the news to Rooster? Wouldn't they assume that's *our* job? Take a look-see at the people you've been associating with up there. Either Mish is crazy (a likely scenario) or someone's fucking around with you. Either way, Di', I'm washing my hands of this. You win—you're too fucking crazy for me. I'll sink no more money in that dump. You can have the goddamn rotting furniture in the joint. *You* deal with the whole enchilada. There, am I taking you seriously now?"

He hung up.

∞ ∞ ∞

Luna was bed-ridden for three days, Dee spoon-feeding her soup and saltines. The poor thing battled with diarrhea and exhaustion. When, near the end of the third day, Luna expressed interest in continuing *Neverwhere*, Diana felt so relieved that she made Luna a milkshake of bananas, peanut butter, and chocolate ice cream, which Luna sipped down through three more chapters of *Neverwhere*, till she fell asleep clutching the shake. Dee prayed the shake would settle her daughter's digestive tract, as an uninterrupted night of sleep would be the best medicine for both of them. Diana was still reeling from the confrontation with Shelly and, despite being exhausted by the past few nights of taking care of Luna, had, when she could steal some sleep, tossed and turned with obsessive nightmares of Shelly and Rooster accusing her all over again, alternating with ones about healing the hideous situation, only to, upon waking up, realize that, no, it all had really happened and that she had no hope of repairing their relationship. In waking hours, she couldn't help but second-guess herself. Should she have told Rooster from the outset that she was renovating the manse in order to sell it, which meant that, sooner or later, he'd be out of a job? Or should she have told Rooster honestly when she first moved in that she really didn't need his and Shelly's help? She was perfectly capable of cleaning the place herself. After all, she was already cleaning up in the wake of her remodeling. That might've been a painless way to cut off the deal with Rooster in the first place, without ever knowing that Shelly was her Mish from years ago. All the while, Brad's words echoed in her head. *"Why the hell would a management company take it upon itself to break the news to Rooster?"*

Or was Brad right in saying that it was a delusion of Shelly's? The only way to discover that was to talk with Rooster, which, at this point, was unthinkable. Dee just wanted it all to be gone, for the reverberations of that trauma to subside and just leave her alone to get this fucking renovation done and sell the place.

Why not go back to Texas right now? Even Selene couldn't stop her from doing that. Yes, it would mean forgoing proceeds from the sale of the manse. But did it look so bad now that she couldn't sell it this moment? She'd always been a perfectionist—maybe now was the time to let go of that. But selling it now was out of the question. Even if she could bring herself to putting it onto the market in its current state, who showed a house in the mountains in the dead of winter? For that matter, who would hike up Laurel Ridge to *see* it? As for Texas, she and Luna would have no place to live. Of course, they could stay with Selene, but Dee couldn't bring herself to do that no matter how welcome Selene would make them. Besides, Selene herself was recovering and far from 100 percent. And Diana simply couldn't face Selene when both of them would know in the back of their minds that she'd left the job undone, reclaiming the house but not reclaiming her never-settled relationship with the mountain and the manse in winter that haunted her adolescence. The eternal nights and truncated, overcast days of no birdsong, accompanied by the only soundtrack in this loneliest of forsaken places—the sound of snow falling off a branch to a heap below. God, that loneliness in the midst of Mom's silence and Dad's eyes of terror still carved a hole in her heart that she now realized she'd not filled, maybe would never fill. She might be destined for life to walk wounded, apologizing to the world and herself for who she was.

∞ ∞ ∞

By the following week, Luna was almost back to herself. They finished *Neverwhere*, Luna too fatigued to go to the library to pick another title. Nonetheless, Dee was relieved to see her daughter on her way back to health, able to walk about, curl up in her favorite chair, and wash on her own. The forecast called for more snow by next weekend. Luna was still not in good enough shape to go with Diana down the mountain for groceries this week. While they had a deep-freeze full of entrees, meat, and frozen waffles, and a pantry of canned goods, they needed almond milk, coffee, bread, cereal, snacks, bacon, other meats, cleansers, shampoo, and toiletries. Sunday or Monday of next week would be the longest they could go until having to make a trip down the mountain to buy enough groceries to see them through a month or more. There were small mom-and-pop grocery stores on the mountain, but their inventory was spotty, as well as their selection, neither of which would be up to the winter-settle-in grocery trip Dee needed to make.

A week passed uneventfully until the following Friday night, when Luna had a relapse of fever, dehydration, and heart palpitations. Dee felt they were snake-bit, the thought of which made her check Luna for spider bites or ticks. If it were Lyme disease, they'd head directly for a hospital in Pittsburgh. "Damn it!" she'd sobbed to herself in the shower, which she didn't dare extend beyond five minutes for fear of leaving Luna alone longer. "Why can't we catch a break? Or are we now paying for

215

the brief time of happiness we had with Selene here? Maybe *I'm* the one who's the carrier of calamity."

After the Steelers' game on Sunday night, she thought it safe to call Finn, as the bar would be winding down. "No worries," Finn said. "The horses' asses were getting trounced by KC anyway. I made last call at the end of the third quarter. By that point, only Allan and two never-say-die fans were left. Lemme put you on hold, so I can take this in the office."

After a lengthy gap, he picked up again. "Sorry, Dee. I had to clear the drawer. My bar-back, Tracy, knocked off at halftime but stuck around to watch the game. She then volunteered to mop up for me. I lucked out with her. So, what's up?"

"Sorry to bug you this late, but I need a huge favor, and I've got no one else to help me."

"Ah, what I love to hear! 'Finn, you're my last resort!'"

She sighed. "You know I don't mean it like that. I wouldn't ask such a favor if it wasn't serious."

"Now I'm intrigued. But I have to warn you that, in childhood, I already gave one of my kidneys to Keith Richard. Bet you've been wondering how he's stayed alive so long."

"The favor's almost as steep as organ donation, but I wouldn't come to you if Luna and I weren't desperate."

"Dee, you're stubborn and proud. You have to see a situation as desperate in order to ask for help. I would know—we're both charter members of the Recovering Perfectionists Foundation. C'mon, spit it out. You know I'll be there in a heartbeat."

"It's not this-minute urgent, but, um, Luna's sick again—"

"Again? Do you need me to take her to the hospital?"

"It's not to that point, but I'm gonna have to if this keeps up. And, through no fault of my own, Rooster's cut off from me

…"

"What?"

"It's a long story of woe I can tell when I see you, but I literally've got no one else. Brad isn't even talking to me anymore."

"Forgive me for observing that's no big loss."

"I'm inclined to agree. But what I'm not inclined to do is starve. If I texted you a grocery list—and it's a whopper—would you be able to go to the grocery store, then haul the load up the mountain? I can't possibly leave Luna by herself in this condition, and I'm exhausted and at my wit's end. I'll Venmo you the money ahead of time, so you—"

"How much?" Finn asked.

"Uh, well, do you think $500 would be enough?"

"No, I mean how much space do you have in your pantry, fridge, and deep freeze, 'cuz I'm ready to rent a 24-foot trailer and empty the store for you. Besides, your money's no good to me. I've been dying to do you a big favor ever since you got here. But, damn it, your hella self-sufficient."

Dee started crying.

"Hey, hey now! Those better be tears of joy. Besides you always sound like Stan Laurel when you cry, which means I'll have to join you to drown you out. And you *know* how *I* cry. Remember in *Rocky III*, when Mickey dies, and Sylvester Stallone pukes up the equivalent of his entire cardiovascular system in body-wracking sobs? Yeah, it's kinda like that."

Dee's crying was now punctuated with laughter. "You big fucking idiot. I don't cry like Stan Laurel!"

"For verification purposes, I'll show a YouTube video of him doing it when I get up there. I'm already recording this call, so we'll have that as a baseline."

"Th-th-thank you so much, Finn. I was beginning to think I'm the kiss of death to everyone I'm supposed to be close to."

"Okay, now I *know* this shit is serious" insisted Finn. "I *have* to come up there and drink some sense into you, Diana Atestesso."

Dee continued to smudge tears from her eyes. "Is tomorrow okay, say, 4pm? After I help you unload, I'll make you dinner. Also, I'll make my famous Atestesso lasagna to take home."

"Phhheeewwww!" Finn whistled. "I haven't had decent lasagna since my mom passed. How about *I* bring up dinner and do the unloading myself? This is supposed to help you, not make you try to juggle dinner, make lasagna for a prince, and care for your daughter. Bud Murphy's pizza, two large pies! Have the oven preheated to warm 'em up. I'll toss in some Chianti, too."

∞ ∞ ∞

By Monday afternoon, Luna had recovered enough to wait by the front window for Finn, whom she adored. "Sweetie, you're only now healing up," warned Dee. "So, you don't need to stand in a cold doorway while Finn and I bring in the groceries. There'll be time to be with him once he and the groceries are in."

She'd blushed to remember that 'bringing in the groceries' had first meant Finn's hauling them up the 39,000 Steps, because the driveway had become impassable when the temps dropped to 20 degrees and froze the then-melting snow. She'd not calculated *that* into the vastness of the favor she'd asked of him. However, Finn seemed intent on showing her that hope and grace hadn't died with the onset of winter. Around 11am that morning, she heard scraping outside and looked out to see four parka-clad guys clearing the driveway, stairs, and walkway, and spreading magnesium chloride to melt the ice. She ran outside, fearing they'd come to the wrong address, but the lead clearer assured her that it was on the up-and-up. "Any friend of Finn's is a friend of me and my boys," he said, then winked. "And I ain't doin' this for free, just for a reduced cost. You'll have to take up the fee with Finn—he's already paid and tipped us, Ma'am." He doffed his Pens cap to her and went back to work.

Dee went inside and wept again, out of sight of Luna.

"What?" protested Finn after he'd arrived and hauled in the groceries. "It was in *my* interest to be able to get up the driveway and the walkway in one piece. I can't cook or tend bar in traction. You owe me zero cents, Diana." He held up two "0" signs. "All of this is on me, except for the lasagna. A man'll go to any length for good Italian."

Dee clasped herself to him in a hug that he had to finally break away from. "Dee, you're acting like this is a hardship for me. You don't make life hard for me or for anyone else who really knows you. I just want you to see that your thinking otherwise only makes life hard for Diana Atestesso. And *that* I won't tolerate."

They devoured the Bud Murphy's, with even Luna consuming her fair share. Finn had bought her a *Captain Marvel*-themed toiletry set, including shampoo, two toothpastes, two toothbrushes, mouthwash, and floss. After that, Luna became a confirmed flosser, making Dee have to counsel her that she needed to do it just once a day. Dee had forgotten to put kids toothpaste on the list. Not only was Luna's nearly out, Dee hadn't been so sure that it wasn't contaminated with whatever virus had twice waylaid her daughter, so she'd thrown it and her toothbrush and bathroom cup out. Finn had come through on another count.

"Jesus," Dee said as they patted their bellies after clearing the pizza, sipping the wine while Luna watched the *Captain Marvel* blu-ray Finn had bought her. "Are you trying to upstage Santa

Claus? Bit of overkill, don't you think? Uh, not that we don't appreciate it."

Finn shrugged. "I have high standards when it comes to food. Got most of the groceries from DeLallo's in Jeanette. Good imported stuff. The rest came from the Kroger in Greensburg, y'know in that new mega-center? When I saw the huge *Captain Marvel* display, you can understand my hands were tied."

"Uh-huh," Dee rolled her eyes, then noticed that Luna had fallen asleep. She must've still been drained from the virus to have fallen asleep to *Captain Marvel*. Finn cradled her in his gigantic arms while Diana led them up the steps where they put Luna to bed, Dee retrieving the three notes of paper she'd read before she'd fallen asleep the first night of Luna's virus that now seemed an eternity ago.

In the living room, they sat down, and Dee handed him the slips of paper. "What do you make of these?"

Finn examined them. "Old paper," he said. "And definitely old script. I could tell that without the date. Where'd you get these?"

Diana explained their origin story and the vicissitudes of removing early 1900s medicine chests from their moorings. "Ever since, Luna's been obsessed with getting me to read them. It looks like pages from a journal, don't you think?"

Finn nodded. "The question is, *whose* journal? Chester Frick owned this house, so that makes the speculation even more interesting." Finn then read them, Dee drinking down her wine. Finishing the notes, Finn asked, "It's pretty clear that 'Father' in these entries is Chester Frick. But who's 'e.'—a mini-me of e.e. cummings?"

"Obviously, 'e.' is Chester's son."

Finn raised an eyebrow. "Chester Frick had surviving twin

sons who were in their thirties at the time these were written, if the dates of the entries are accurate. And those two sons were real pricks, at least in Chester's esteem. Then again, Papa Frick had just as endearing a reputation with the two of them."

"How do you know so much about the coke baron who built my house?" Dee asked, feeling a little buzzed from the wine.

"It's like I told you when you first came back here in the summer—y'know, my theory about the collapse of the coke industry and the mine fires. I've long been interested in the times when Fayettenam was not akin to a war zone but commanded privilege, riches, and clout." He gazed around them at the house. "This mansion was just a little summer cottage for Mr. Frick. But did you know that this is where he died?"

"Yes, and eww," she scrunched her eyes and moved closer to Finn. "I hope it wasn't ghastly. I've been hearing suspicious noises around this place, and Luna's convinced it's haunted."

Finn gazed down at her as she nuzzled into his shoulder. "Not to make you feel any creepier, but there was some debate at the time as to whether it was something other than suicide. He was found dead in the bathroom with a pistol and a clean shot through the heart that the County Coroner tentatively concluded was self-administered. But the gossip rags of the era speculated that it was the murderous work of one or both of the aforementioned prick twins. From all accounts (of both reliable and yellow journalism), the sons had sufficient motivation. But the DA's heart wasn't in it. He wouldn't pursue a grand-jury indictment for murder, despite the coroner's never being explicit as to whether the shot had been self-administered. And the forensic records weren't released to the public till decades later, after the twins themselves passed on. As you can imagine, with grand-jury members, DA, coroner, law enforcement, and general public alike, it was hard to find a person in the County who wasn't either enamored of or beholden to the Frick estate.

So, it might not have been all that arduous to secure the cooperation necessary to sweep under the manse rug any dirty deeds."

"Double eww," she said, fingers on his chest. "You know so much, you oughta write a book about it. I could submit one of the chapters to the *Journal of Creepy Nursing Stories* for you."

Finn snickered. "I *could* write a book. But it's already been done—a detailed bio and history of the rise and demise of the Chester Frick empire. It's one of my sources, though it's been years since I read it. The Penn State Fay-West campus library doesn't have much of note on its shelves, except for it's Fayette-County history collection, happily financed by the Chester Frick Endowment, which is apparently still administered by the descendants of the prick Fricks. In fact, though not many people except nerds like me care about it, the *Connellsville Daily Courier* ran an article a few years back about the entire collection being digitized and the original tomes sent to the Penn State main-campus library where they have a refrigerated book repository for all the antique books and manuscripts that didn't hold up so well to a Chester Frick by-product—coal-induced acid-rain humidity. The ultimate irony. Wonder how much the prick Frick Endowment gave to build that ice-box book silo?"

"Hee-hee," she giggled and stroked his chest. "'Prick Fricks!'"

He kissed her hair. "Though most mere mortals couldn't get the digital version online, I bet you, with the academic library permissions you have, could access it. You oughta read up on his life, to see what connection it might have to this confetti journal. Chester Frick remarried later in life, and I think had a son, which may be the source of his two older sons' prickliness—they might've been afraid old Chester was going to do an end-around and give his estate to the upstart. Maybe his second wife or their missing-link upstart son is the mystery 'e.' of these pages."

She was kissing him, her hands on his face and in his hair. It had been so very long since she'd felt this kind of release. And, well, *Finn.* They'd hooked up once in high school but couldn't look each other in the face the next day, though she never understood why. Maybe it was because they were indeed such friends that breaching a new stage in the relationship threatened to overwhelm what they had.

He returned the passion. She was trying to get her blouse open when Finn gently took her wrist. "Diana," he whispered.

She paused, stroking his face.

"Honey," he mumbled. "Don't get me wrong—I'm all about this, and you know I'm no gentleman. So, this isn't about honor. But you've had a helluva time of late, and you're vulnerable."

"You're damn right I am," she said, putting her lips to his.

She could tell she was winning him over, but, damn it, he paused again. "Dee, it's gonna get to the point of no return. And by 'vulnerable,' I mean that you're lonely enough to want any affection right now—"

"You mean I'm horny, Finn. And you're right!" Her hand was searching for his belt buckle, but he took it again.

"Dee! You *know* I want this, but I need you to want it for reasons you're sure about. Wine and your friend having brought Christmas cheer may not be the best basis for such a decision." He paused to look away, almost disgusted with himself. "God! Listen to me! I can't believe I'm saying this, because you don't know how many nights and days long before you ever came back here I've fantasized about having you. And renewing our friendship hasn't exactly turned a cold shower on that."

"Then it should be no problem," she said, quite happy with herself. "I'm a big girl. I can show you."

He held onto her wrist. "Dee, please. I—I don't know why,

but I don't feel right taking it further, at least for the moment. You just lost Selene, Luna's been sick, Shelly went apeshit on you, and your brother has all but abandoned you."

"All the more reason I need you, Finn. Now c'mon, let go of my hand so I can show you."

"Diana, that's what you want right now, and Lord knows it's what every fiber of my being wants, but I don't want *us* to pay a price for it. Let's nurture this. Slow it down. I'm not gonna abandon you or up and die. Let's do this the right way. We can spend Christmas together—you, me, and Luna. I want you, but I want every bit of you, and right now I'm worried that the wine and the recent craters in your life aren't speaking for all of you."

She pulled away, angry at him, but more at herself for being angry at him. He was right, she knew. Yet another area in which she was amply demonstrating impaired judgment. She started crying. "Oh, Finn. I'm so sorry," she said and wept a long time into his shoulder.

Hours later, she was with him at the door, the two kissing, one not wanting to leave, the other not wanting the departure.

"You alright, Dee?"

"Yeah. Thanks to you."

"No, Dee—thanks to *you*. You've known me too long to confuse me with a knight in shining armor. I'm a dude just like all dudes. But I care about you."

She felt the tears coming on again. "I don't want you to leave. I'm … I'm worried you won't come back."

"Like that's gonna happen! Let me get back home and check my Xmas schedule. I know I had a Yuletide tea scheduled with the Queen, but I'll just have to tell the bitch that the chance to get more of your lasagna pulls rank on her sorry royal ass."

"Oh!" she said and ran back into the kitchen to pull the

lasagna from the freezer.

She laid it in his hands. "It's not that I think you won't want to come back, Finn. It's just that, well, I don't have a good track record of people leaving and being *able* to come back to me. I'm Rappaccini's Daughter—one kiss and you're poisoned."

Finn smiled at her, then kissed her long. "I think we've had more than one kiss tonight. If I could bottle you, I would swallow the contents as my cure-all. I *will* be back, even if I have to, *a la* Aragorn, walk the paths of the dead."

She wanted to melt into him, but he made sure to kill the moment. "Now let a man go home to make love to his lasagna, will ya?" He kissed her forehead and tramped to his Jeep, her heart lying frozen on the porch step.

∞ ∞ ∞

The next morning, Finn sent her a mushy e-card, then texted her the name of the Frick history and its author.

The snow was coming down thick, and she had little to do while Luna watched *Captain Marvel,* so Dee accessed the Penn State library digital database to find the 1957 title, *The Life and Demise of Chester Frick, Southwestern Pennsylvania Coal Magnate.*

This was no tall tale nor homage to the memory of Chester Frick, unless such had been bidden by his sons, decades after, unaffected by his legacy, except in terms of how it padded their own. The author, one Darcy P. Lullbright, had been a Professor of American History at the University of Pittsburgh. Perhaps this volume had won him tenure.

Diana parsed through the early chapters dwelling on Chester Frick's childhood at the mercy, or lack thereof, of his father, Alesso Fricci, a hard, unfeeling Italian immigrant from the Marches region of Italy, who worked his way from back breaking coke laborer in the mid-1800s to the master of 100 coke ovens in Fayette and Westmoreland Counties. Eager to be free of the stigma of "greasy guinea Italian" in a realm colonized a century-and-a-half before by English and Scotts-Irish, Alesso changed his surname to "Frick," married a woman of English stock, and, though he'd named his only son, born in 1869, after the Italian cognate of Caesar, "Cesaré," insisted on his child being called "Chester." Raised in the ruthlessly dogged work-ethic of his father, Chester also saw beyond his elder's ambitions, understanding intuitively that his father's holdings and means of production were limited and unsophisticated. Taking his earnings as a foreman in his father's company, Chester bought his own coke ovens and converted their process to a more efficient method—an ingenious late-1890s innovation that would lead to his empire and its ultimate collapse.

Coke was a lighter, airy carbon derived from smoldering coal to free from it "non-essential elements" that burned off as gasses and tars. The original coke ovens had been a mini-industrial revolution from the old process of burning coal underneath a layer of sod. But Chester saw something more than the beehive ovens of his contemporaries. Why let the gasses blow away and the tars run off? Instead of beehive ovens, why not create the coal-industry equivalent of a rendering plant? *Trap* the gasses and *collect* the tars and other byproducts in compact ovens that produced increased coke per ton-of-coal *and* harvested byproducts marketable for other industrial applications. Team this with a railroad conveyance network of coal to oven to steel mill, and the production and yield of coke became not just quicker and more efficient but turned what before was waste into marketable commodities.

By 1893, Chester Frick sent his father into retirement. By 1897, Chester operated 8,000 new-fangled coke byproduct ovens. By 1905, no coke producer owned anywhere near the 36,000 ovens of the Chester Frick & Sons Corporation, who also oversaw rail, telephone, oil, and smelting concerns as the largest employer in Fayette and Westmoreland Counties, public or private.

Here was where Dee began to read in detail. *Frick was a ruthless and cutthroat monopolist, driving down his prices to gut his competitors and buying their concerns for pennies on the dollar. But he was rapacious beyond the boundaries of the coke industry. The growth of electricity as a power source saw Frick buy utility providers and state and congressional representatives to ensure that electric would stay primarily a residential and municipal source of power, even as technological advances increased electricity output, making it more cost-efficient and attractive for industrial applications. As he improved the efficiency of his modern coke ovens, however, he laid the groundwork for his ultimate demise, as his own engineers began to leave his employ to port the byproduct-oven design in even more compact and innovative applications to the steel mills themselves. Why wait for coke to be refined and shipped from Connellsville, when the more ample rail lines of Allegheny County could move raw bituminous coal directly to the steel mill, where coke could be processed in-house and, while still hot, be used in steel production, cutting out the middle-man Frick, who had built his reputation and riches on his implacable dictation of the terms of his coke-enterprise relationship with steel producers?*

"… From his unhappy first marriage, Frick's twin sons, Alesso and Adesso, had foreseen both the rise of in-house coke production and the advent in later decades of electrical firing in the steel process that could provide higher and more easily regulated temperatures than the burning of coke, with appreciably less waste and effort …

"So entrenched and confident had Frick become in the purity and efficiency of his coke production that he scoffed at the idea of steel mills taking the process in-house. Further, he thought he held the reigns of the electrical utilities but was so blinded by his own companies' lack of interest in industrial applications of electricity that he could not see both governmental and competing firms' innovations to expand electricity output in ways hitherto thought impossible. So adamant did he become in these matters that he rebuffed his sons' urgings to divest of his coke holdings and invest instead in new means of electrical production, especially hydro-electricity. This, in turn, turned his sons against him, playing cat-and-mouse games in the management of Frick holdings to the point that his sons

wrested from their father control of a good portion of the enterprise …

"Much of their animus could also be explained by Frick's divorce and abandonment of their mother, as well as his wooing of a younger woman who would bear him a third son, Emilio, whom Frick immediately vested with direct inheritance of the entire Frick empire …

"In his later years, with the day-to-day management of the very company he'd founded as the bedrock of his vast holdings now slipping from his control, Chester Frick increasingly retreated to his mountain-mansion enclave to take care of his chronically ill bride (who some sources claim was irretrievably damaged by her pregnancy with Emilio) and raise his son in mountain isolation …

"Frick's hermitage was increasingly breached by the inroads and demands of his elder sons who now saw him as falling into early dotage and sought to have him declared mentally unfit …

"Chester armed himself with batteries of attorneys to circumnavigate every attempt by Alesso and Adesso to wrest his dominion over the holdings left to him, and rebuff their efforts to institutionalize him, which, increasingly, they sought as their final means of claiming not only what they saw as rightly theirs but to oversee that empire through the upheavals occurring industry-wide. None of his former associates and business partners, now increasingly alienated by Frick's retreat to the mountains, ever previously noted his slightest inclination to be a philanthropist. However, his tenacious and assiduous establishment of charitable, educational, and medical foundations not only afforded him shelter from taxation but effectively placed out of reach of his elder sons much of his wealth. With few or no records of Chester Frick's state of mind through the period of 1923 to his suicide in 1929, a shroud of mystery veils his true intentions, but his sons interpreted his actions as those of 'If it will be taken from me, you, at least, shall not have it either.' What was to be left to young Emilio beyond a lifetime of managing philanthropic concerns remains a mystery. However, Alesso's and Adesso's intrepid legal maneuverings seem to indicate that they feared Emilio's one day being able to seize the Frick empire from them …

"All that has been reported and committed to print as to the fate of

Emilio Frick could fill another tome, lengthier than this one. Suffice it to say that, to this day, no party, person, or governmental entity has been able to confirm his ultimate denouement. The months spanning 1928-29 are critical to understanding whether he was kidnapped by his elder brothers or otherwise spirited away (though no legal or investigative proceeding has been able to establish their culpability in his disappearance or potential murder) or whether he fell to the same fate as his father. Little if no documentation exists, as, in the years following the death of Chester's wife in 1926 to her chronic illness (which some liken to tuberculosis, though Frick allowed no autopsy), Chester limited himself and Emilio exclusively to the mountain residence, seeing no one but his primary attorney, J. Eldon Wadsworth, Esq., whom he afforded no further egress into the domicile than the front parlor. Indeed, so rebuffed became Wadsworth at Frick's seclusion and secretiveness that, despite what must have been a lucrative remuneration, he separated himself and his firm from Frick's retention in late 1928, after which no record persists of Chester Frick's having secured legal representation …

    "Some more romantic accounts speculate that Emilio chafed at what effectively was his imprisonment, and eventually escaped the clutches of his father. That young man's years-long isolation and the greater world's utter ignorance of his visage and identity, as well as the funds at his disposal, enabled him, as those accounts purport, to assume an entirely new identity, free of the familial feuding that must have made his young life unendurable. Indeed, those reporters of more yellow journalistic penchant attributed Chester's death neither to his elder sons nor to suicide but to Emilio, who, it is conjectured, thereby freed himself of the surly bonds of his imprisonment by striking down the tyrannical rule of his father and pursuing life on his own terms. Such farragoes speculate so far as to say that the ultimate collapse of the Frick empire was not so much generated by the Great Depression or Alesso's and Adesso's and their heirs' later inability to sustain their forebears' initiative as to the invisible handiwork of one Emilio, who, having disposed of his father, also sought to wipe away what he deemed the Frickian blot as represented by the rapaciousness of his father and elder half-siblings. These untenable sources assert that the veracity of their conjectures is confirmed by the fact that the remaining vestiges of the Frick presence that once dominated Southwestern Pennsylvania are the

surviving charitable institutions that yet bear that name. For such purveyors of purple prose, the Frick fire still burns underneath the ruins of an empire that had once remapped the western half of the Keystone State and the Tri-State region.

Dee closed her laptop and rose from her seat, looking about her at a home that now took on a more sinister mien. "Jesus Christ, no wonder this place dragged me down when I was a kid! Depressing a teen is like shooting fish in a barrel, but this is misery-loves-company to a new sadistic low," she whispered.

Maybe Luna's insistence that she'd seen a ghost had more to it than Dee realized. Chester Frick had offed himself here. When in her remodeling was she going to strip wallpaper to reveal more bloodstains in addition to those on the bathroom floor? And it seemed that Emilio was indeed the "e." of the journal entries. Chilled, Dee wrapped her arms around herself. She suddenly felt an isolation that had snuck its way in, right under her nose, a visitor unbidden, uninvited, whose presence made her question all her best-laid plans. She didn't belong here and had been mad to think she could make this place anything other than the prison she'd always known it was. The walls rose about her, emblematic of the failure of her every ambition. Her whole shambling life had been a vain attempt to renovate a haunted past, amounting to a peeling veneer layered over futility.

She shook her head. "Talk about purple prose, damn it! How did I get into such maudlin thoughts? There's more to this story than what some blowhard historian scribbled in the 1950s. I've done something right—look at Luna!" The thought of her daughter reminded her of the labor Luna had assigned her—to read the journal slips. "That's gonna fill in some blanks, and not just in Frick's story. Maybe in mine as well!"

Part IV

Emiliana

She's singin' "Knick-knack, paddy-whack,
a broken glass of cognac,
I bet he can't hurt me from the grave"

Big bad wolf in pretty sheep's skin
showed his teeth when he took to the drink,
Little bitty girl is capable of terrible things
when she's pushed to the brink
—"Beautifully Sewn, Violently Torn," Lincoln Durham

Dee hadn't heard from Finn after his e-card and text, which was strange, given the intimacy they'd shared Monday night. "Did I scare him off?" she wondered. "No, wait a minute. This is Finn we're talking about." Connellsville had gotten its share of snow, though not as much as the Ridge had. Maybe he was digging out and simultaneously dealing with holiday parties booked at the bar. But every time she tried his phone, it went straight to voicemail, which was full. Finn ran a business. It wasn't like him to not answer messages or emails.

She tried the bar, but Tracy, the bar back, and not Finn, answered. "Can you get Finn, please? Tell him it's Dee."

"Hon', I wish I could, but Finn's in the hospital, and I'm up to my eyeballs here trying to keep the bar afloat, me and the backup cook, Todd."

"What? Oh my God! Why's Finn in the hospital?"

"I'm not for certain, Hon'. We'd love to know, too. Allan's

been my source of information. He's the one who found Finn."

"Which hospital, Tracy?"

"Todd!" She yelled. "Where's Finn laid up?" Pause. "Oh, yeah, that's right. He's at Excela Frick in Mount Pleasant, Hon'. If you're going to see 'im, tell 'im we miss him."

Allan was the only person in the ICU waiting area when she and Luna arrived 10 minutes before visiting time, and he looked like a dog who'd lost his human. "Hey, Dee," he murmured, and hugged her. "Helluva way to renew an old high-school acquaintance, huh?"

"It's been years, Allan," said Diana. "But, nothing against you, I could've gone another 20 years if it meant not seeing you under circumstances like this."

"Yeah," Allan said, looking down at the floor and shuffling his weather-worn boots.

"Allan, this is my daughter, Luna." Dee turned to Luna. "Luna, this is Mr. Franklin."

Allan looked more the child in this encounter, his eyes wide, as if, in shaking Luna's hand, he might break it off. Luna smiled and showed him the Captain Marvel sticker she'd applied to her wrist. "Hey there, little girl. I ain't kept up with m' comics since I was young, but that one looks like she can handle herself."

Luna emphatically nodded her head and gave Allan an enthusiastic thumbs up. Allan looked back up at Dee, his eyes like saucers—the thought of bringing a child into the world seemingly epic beyond his imagining. "You done good by yourself, Diana."

"Actually, she does all the good for me. What's the situation with Finn?"

Allan scratched his head and again shuffled his feet. "Well, it takes some tellin', if yinz don't mind sittin' down to hear it."

Dee set Luna up with the iPad and a ginger ale that they'd gotten from the vending machine. Then she turned to Allan "What's his condition?"

Scritching his neck, Allan searched for words. "The way I can figure it, he's in a coma, though I ain't heard no doctor say that."

"Coma? What happened to him, Allan?"

"That's what I wuz 'fraid you'd ask. I don't really know, and I was the one who found 'im."

"When?"

"Lessee. Today's Friday, the 20th of December, am I right? I've kinda been in a time warp with the excitement 'n 'at."

"Yes, it's Friday."

"Then it wuz Wednesday. Two days ago, in the morning, 'round 10am."

"Where did you find him? The bar?"

"Naw. In his apartment behind the bar. See, I like to get my drink on early, an' sometimes Finn, he'll let me in early-like, 'cuz he an' I've known each other since kindygarten. But he wuzn't in the bar. The place was dark like it'd be at 6am, an' I wuz worried he wuzn't gonna open. So I went 'round back to his place an' banged on the door. No answer. An' I thought, 'Now, Allan, what if he went outta town for the holidays 'n 'at?' That got me worried, 'cuz Finn's kinda m' only friend an' keeps me from spendin' Xmas alone. So I pounded his door to beat the band, then I see his truck's still there, so he's gotta be home. Did the lunkhead sleep in, or what?

"Well, shit, I wuz worried now, so I found his magnetic key holder where he puts it under the brushes drawer o' his barbecue grill—it's a big ol' thing you could cook a buffalo in. I feel kinda sheepish tellin' yinz this, but I told the EMTs the same thing—see, I snuck in with his key, but I figure m' hands were tied. Anyway, the EMTs didn't bat an eyelash at me doin' that. They just wanted to know what I found."

"I do, too, Allan," said Dee, growing impatient. "I saw him on Monday, before the snow, and he was in perfect health. What could've happened to him?"

Allan wiped his mouth with the back of a trembling hand. Dee looked at her watch—it was 8:24am, and six minutes to ICU visitation. "See, I don't know, Diana. I found him collapsed on the floor, in the hallway 'tween his kitchen an' the livin' room. TV had NHL Network on, y'know how he loves his hockey. I turned 'im over and put m' finger to his throat, an' he had a pulse an' was breathin' but it was labored 'n 'at. I tried that CPR on 'im, though I ain't sure I got it right. Seemed t' help, so I grabbed the phone an' called 911. Wuzn't much I could do. Pardon me, yer a nurse, I sat there an' wondered if he had anythin' that was catchin' 'cuz, y'know, I put m' mouth to his 'n at for the CPR."

"No, Allan. I don't think you'd catch anything from him, as he seemed in great shape when I saw him. You did the right thing with the CPR, and I'm proud of you—you saved his life."

Allan looked down at the floor, and his cheeks grew redder than his nose. "I don't know 'bout that, but I did my best. Damn'est thing, though. I ain't never had no herp m' whole life, an' I ain't lived 'xactly the best life, y'know. But it wuzn't till yesterday mornin' I noticed I got this here fever blister somethin' fierce." He pulled open his bottom lip, and in the corner was a nasty blister. "Itches and burns like I got fuckin' poison ivy." He paused and looked wide-eyed in Luna's direction. "Oh, Dee, I'm sorry for cussin' 'round yer daughter."

"Don't worry, Allan. She's heard worse from my mouth. I can recommend some over-the-counter cream to help you with that cold sore. I'll write it down for you before I leave."

"Thank you, Dee. You wuz always a decent person in a pretty shitty high school. Always looked fresh as a daisy, even in the dead of winter."

It was Dee's turn to blush, but she redirected Allan. "Did you notice anything else about Finn's condition?"

"While I waited for the EMS, I looked 'round an' saw a broken plate and some spilled food. Guess he'd been carryin' in some o' the lasagna I saw on the kitchen table when I took in the pieces of the plate an' the spilled food to the garbage. The lasagna was still warm so I put it in the fridge, 'cuz it shouldn't spoil, y'know."

Diana held herself back from a worried look about the lasagna and the fact that Allan, in his between-binging spurt of conscientiousness, had removed indicators that might've helped the EMTs piece together what had happened to Finn.

"Then I went back to Finn, to keep 'im company 'n 'at, in case he … y'know … died. I'm sure glad he didn't. I owe him a huge tab, an' I don't feel right not payin' it."

"Allan, what did the paramedics do when they arrived?"

"They checked his vitals 'n 'at. They asked me if I'd done the CPR, an' I told 'em I did. Then they barked stuff inta their radios and brought in a stretcher an' wheeled 'im out. Wasn't nuthin' for me to do, so I took 'is phone an' his truck keys an' drove to Frick here. Waited forever in th' ER, so I used his phone till the battery went, 'cuz I couldn't find his charger when I took the phone. I called Tracy an' Todd an' th'other bar employees an' told 'em we had to keep the place runnin' 'cuz he might go bankrupt, like I did with m' daddy's old propane business eight years ago. Tracy an' Todd've been doin' a bang-up job. I know Finn's like the back of m' hand, so I've helped 'em with decision makin' an' orders for supplies 'n 'at, when I ain't here for visitin' hours. Makes me feel like I'm repayin' Finn. He's always been good to me. Finally, the doctor comes out an' asks if I'm next-of-kin, an' I lied that I wuz Finn's brother 'cuz they might not tell me nuthin' if I wuzn't family. Doc tole me Finn'd some 'llergic reaction, an' asked if I'd seen anythin' mebbe allergy-causin' when I found 'im. I told him I found some food but the Doc, he said it wuzn't no food allergy 'cuz o' the blood tests they did 'n 'at. Doc said the reaction closed Finn's throat an' put stress on his heart an' that mebbe his brain didn't get the right amount of oxygen for a time an' that m' CPR helped save 'im. But Doc said Finn wuz still unconscious an' might be for a while but that I could visit 'im. But you go in first, Dee," said Allan, like he was ICU maitre'd. "I seen 'im every day. It ain't much. Looks kinda awful. He don't say nuthin', but I talk to 'im like we're talkin' over the bar, an' I tell 'im 'bout the Pens last game an' how many goals Crosby scored, even though I ain't sure he can hear me."

The overhead light flashed, signifying that 15-minute, one-person-at-a-time visiting had begun.

Allan looked over to Luna. "Oh, you can leave her out here. I'll keep an eye on her." Then he paused, staring down at his boots again. "I may be a lush, but I wouldn't harm a hair on a kid's head. You can trust me."

A tear came to Dee's eye. "Of course I trust you, Allan. If it weren't for you, Finn wouldn't be alive. So I'll take you up on that waiting-room babysitting. She's pretty self-maintenancing."

Allan looked up at her. "Thank you, Diana. You wuz always decent to me."

"I've another favor to ask you," she said. "Do you still have Finn's house key?"

Allan felt around in his pocket. "Matter o' fact, I do."

"Would you mind slipping it to me. I'll return it to the key holder. I'm no detective, but I am a nurse. I might be able to learn some things about what happened to Finn."

∞ ∞ ∞

As she drove from Frick Hospital to Finn's place, she wept over what she'd seen, growing ever more anxious that *she* had been the cause of it. Again, the poison kiss. Finn's face was swollen beyond recognition, and he was intubated. Conversation wouldn't have been possible even if he hadn't been, as he was still unconscious—his body's efforts to recover from shock versus the coma Allan had speculated. Through his picc line flowed a drip of glucose, antibiotics, and steroids, the last of which was to bring down the swelling. Dee had left almost as soon as she saw him, barely able to keep her composure in front of Allan, who had to have guessed her distress. She thanked him and swept up Luna, who was solemn about Dee's weeping, laying her hand on her mother's thigh as Diana cried all the way to Finn's.

"You stay here, baby, and keep the doors locked," she cautioned Luna, the engine running, with the heat on. "I won't be long."

Inside, Dee found the place as Allan had described. There were still potholders on the kitchen table from where she guessed Finn had set the lasagna to cool. She opened the fridge and pulled out the casserole dish. Allan, in his own shock, hadn't thought to cover it, and the top layers of pasta and sauce had hardened. By the massive rectangular gap, Dee could see the section Finn had cut out. She smiled, thinking about how he'd eat the corners only if they were all that was left. She took a fork from his dish rack and poked around—she wouldn't dare touch it, given what had happened to Finn. If what she suspected were true, she had to get back to the manse before that bastard had booby trapped the entire joint with poison and whatever other nightmares he could think of. Clay was insane or evil enough to have followed her to PA and had holed up somewhere in the area in the attempt to make her life living hell, as he'd done when they were married. Would she never stop paying for her mistakes?

As she pushed around the lasagna, in the back of her mind, Diana saw a vision from one of her first nursing floor shifts, of a patient who'd come into the ER after a severe allergic reaction. Like Finn, he'd had a beard. Under that beard, he showed the same swelling and skin pocked with pus-and-lymph-filled blisters. The poor guy had been chain-saw sectioning a downed sycamore and had hit a poison-ivy vine hidden on the bottom side of the trunk. Poof! Instant vaporization of the urushiol, the culprit venom of the plant, that he inhaled and got into his mouth, nose, ears, and skin. He was a kid, really—just 21 and doing his first timber work on a summer job. He'd never come into contact with the ivy till that moment, so he never knew that he was allergic to a point far beyond which calamine lotion could treat. Just one nanogram of urushiol is enough to cause a rash in the general population, and, with ¼ oz of that shit spread evenly across the globe, you could raise a rash on every person on the planet. 100 Nanos was the typical exposure most people got. Who knew how much her hyper-allergic bearded patient and Finn got? And what EMT or doctor would think of poison ivy at Christmas time? Hell of a mistletoe kiss-of-death.

She flipped over a large chunk of lasagna to reveal an oil slick at the bottom of the dish. Could be just fat from the ricotta and sausage. Then she sniffed it, yanking back her head—a smell of hot plastic and bleach immediately nauseating her. Buried under all those noodles, sauce, and cheese, Finn could never have detected it. But she had smelled it before, oozing from the pores of her bearded young patient. Urushiol. Probably synthetic, though, where Clay had gotten it was impossible to tell.

Finn had been poisoned.

So had her life ever since that motherfucker had walked into it with a cheeky smile and a cable-company clipboard.

∞ ∞ ∞

As she drove back up the mountain, a sardonic determination took hold of her. She couldn't allow herself to think in such a way—she had a daughter who depended on her.

Yeah, a daughter. One who'd been scarred so much by that bastard that she could barely talk

"If I don't make a stand here, he'll hound me the rest of my days," she whispered. Luna stared at her, but not, it seemed, in fear. There was a look of assurance on her daughter's face that endorsed whatever Dee was planning. Two against the world.

In the manse, Dee trotted out the new locks she'd bought in the summer and installed them. She double-checked every window casing to make sure the storm windows were fully in and the windows locked. Luna trailed along with her, carrying tools, helping where she could. In the attic, Dee inspected all the vents to make sure they were in place, then, in the hallway, boarded up the attic ceiling door. In the basement, she gathered the two dozen hurricane lamps and paraffin fuel her father had bought years ago in case the power went out in the winter. She then put a filled lantern in every room. Down at the tool shed by the creek dam, she checked the interior for any signs of Clay's having been there. In the corner, she saw the sledgehammer Rooster had left. She made a mental note to kiss that old coot the first chance she got. "Shelly was right, in a way—none of us deserve him," she whispered aloud, breath trailing from her lips, Luna looking solemnly at her.

∞ ∞ ∞

Diana didn't know if Clay was armed. In Finn's and Selene's cases, he'd already attempted murder, and he'd made sure that Rooster wouldn't be around to check on her and Luna. So she didn't think him beyond any extremity. How he had gotten in and sabotaged the wood screws and poisoned Finn's lasagna was anybody's guess. She felt crazy for not jumping in the car with Luna and driving to a hotel or straight to Denton, but she knew that she was just as much, if not more vulnerable on the open road as she was here in the manse. Dee knew the manse, inside and out. Clay didn't. He could set booby traps, and she could defuse them, till he murdered her and Luna, to get his way.

But was that his way? Murder them, and he'd lose forever the chance to permanently carve his mark into their lives—their existences forever beholden to him and the shadow he cast. Clay had always wanted to make a mark on the world. The problem was, he could never conceive of himself as anything other than a stain. And if he couldn't blot out that dark self-assessment, he would be intent on forever casting Dee and Luna in the same blood-red hue. To make Diana know her limits … *his* limits. Know that not only was her daughter *his* but that Diana's own life would be lived at his whim, under the terms he dictated, in the shadows he haunted.

Dee wanted to puke the gall she tasted, but all she could muster was intense hatred. For the first time in her life, she knew a reason for pure, clean hatred—an acidic emotion, but, like any emotion, value-neutral, like a spark is neutral. The fuel it inflames was the stockpile of the vanities, the fears, the self-loathing. Her intense, burning hatred smacked of no self-abhorrence but smoldered like coke under sod, its energy to be released at the right time, blasting a furnace into veritable hell. This was her house, goddammit. When he next set foot in it, she would know. Now was the time to again get in tune with this place, this one-time curse upon her existence. For she was learning something. A curse will damn you, only if you let it. She was feeling some beast slowly uncurling inside her, stretching its muscles. And that beast was not in the mood to *let* anything happen to her anymore. But she was not the beast yet. Give it time, she thought. Christmas was almost here. And it would be Clay's way to leave his indelible trench-deep wound on that feast. Maybe, just maybe, he wasn't accounting for something else to be born that day.

"Mommy," said Luna in her clearest voice yet. Dee turned out of her reverie on the window seat to look at Luna standing there in her pajamas every bit as poised as a vestal virgin. "The Fire Golem is coming."

"Where did you hear about the Golem?" Dee asked her.

"Daddy told it to me when he was sick in his heart. He told me it was a monster inside him. I tried to tell him he was wrong, but he kept saying it. I need to brush my teeth now, and I can't get the safety stuff off the Captain Marvel push-pump toothpaste."

"Since when did you get so earnest about brushing your teeth, you little bug?" Diana asked her. Luna just cocked her head. "What's 'urnst'?"

Dee paused. "Earnest was a little girl I once knew, who'd gone away a long time ago. But I think she's coming back. You remind me of her."

"C'mon, Mommy. Let's brush our teeth to get ready for the Fire Golem."

Diana's stomach dropped. No amount of bravado or words could take the bitter metal taste off what was coming. "When is he coming, baby?"

"Who, Mommy?"

"The Fire Golem, sweetie. You said he's coming."

A puzzled Luna stared at her. "The Fire Golem's not a he. Don't you know, Mommy?"

Dee wondered. "I guess I don't, dearheart. Can you tell me the closer he—uh, I mean *it*—gets?"

Luna shook her head. "Mommy, you need to read the papers from the bucket, like I showed you. I won't let you read books to me till you read those papers. Right now, though, Mommy, we have to brush our teeth."

Dutifully, if lacking clarity, Dee followed her daughter into the bathroom. "See, Mommy? I can't tear off this child-proof stuff. Guess that's why they call it child-proof."

Dee laughed despite the gnawing fear that was growing in the backdrop of her heart. "Sometimes I think these things are mom-proof as well. It's takes a bear-grip to open them. But wait a minute! We already opened the other one that Finn brought you. There's got to be loads of toothpaste in that. Why are we opening a new one?"

Luna looked suddenly solemn, dropping her gaze. "'Cuz I don't like that one."

"Where is it?"

Luna clammed up. "Oh, come on, baby! You hardly say a word for months, then, just when you get positively chatty, you stop?"

Luna kept looking down. Dee followed her gaze to the bathroom trash can, where the other toothpaste had been deposited. "Sweetie, this was a gift from Finn. Why would you throw it away? It's the same flavor, with all the same Captain Marvel logos on it. Honestly, what a time to become prodigal."

Dee retrieved it from the can, while Luna watched, all the time shaking her head. "I don't like it, Mommy."

"Well the dead have spoken! Glad to see you're still here. C'mon, Luna! Let me show you that it's the same stuff." Dee squeezed the pump, but it wheezed and hardly emitted anything onto Luna's toothbrush. "Once I get the stupid thing working, I'll put it onto *my* toothbrush and use it, to show you it's okay."

"No, Mommy!" commanded Luna in a voice so loud Dee thought it had to be miked.

"Excuse me? Since when did you become a petulant brat? Here, I think I'm getting it to come out better." She pumped repeatedly, but the device still wheezed and bubbled. Dee could smell its fragrance. She could've sworn the label said bubblegum flavor, but she wash smelling Amaretto. Wow. They were making kids' flavors more sophisticated since she'd been Luna's age. Then Dee felt something wet on her hands. Ooze leaked from the side of the pump cylinder, through what had to be the tiniest of holes, given the micron bubbles the leak was emitting. "What? Did you not wanna use this because it's defective?" Dee smelled her fingers, the Amaretto smell accentuated by the bubblegum undertones. She was putting her finger to her mouth when Luna pointed to the clawfoot tub, "Mommy, the ghost is here again."

Dee turned and dropped the toothpaste to the floor. It clattered and rolled almost underneath the tub, resting over the largest of the blood spots there. Standing in the tub was a young woman, late adolescent. She didn't look like a ghost was supposed to, at least to Diana. The specter was as substantial, it seemed, as she and Luna, but the young woman could not be touched by them in their space-time continuum, like she was a nighttime radio signal beamed from leagues away, snatched from the night sky by chance, from another land, another time, to fade as soon as it had come. She was tall and brown-eyed, an intense sadness in her gaze that belied the lightness and insouciance of her movements. Whatever had once burdened her was hers no more, but Dee's and Luna's world would not abide a vision of that lady that wasn't scarred. From the tub she stepped, clad in a flapper's dress, long beads hanging, skimming the rim, gently tapping there like dancing fingernails on immobile piano keys. Her deep-brown wavy hair was shoulder-length and not in the flapper style, but it somehow matched who this woman was. A brooch of pearl shone on her bodice, bearing a simple "E." She lightly bent to the toothpaste, picking it up in a single motion, alighting back into the tub. Then she and the toothpaste were no longer there.

"I told you I didn't like that toothpaste, Mommy."

Dee's fingers were still an inch from her open mouth, the smell of almond still overpowering. But the almond trailed off with a horribly bitter afternote, and Diana remembered, oh God! She remembered that smell! Peach blossom and bitter almond. She quickly jammed her hands under the faucet and viciously scrubbed them, then took a washrag and pumped globs of soap onto it, scrubbing the counter, the mirror, the faucet and handles. "Oh my God, Luna! Did you ever use any of this?"

"No, Mommy. I didn't like it. It had the smell of the old toothpaste that made me sick. And E. told me not to use it ever."

"Made you sick?" Then it thundered down upon her, and in the back of her mind she heard a creak. But this time of a door opening. He had poisoned his own daughter. With cyanide.

Diana ran from the bathroom, down two flights of stairs, into the kitchen, yanking from the refrigerator any food that could be injected with poison. Bread, a tub of ricotta, a packet of bacon, Yoplaits, fruit. Then she went to the pantry and flung out any open box and unsealed bag. Dragged out whole cases of Coke Zero and grabbed the washrag to scrub the cans clean of any potential poison. Back to the kitchen proper, she grabbed the Keurig and emptied it of water. She unscrewed the Pür filter from the kitchen faucet, checking for any sign or scent of its having been tainted.

She rushed into the parlor, ripping off couch and seat cushions for snakes, explosive devices, broken glass. She unplugged her computer and Luna's and would've unscrewed the wall plates if she had a screwdriver at the ready. She scanned ceilings and walls. Who knew what could be behind them? Ghosts. Poison. Incendiary devices. A stealth intruder had been here, in her home. Where could she turn? What else could be poisoned or booby-trapped? She had no gun, no blade except the kitchen cutlery, and what if he had sabotaged those, as well, so that their blades would fall out of their handles at the slightest nudge?

Running to her purse, she pulled out her car-key fob and feverishly pressed the remote-start button, then saw Luna beside her. "Mommy, I told you the Fire Golem isn't here yet."

Dee knelt down and stared into her daughter's eyes. "Sweetie," she held back tears, "Mommy's confused and scared, and she needs to know she's not going crazy. Tell me, baby, how did you know that you shouldn't use the toothpaste?"

Luna replied patiently but pointedly. "I told you, Mommy—E. told me not to use it, that it had the same stuff in it like the old toothpaste that made me sick."

Diana swallowed hard, nodding her head. "Honey, who is E.?"

"I told you that, too, Mommy. E. is the ghost. You saw her before, up in the bedroom, in the face of the Fire Maiden I painted on the wall, then in the tub. I thought you knew. She wrote the slips of paper. You need to read them."

"S-so you saw the gh—I mean, E., too, just now, in the bathtub upstairs?"

"Of course I did, Mommy. This is her house. She likes you. She says she knew you when you were younger. She says she saw the times when your daddy hurt you bad."

Dee blinked. "Hurt me? Dad hurt me? No, sweetie. Your late grandfather was the one hurt, by a saw. Later he had a stroke. I took care of him."

"E. saw you take care of him. She saw your mommy, too. E. told me your mommy didn't talk, just like me. So that's why I talk now. Because you need to see things."

"*What* things, Luna? I don't understand! I'm scared … and

you aren't."

Luna looked at her with ancient eyes. "I'm not scared right now, Mommy. But I will be when the Fire Golem comes."

"*When* will he come, Luna? What is he? I need to know, to protect you."

"The Fire Golem's not a 'he,' Mommy. You'll know when the Fire Golem is coming. You'll know what to do. But the Fire Golem's not here yet. You need to read the slips of paper E. wrote."

Diana broke into sobs. She felt displaced, floating above the two of them, seeing but a shell of herself crouched down beside Luna, powerless to save those two from what was coming.

Luna grabbed a paper towel and dabbed Dee's face with it, then led Dee by the hand, upstairs, to the window seat, where she bid her mother sit down and put into her hand the next slip of paper. Then Luna curled herself into bed to fall asleep. Over the next evening and Christmas Eve day, Dee read the slips of paper.

25 December 1928

Father and I spend a cheerless Christmas. He will not let me turn on the wireless or play the phonograph, and he will not speak to me. He mourns because mother died on this day two years ago, and he blames me. "She had been gay and light before you, you stillborn," he told me once, when I was younger and asked him why mama was so unhappy. "Doesn't she have you, Papa, and me and this best of houses you built for her?"

He sneered at me. "Houses are no refuge when the evil you've fled lives with you." He said no more to me that day. Mother had been unhappy since I first could remember. She would give me a wan smile and touch my curls. I could even get her to forget her sorrow by letting her curl my hair until Father, on one of his few times home, found her doing that. He'd bruised my wrist that day when he yanked me from her and locked me in the nursery that is now my prison cell. "That is our son! Emilia, I know you are unhappy, and God knows I've tried everything I know to bring you peace, but you've not stirred since he was born! I come home to this place I built, a refuge for us to shut out the travails of the world, and you are here primping and pampering him like he's your damnable doll! Well, he's not, I tell you! He is the one hope to right things from the clutches of my ungrateful sons. Damn, woman! I can give you anything and everything to be happy — but not this ... coddling *of him. He already cowers from me as it is!"*

"Cesaré," she wept to him. "I am unhappy because you *are*

unhappy. I weep because you refuse to. And I nurture Emilio because you won't. Don't you see? My love, the world is not the barren place you make it in your heart. Open your heart to me."

"Enough of that!" he roared. "Happiness is not why we're here, damn you and your coquettish ways! We're here to wrest a life from the clay and to leave a mark, so they'll know we were here. No wonder you're of such melancholy bent — you've no sense of dignity and duty, woman. I opened my heart to you from the very first, and you close yours to me behind a veil of sadness. What would you have of me?"

"Just you," she whispered.

Father was out the door, not coming back for three weeks. Mama let me out of the nursery, and we walked the mountain paths, till Father returned home, and Mother's face dropped, when, with hope, she had gone to the parlor to greet him, only to see his visage, glowering over some new depredation worked upon him by Adé and Alé.

This yuletide morning, thinking Papa yet asleep, for he sleeps late these last months, I went into Mother's bedroom, still looking as it did the day she passed — no, <u>killed herself</u> — I'll have no lies in my journal. There I took her brooch, the one her own father had given her long ago when she debuted, a simple "E" that clasps the fabric between the breasts, put it on myself, and looked in the mirror, as I have done many mornings. The door creaked open. Father stood there amazed, then enraged. I thought he would kill me or at the least tear off the brooch, but he is so loath to touch me that he paused, stared at me savagely, then left, slamming his bedroom door, not to come out till past dusk on this foul and cold day of rain on what should be a holiday. He sat in his chair in the parlor, pouring himself whisky and muttering. I held Mother's brooch to my heart, knowing the gloom she clutched there while she lived.'

5 April 1929

Today, spring has truly arrived on the mountain, and I even

persuaded father to fly fish in the stream with me. Winter's fleeing has seemed to lighten his soul, and he even jokes with me. I have tried much to share with him the things he treasures, even to the point of asking him to explain to me the fortunes of the company and his hopes for it. And hope indeed he seems to have. "Ah, but your father is more clever than your brothers account, Emilio! Things are looking up! Wadsworth has told me of several new initiatives to make inroads into the betrayals those two scoundrels have wrought upon me. Despite their doom and gloom about the business, we will soon contract with a new Canadian steel firm! Ah, their tariffs be damned, Emilio," he smiled and winked at me, "We may have in our pocket an influential MP from a riding due north of Erie. Pittsburgh be damned, son! We'll make Hamilton the Pittsburgh of Canada, eh?"

Father crowed when I netted a fat trout on his line, and we filleted and pan-fried it in butter tonight. Is this the happiness Mother sought for him?

12 May 1929

Father has returned from Hamilton, Ontario, and he is beaming!
I see in him a delight that must have charmed Mother and so many
others when he was a younger man with dreams. If only he could
forget about Adé and Alé and blaze for himself a new trail, like
he did when he was a youth who took the world by storm, as he
accounts it. I believe him, but Mother too often talked about the
peace of mind he'd sacrificed to pay the price of his rise in fortune.
"He is," she once whispered to me, "my dear sweet Emilio, not the
man he was. The empire he built consumes him. When I met him,
he said I gave him such joy that he could be a new man, free of the
chains he'd wrought in the building of empire. I believed him, or
better say I believed I could bring him some small peace. But that
one is gone in me now. And that one is gone in him, if it ever was,
Emilio."

"Call me 'Lana, Mama," I'd begged her then, for her voice
sounded like music when she said my name, and I was young and
heedless, with Father not home enough to levy a tax on my dreams.

"You must not be called that, Emilio, for you are not a child anymore. You grow into manhood." So, I smiled at her, for I knew she delighted in those times of my childhood when, with Father gone, she felt carefree with me. And I couldn't bear her sorrow if it were because I did not smile at her. But my heart died a little, for I have never wanted manhood. It's a poison in my veins and a fever in my mind, what I see in the mirror putting to the lie what I feel in my heart. She would not let me talk to her about E., for she feared the price of those words, words that were always hushed in his company.

1 June 1929

"The plan is afoot, Emilio!" crowed Father. "They cannot halt it, for my charitable enterprises and foundations, and not my holdings bear the mark of this Canadian venture. To the world, we do it not for money, eh, Emilio? We do it for the grand philanthropy and the legacy and a name that will last. But our taxes will see a benefit, to be sure, and not a penny of it will your avaricious brothers ever see. And do you know what's best about it, Emil?"

I smiled, though my heart was not in it. "I will run it, and it will be in my name, Father."

"Ha-hah!" He cackled jubilantly. "You're damn right, and Adesso and Alesso will know that it is _my_ doing! Will know they've been beaten at their own game, eh? They'll see my mark and 'ware me, and 'ware you! You will be of great expectations!"

I don't want anyone to 'ware me and cringe in fear of me or be my lickspittle because of my money, stature, name, or mark. I want to be loved as I am. And, as I am, I will never be loved. Why is Father's joy my invitation to gloom? I bear much of the melancholy of Mother, and only now do I feel the creeping nightshade she felt. But I smile at Father, for he is happy now, and does not curse me. May he forget his grief over Mother and know some joy, even if it is the joy that comes from spiting his enemies.

20 August 1929

I will no longer nurture a joy that sucks the blood of others, even one's enemies, for it is the vain hope of a desperate person. Wadsworth has left Father's employ, and Father is enraged as only he can be. "The traitor!! He quails that Hamilton will not be ours, damn it! But when has a momentary defeat paused Wadsworth when money is still in the offing? What does he mean he'll no longer countenance my plans? He dared to say they're fueled by passion, vengeance, and intemperance, and not by sense! What sense does *he* make? Ah, it's the cents, and dollars, he fears he *won't* make, for he's lost faith, joining the bandwagon of those who find it fashionable to see me on the outs! Don't trust people, my son! Oh, the bastard never hesitated a second at my so-called 'ruthlessness' when he saw money come hand-over-fist the way of his firm, making him the most powerful attorney in the state! Now the reputation that my interests and capital built for him is too refined to be associated with me. I'll break him, damn it! Just like I'll break your blood-traitor brothers."

"Father, I know you're wounded, but is there not some prudence in what his leaving forebodes, even if his is nu abandonment of you?"

"Eh? Damn you, boy, I'm not wounded! But don't corner a beast at bay! He'll scar you! Wadsworth's betrayal reeks of prudence indeed — safety, caution, the whispers in his ears of his peers who follow the madding crowd of opinion and not true insight into what's happening here! I've been targeted, Emilio! For being too damned successful! Too damned independent. Too damned courageous where they've wallowed in the shit of their drawers. Cowards! I'll have them yet!"

2 September 1929

I must be short with this entry, for I am in pain and must attend to myself. Father beat me till I swooned. Without warning, his febrile obsession classes me in the ranks of those who have betrayed him. But I am worse, for, in his mind, I betrayed him at birth and have been at it since when I was little and asked to wear one of Mother's dresses. Father overheard me, for I had been too young to be temperate in this matter, as Mother had cautioned me. He beat me then with a strap and forced me into starched collars. This day, he beat me with his fists, kicking me while I groaned on the floor. I cannot survive another beating. I must give him reason to pause.

10 September 1929

Things grow dark for Father's business fortunes. Today he chased away with his cane a constable who came to serve him and nearly struck a doctor with an order for Father to go to the sanitarium.

Seeing me in the hallway watching, bent over as I am from the ribs he broke last week, he turned to bear his wrath on me. I know not from whence it came, but a fury rose in me, and the cub bared fangs larger than the brute imagined. In my hand, a stiletto letter opener I sharpened on a whetstone slit open his wrist and scored his throat. He will corner me no more. As he fell in shrieks of pain,

I stood over him and gritted my teeth. "My name is Emiliana. And if you harry me, you will have to kill me, for I will not abide your tyranny, Father."

29 October 1929

The wireless speaks doom. Father sits in the parlor chair. "Adesso and Alesso are mortally wounded," Father whispers. "And so am I. My sons! Why have you abandoned me? Did I not give you everything?"

I eye him, my stiletto in hand. He will not class me with his sons, and I am resigned to that fate. I will be who I am.

28 November 1929

Father will hear nothing of thanks this day. But I am thankful to know who I am. I am no abomination. Soon, I will step into a wider world to show myself.

14 December 1929

Father has not stirred from his suite on the second floor for two weeks, except to climb the stairs and soak for an hour in the clawed bathtub he finished himself with a coating of porcelain. Cans of it are still in the bathroom, as if he wants to paint himself forever into that tub. The place is deathly silent. The larder is low, but I make do, for I need little. I want little, just my freedom.

I will be born.

19 December 1929

Father has broken his silence to bring up bottles of wine from the cellar. He is emaciated, rings under his eyes, but he bears a giddiness that will not be brooked. He says he and I are at peace. "We share more in common than you think, Emilio," he says as he pours himself wine, the only thing that now passes his lips. "You have my eyes, and you hunger for more than this world can give, eh?"

I will leave him when the frigid weather clears, for his ramblings bring no peace but unsettle me. I see in his face a mirror of what I would be if I am not born anew.

"Come, drink wine with me!" he insists. I only watch him. I should leave, but my heart will not allow me. For is he not my flesh and blood? He and I both grieve mother, and too many others have abandoned him. But I will not drink his cup.

24 December Christmas Eve

I awoke with the brute's hand on my throat, his other arm clenching the stiletto from my grasp. Breath reeking of garlic and wine, he sneered at me. "So, you want to be who you want to be? You won't be my son, but you'll be a son of a bitch or a bitch herself! Hah!!" He licked my cheek, and I would have vomited, but I could barely breathe.

"You won't squirm away from me this time, little mouse. The cat has you in his claws. But you will not die from his fangs, oh no! You will drink his joy, the joy of the absolved, the mindless, the dead!"

He wrested the blade from my hand, his knee pinning down my other, then threw me like a rag doll from my bed, across the room, my head crashing into the side of the window seat. I saw blotches in my vision even as the snow fell outside, the moon's last quarter smiling down on me. I tried to gain my feet, but he smashed my mouth, and I fell again, my head hitting the window seat ledge.

Half-conscious, so that I thought it a dream, I felt him grip my hair, forcing back my head and jamming a goblet's edge into my mouth. I gagged and sputtered, the wine pouring down my face and mouth till I had no choice but to drink or die.

When he'd emptied it, he threw it to the floor where it sprayed glass that flickered my face. "There!" he said, falling back. "We *are one, little mouse! You are not in my belly, though you might as well be, for our bellies share the same draught. You will know my fate." He stumbled from the room, and I heard the bathroom door open and the tub fill with water.*

Diana felt everything rise and converge. It was Christmas Eve, and the last bit of moon crowned the sky. She looked to the Fire Maiden, who stared at her with certainty, pointing to Dee and the window seat on which she was perched. The Maiden's face merged with Diana's own—with pictures she remembered of herself from childhood, the face of her mouth with her face of the ghost, all blending into the face of Emiliana who nodded at her, letting open a floodgate of memory. The dam burst.

"Come here, Dormouse!" Dad had said to Dee. "You're old enough to learn. You're 12 going on 13, and you don't know how to tread water?"

"Who cares, Dad? I can swim!"

"You swim like a battleship anchor with water wings!" he'd said. "Brad-a-doccio was swimming like a seal at age three. You don't want him to show you up."

"Brad did a lot of things before I did, 'cuz he's older. Bet he'll never spell 'Antidisestablishmentarianism' no matter how old he gets." She paddled to the shallows.

"Ah, he's the brawn not the brains of this outfit. That's you and me, Dormouse. But you gotta learn to keep your head above water! Connellsville's swim program'll teach you. They've had state champions. But that won't be till you're at the Senior High, little Dormouse. Here, I'll show you."

"Dad! I'm in Junior High. Nobody's parents teach them how to swim when they're that old!"

"C'mon," he snatched her from the shallows. "I'll teach you."

Her hands were swallowed in his callused bear paws before she could jerk them back, pulling her inexorably to the deeps. "Daddy, no! This creeps me out! You know I don't like the deep end! The fish nibble at my legs, and I hate it!" Her breath was coming out in pants, as was his. She could feel the swishing of his legs, keeping his head, shoulders, and her above the surface.

"Dad, I'm not kidding!" Her voice was shrill. "Let me go!"

"Little Dormouse has to learn how not to get swallowed by the cat!"

"Jesus [pant] Dad. [pant] I'm not—[pant]—a kid anymore. Stop—"

She was going to say, "Stop calling me that!" but he'd pulled her close in to him.

"Ha-ha! The panther has the Dormouse!"

She beat him on the shoulders. "Stop it, Dad! I don't like this!"

Her heart was racing, and her stomach screamed a panic she'd never before felt.

He ignored her hapless pounding and his legs swished her across the deep end. "Noooooooooo-aaaa-ooooooh! Daddy!!!" Her screams came in high-pitched trills that bounced off the trees, the hillside, and the looming house atop it. She scratched at him, trying to tear herself away, but he ground himself to her. She could smell whiskey fumes on his hot breath.

"Come here," he whispered. "Come here, Dormouse." They were on the rock shelf in the deep end. His legs had stopped swishing, but her toes couldn't find the rock. He gripped her hips and sat her down on him. She could feel his thing poke her thigh. Before she could act, his bear paw tore off her bikini bottom. "That's it, little mouse," he panted. "Right there. I'll show you."

"Daddy!" she'd wanted to scream but couldn't.

"Open up. Relax, baby," he said, kissing her neck. She tried to twist out of his grasp, but his other arm vised her. She beat at his face, but he *smiled, like he relished it. His thing was touching her there. Wrenching, she tried, vainly, to knee him, but she was barely a third of his weight, and her wriggling excited him.*

"Just a little more, Dormouse."

She felt herself split open. Then felt nothing, because she was no longer there. She separated. Diana was gone. She saw two other people, one who was a daughter, the other a force that thrust and tore, her riding its rollercoaster teeter-totter, trying in every way to not be there, to not move, to not give him the satisfaction. That was the word, she'd thought. 'Satisfaction.' That's what it means in context,' her mind had said to her then in that most desperate of seconds. She learned a word.

All was a pain was a force was a jolt up her spine, electrocuting her, her father moaning till he stopped and was out of her.

"It's … okay, Dormouse," he mumbled. "I've been snipped. You won't get pregnant."

But she was already drifting in the deep end, far off the rock. Oh, how she wanted to drown. But she floated.

That night, she didn't stop bleeding even after she'd showered. As she lay in bed, wondering if she could sneak into Mom's room to see if there were any pads, a picture floated into her vision. A woman. In the third-floor window. Looking down on the two of them, in the pool, from far above. Watching them do what they would do every time her father took her out to the pool after that. Then in the big claw bathtub in the winter. Three years. It stopped when Diana took the stiletto letter opener into the tub with her and made sure he wouldn't touch her again.

She watched herself from afar, as she carried out the stiletto ploy—that's what they called it in the goth novel she was currently reading—through to when she surgically slit him open. Having been forced to watch herself do everything since that first time in the creek pool, she'd gotten down the technique of withering self-evaluation, playing this anticipated scene again and again in her mind like a batter watching the last at-bat, perfecting the swing, balancing the wrists, swiveling the hips, and that oh-so-subtle-and-satisfying last flick that lit into the ball for maximum exit velocity. She'd replicated her video perfectly, as the blood clouds in the bath water attested.

She hadn't castrated him, just made sure that the member would stay attached and useless, inserting the stiletto lengthwise and swishing it through what thereafter remained of his genitals. Retracting the blade, she held the dripping stiletto to his face. "Listen, you daughter-fucking shred-dick," she said. "I'm going to shower your shit-blood off me. When I'm clean of your filth, I might drive you to the hospital. And I swear, if you call the police, I won't hesitate to do to your nose what I've already done to your dick." Then she stepped into the shower as he bellowed. But Mom, whether she'd heard him or not, didn't respond. Brad was out drinking with his football buddies, tipping cows for all she knew.

At the hospital, she carried out her role just like she'd seen it in the video that had played in her mind for three years—the shrieking, freaking-out, concerned daughter. "O'm'godO'm'godO'm'godO'm'godddddd! Please help my dad! He was trying to cut an opening for the doggy door we were installing, and the saw bucked. There was blood everywhere! O'm'god, is he gonna die?"

By this time, her father's face was ashen. As the orderlies ran about, she whispered in his ear, "That's the story, cheese dick. Got it? I won't hesitate to shiv the fuck out of you in your sleep if you say otherwise."

The memory rose from her heart into her mind, converging on this moment now. There never had been a saber-saw accident. His eyes of terror till he died four years later told a different account.

It had been her.

After that, they'd had a pleasant father-daughter relationship, Dee—not 'Di,' not 'Dormouse'—seizing the lead, sharing their passion for remodeling, taking care of Mom's needs, seeing Brad off to Penn State. This daughter and her father were everything they should be. They understood one another, respecting each other's space. He encouraged her in her interests, via both loving participation and generous funding, like a good father should.

Dr. Palao had said that her father had suffered severe shock, from which most patients recover. If accompanied by severe and prolonged blood loss, however, there could be irreversible brain trauma. She'd read about that well ahead of time, during the years of being ripped open by him. After estimating the drive time down the mountain and her father's anticipatable flow patterns, given his blood pressure, as well as his statin and lisinopril dosages, she calculated to a nicety (she liked that word) the requisite amount of blood loss. Thus, he'd been in the right frame of mind to take all her words to heart and ensure a thereafter functional father-daughter lifestyle.

She hadn't remembered the Diana who did that. The Diana who looked, lived, and calculated long before her Clay had crafted his plans and mark in her life. That Diana had been long gone, maybe closeted in the third floor through twenty or so mountain winters.

The morning her father died of his third stroke in three months, when her sophomore year at Penn State was now a forgotten wisp, she noted in his fading eyes a reflection of herself. She saw, as he expired, that the little Dormouse would eventually reassemble herself. All it would take would be a few small repairs and a long stay in Texas.

∞ ∞ ∞

25 December 1929, Christmas Day

I am lost unto this world.

The rest of the page was blank, but Dee furiously snatched up the last page, feeling an urgency she couldn't explain.

The handwriting was not as steady but still legible.

He has poisoned me. He has entered me unbidden and filled me with his venom. I wretch and convulse and sweat. Rat poison. Arsenic for his mouse—

Here, the writing trailed off, the pen strokes jagged and bleary, finally resuming two thirds of the way down the page.

I will not die without a resurrection. I will rise and go now. To Mother's wardrobe. I will don her clothes, her brooch, her pearls, her beads, her shoes. I will get Father's dueling pistol and finish what I started. Then I will sleep until I resurrect. Till that time, I will keep watch. It will be done unto me according to that word.

The page ended, and Dee frantically searched for one more sheet. *"O'm'godO'm'godO'm'godO'm'godddddddd! Please help me find it!"* she cried to the room.

The lights and power went out.

"Mommy!" Luna had risen in her bed, eyes wide open. "The Fire Golem's almost here!"

"Oh my God!" she screamed in her mind. "He's coming. I need a weapon, anything! I will not let him do this! *I will not die without a resurrection!"*

She gazed around the room for something, anything. The curtains smiled back at her. Outside the snow was falling, the last waning crescent of the moon gazing back at her. So thin. She'd called it God's fingernail when she was Luna's age. Now the divine fingernail was pointing down. At Diana. At the window seat she knelt beside.

She heard a creaking overhead and recognized the sounds for what she'd always known them to be but had denied to her waking mind. He wasn't *coming*. He'd been here all along. In the attic. In the footprints. In his poison. Watching. Waiting. Leaving his mark, the cloying scent of which now gagged her nostrils and throat with acid-rain downfalls of cyanide, urushiol, and arsenic.

"Mommy! Don't you see?"

The attic ceiling door was rattling. Despite her having boarded it up, it would not hold him.

Looking wildly about, she saw the Fire Maiden pointing. To Diana. To the window seat.

She braced her hands under the lip of the seat, planted her feet, and drove upward, bellowing even as the nails of the window seat screamed against century-old wood. Wood that Diana herself had reinforced so long ago, when she'd taken the hammer from Dad's bear paw and drove in the final nails on all memory that would dare resurrection. Dare leave its mark.

It opened to a mummified skeleton in a desiccated flapper dress, pearls floating on her throat. Emiliana.

An old-fashioned, marble-plate-covered journal with an "E" engraved on it, gutted of its pages, lay beside the form, and clutched in the skeletal fingers were a slip of paper and an old fountain pen, dry of its ammunition.

Dee seized the paper.

It is finished.

He was in the bathtub, seizing and shaking in the water, imbiber of the poison he'd forced down my throat, as he had done to my mother and to me and to himself all his days.

"I am not your victim," I said to him.

He looked at me and smiled, ready to say something.

I raised the pistol, and his face dropped.

"I am Emiliana."

I fired straight through his heart and watched the blood stain his nightshirt, flow down his arm, and drip from his fingers onto the floor. I dropped the pistol into the tub with him.

I opened the medicine chest, tearing out the pages of my journal and slipping them into the razor disposal, one by one, while his bathwater turned red. Then I took the porcelain paint and brushed it over the slit. My shaking and convulsing coated the whole chest, locking into place my story for another to find in a better day. Or none at all. My story is told even if none witness it. Today is that better day.

I am born even as I die. There _is_ absolution. Yet, there is nothing *ever for which to be forgiven. I am my own. I will rise.*

As the words trailed off in her mind, Diana couldn't believe them, seeing herself from above, kneeling by the window seat, a piece of ancient parchment clutched in her hand.

"Mommy, I need you to hear me," said Luna. *"Hear me!"*

This eloquence from one who had been mute till the hour of the storm.

"Make things right, Mommy. Things have been wrong for so long."

"I don't understand, sweetie!" heaved Diana, overwhelmed by what was happening, she and her daughter about to be seized by him. Her last anchor to the past, the past of the life she had sought to leave in the ashes, to bury that old life, had reached out to her in a skeletal hand with a message on yellowed paper. All indeed would be ash in movements too swift to comprehend if she didn't dare to be herself. Now. In the midst of the storm.

"Do not *understand*," said the voice that was Luna but was not but was more. "Listen. Be still. Be. *You!*" whispered the breath that caressed Diana's ear.

Diana hushed, the moment hers to grasp. Then she was back with herself, as herself. Diana, Queen and huntress, chaste and fair. She raised the empty journal and hurled it through the window, in that moment, the waning Christmas crescent moon dropping behind the trees.

She needed no weapon.

"Mommy!' Luna exhaled with one last supreme effort. *"You are the Fire Golem! You are the Fire Maiden!"*

She had always been enough.

"Bring it!" arose Diana with a roar, setting into motion the falls and fells that would crash the universe around his ears. "Come out of hiding!" she yelled, "And I'll teach you something about freaky, you cunt!"

Her voice thundered, rattling the walls and beams and joists and every room and every last step of every last stair. And for a moment—she *could* feel it, *see* it, *hear* it—her accuser paused his rattling of the attic door, wondering if he'd prepared for this extremity. Only at the last did his proud-flesh heart dare ponder, if for a flash, that he had never been the pursuer. She felt the thought flee his mind as soon as it was conceived.

"Mommy," said Luna. "I'm not afraid of him anymore."

In that word, "him," Diana saw her father, Emiliana's father, Brad, and the hapless specter that had always been Clay. She had never had to be afraid, least of all, afraid of *them*. Her greatest fear, her one and only fear, ever, she realized, had been terror of herself, of what she might let loose when she finally understood that the last and only bond she had to break was the gossamer one she'd tied around herself at their bidding. They'd convinced her it was made of steel.

"Neither am I," said Diana, "Luna, I need you to do exactly as I say."

The generator kicked in, restoring power and dim lighting.

When she had told Luna all, she put her into the dumbwaiter, pressed the button, and watched her daughter begin her descent to the basement. Something was bludgeoning the attic ceiling door, beginning to splinter it. As the compartment top of the dumbwaiter passed into the depths below, Diana clutched the ladder she'd years ago built into the shaft and ascended to the trapdoor to the attic.

Part V

The Fire Golem

The war you fight is underneath
the water, getting deeper.
The wall, the wall, the falling wall,
the wall is busting open.
The wall is busting open.

In like a dull knife
pulls out all the stops
I fall out like
time running out
—"The Fool," Warpaint

She peered beyond the trap door, into the shadows of the attic. His back was to her, a bulbous, monster-shadow form, lifting heavy things and hurling them down onto the attic ceiling door.

She never paused.

As she sprinted toward him, she saw it all, perfectly. He reared a huge trunk over his head and thundered it down onto the attic door that exploded.

Then he exploded.

She could smell his sweat as she felt the crashing jar of her shoulder into the small of his back. Splinters in their faces, they fell through the wreckage to the third floor, she landing on him, hearing his ribs crunch.

Before he could rise, she bolted into the bedroom and

grabbed the wand lighter to fire the hurricane lamp she'd set aside for such a night as this. He stood in the doorway, a hulk gripping the lintel as if he'd shake the house to its foundations. It wasn't foundation-shaking Dee had in mind.

She swung the lantern by its handle for his head and released it, he in the last instant deflecting it with his forearm. It smashed into the wall, igniting into flames that licked up the wallpaper. He grabbed at his eyes, and, as Diana raced towards him again, she saw him clutch a bleeding sliver of glass from his eye and stare at it in awe.

But she demolished him again, hurtling him into the open bathroom where he stumbled backwards, cracking his head against the tub. Blood trickled down its ivory coating. He struggled to his feet, clutching at something in his belt. Diana gave him no space to breathe, again arrowing herself into him, he slipping in his own blood, tumbling into the tub, a blade spinning into the air from where it had left his hand. It fell to the floor and stuck there, tremoring. The stiletto letter opener.

Dee tramped it, breaking the blade at the hilt. A heap of Clay lay crumpled in the clawfoot tub, his feet dangling out. She didn't pause to look at his face, for she knew this wasn't the end of him.

Sprinting down the stairs to the second floor, she felt a searing pain up her ankle and knew it to be sprained. Her shoulders ached from their battering-ram labors. Dee spit glass fragments from her mouth and relished the taste of her blood. She prayed Luna was doing as she'd instructed.

In Chester Frick's old bedroom, she grabbed a lantern. Then, as her would-be bane thumped down the staircase, she looked up to see a golem. He'd achieved his ambition. So nice for him. As his foot landed on Selene's step, the next lantern hurtled into his chest, knocking him backwards. The lamp shattered on the steps, spewing flame as its shell clanked down to the landing.

Before she could move, he'd launched himself from the stairs down at her, flames licking at his sleeve as he landed on her legs. A wrenching pain felt like it was shearing her left leg off at the knee. She rammed her right heel into his face repeatedly, feeling his teeth sink into it. Diana reared, bringing down her elbow against his skull, and his bite relented. Scooting back, she got to her feet and scrambled down the hall, to the guest bedroom.

In the dark there, she could hear him flailing, beating at the flames that had caught his pants and shirt. Then he was lumbering down the hall towards her. "Wait for it," she thought, and wondered that she was no longer waiting for fear to engulf her. She had no time to fear.

Dee swung the lamp into the dark doorway, into his face, glass, blood, and fuel spraying and catching in drops of fire as the golem crashed backwards, clutching his face. No time. She hobbled over him, her knee in excruciating pain. Despite it, she took the steps three at a time, like in the stairwells of the Junior High, her hands gripping the railings, a gymnast on the parallel bars. Then her arms buckled, and she rolled into a protective ball, crashing into the back of the parlor sofa. No time. She scrambled to the lantern and lighter on the coffee table, sparking the lamp and flinging it into the staircase that went up in a curtain of flame.

She didn't pause to see him emerge from the licking tongues but dashed to the kitchen, hoisting herself up on the chopping block to pick the shards of glass out of her heel, among which fragments were two of the serpent's teeth. "Fuck! I'll have to get a tetanus booster. Maybe one for rabies."

She tore open the ricotta container she'd left out from her panicked evacuation of the fridge and spread cheese on the floor. Snatching the kitchen lantern and lighter, she went to the beckoning basement doorway and waited. She wanted him to see her.

Slouching from the parlor, he smashed himself against the walls leading to the kitchen, trying to put out his own flames. He was a brand who'd plucked itself from the burning, seeking to seed fire over the earth. As he reached the kitchen entryway, she lit the lamp, holding it before her, a priestess of Artemis with a bow of fire, illuminating her face in all its splendor and fierceness. Hot, fresh hell was upon him, she would leave no doubt.

He stood there, as Clay as ever. For a second, immobile and passive in the light of her debut, he regarded her, a hideous smile cracking his charred, lacerated face, one eye gouged and leaking, but the other quite functional, taking her in, head to toe. He spit out blood and a tooth, then wiped his nose on the back of his singed sleeve, the fire behind him seeming to follow his beckoning.

"Damn, Di', you look fine!"

He stood there, expecting her to answer, but she held aloft the light, till a drop of sweat rolled into his eye, stinging it. He winked it away.

"Daddy's back, baby! Look at what he done made, up here in the mountains! He made good, Di', didn't he? Time to give Daddy his due." He stepped forward, slipping in the poisoned ricotta and falling backwards. Diana shambled down the steps, her light the flame to which a crumbling clay moth would flutter.

"You abandoned me, Di'! I told you not to!" His voice echoed behind her, stumping out of the kitchen to the basement door. "Nobody leaves me, Di'! I'm with you for life, and even after that, I'll haunt your dreams. I'm yours forever!"

Dee smiled to herself. She didn't believe in ghosts.

At least not the kind that drip with ricotta.

In the basement, she found Luna, still pouring paraffin on

the floor, the workbench, tools, and the coal Rooster had put down the chute for them. Dee would definitely have to kiss that good man. The two had cleared the top of the coal heap, Dee pushing Luna through the chute, then handing the lantern to her, as Clay found the bottom of the cellar steps.

"Oh, a coal chute, Di'! I didn't know this joint had one of those!" he yelled. "You think you're gonna escape me through there? Haven't you learned by now that I'm smarter than anyone you'll ever know? I've got craft and power, Di'!"

Above her, Dee heard rumbles of thunder. But there was no thunderstorm—it was snowing. Must've been the third-floor sanctuary of Emiliana and Diana, calling it quits, having expended its century-old magic.

As she scrambled through the dark birth canal of the coal chute, she heard his old-born cries. "It's me, Di'! Your Clay! I'm never giving up on you. I'm tried and true. You're my challenge, baby!"

Diana took the lit lamp from Luna and threw it into the coal chute, clamping shut the cast-iron door. She looked at Luna. "Two against the world, huh, kiddo?"

Luna beamed at her. They shambled away from the house, trailing snow angels after them, sparks from the eroding third floor raining a sizzle in the drifts. Dee fell to a crawl, her knee and ankle giving out, the blood from her heel leaving a dark scar in the snow.

Luna came back to help her. "No, honey! Do what I told you. Down to the creek pool. Into the shed." Luna nodded her head and scampered down the 39,000 Steps.

The manse roared as the blazing third floor and attic collapsed into the second floor. A hell's glow peered back at her from the two cellar windows, flaming eyes that would not leave her. She slid backwards, to the top of the steps, awed at what she'd done. Kinda proud of it, too, now that she had time to admire her work.

"Here's to your resurrection, Emiliana," she whispered.

Her father had once told her that old houses burn fast. "It's the old, old wood in them," he'd said, as the two of them installed smoke and CO detectors in every room of the manse, years before he'd raped her. "The years cure it, dry it out, till it's as ripe as straw. And the heat! You can't imagine it. You could sit 200 feet from an old-house fire in the dead of winter, and toast marshmallows, Mouse! But you won't toast 'em long, if it's a place as old as this. It'll burn quicker than light!"

So it did. The second floor crumbled into the first, a lava-skeleton of the frame still lighting the moonless Christmas darkness. The snow had stopped, clouds parting to reveal Orion's Belt. She watched the stars a while, then jerked up, realizing she'd dozed. Her muscles were stiff in the cold, her knee a frozen rock of pain. The first floor was now down, the frame of the upper stories crumbling, support-beam-after-support-beam bending under the will of flame, reaching a tipping point, poised at the edge of the abyss, and, slowly, ever so slowly, bowing to her, Diana, before it fell into the conflagrating pyre below.

The fire roared a finality, the heat of the engulfed house burning her bleeding cheeks. It was done.

Then a dark blot reared in the flames and stepped toward her.

∞ ∞ ∞

She was sliding down the 39,000 Steps in nightmare, the golem behind her, clutching at her, hollering inchoate syllables. It beseeched her, cursed her, howled for her.

Her knee and ankle couldn't hold on the steps, so she clawed her way down over the snow-draped, splintered wood that her father had laid decades ago, now her graven gauntlet. No time. To look back. No time. To think this was just a dream. No time, but to scrape and skitter, her body wracked with the blow of every step. His flaming skeleton melted the snow that washed down on her in a sooty penumbra.

He had stopped the cries now, fixated only on having her, clutching her to his breast in a hellish embrace, to meld her to himself forever. She heard beneath the roar of the fire at the top of the slope his breath wheezing through the holes in his face, the beast slavering for her.

Then she was at the bottom and, screaming with pain, forced herself to her feet and found that, in the right moment, you can do the thing you thought impossible. Agony rippling up her legs like thorny vines clawing for her heart, she stumbled, then walked, then made those two steam-screeching motors that were her lower limbs run toward the creek pool.

He was behind her, but took his time, the cat toying with the mouse. She smelled the stench of his flesh cooking in the flames that were now more him than he had ever been. Not looking back, she felt his smile, his hunger. "I will swallow you," his whisper came to her.

She was at the shed, the beast twenty paces behind. Dee found Luna there, dragging the sledgehammer from the corner. Diana took it in hand, then raised a finger to her lips. "Shhh …" she blew a kiss to her daughter and closed the door as she left the hut.

She ran onto the dam. The pool had frozen over, but she knew it wasn't solid. That would come only in January, if at all. She'd spent years on that ice, skating, in some years wishing the ice to crack beneath her and drown her in a frigid tomb—the years her father had broken her, enslaved her. But now as she stood at the center of the dam's crown, she looked into the ice and realized that she hadn't back then wanted it to crack so that she could die. No. Something had been moving under that ice.

That something was her. It was time to blow up the prison.

She turned, and he was edging the creek below the frozen spillway, his glow sizzling naked tree branches the snows on which fizzled out the nascent flame. She kept the sledgehammer resting on the damn, hidden behind her leg, her feet straddling the largest of the cracks Rooster had shown her. In a frozen sheath, the stream was quiet, but still might have something to say.

At the bank, he paused, as if looking at her for the first time, her shadow form tossed against the background of dark forest and peering stars. If she had been able to see from his angle, she would have witnessed the belt of Orion the Hunter graze the top of her head, bejeweling her with a crown. But even Clay didn't see it because he was looking only at himself, beyond all pain, beyond all desire, burning up.

"You've got a limited shelf life, fucker," Dee whispered to herself. "You aren't gonna burn forever. Come to Mama."

Clay stepped into the frozen creek, his fire gait melting the ice, sinking his feet with each step. Bit-by-bit, he moved toward her, toward the center of the stream. "Come on, you bastard," she said silently. "One more step."

He reared back as if to hurl a fireball at her, when she stepped aside of the crack and brought down the hammer on it in one clean blow.

It was all she ever needed.

In a torrent of water, Diana flew off the dam, letting go of the hammer and watching herself launch toward him. Her heels crashed into his jaw, his head tearing off, body crumbling beneath her. She rode a frigid wave in exhilaration. If this was death, bring it!

∞ ∞ ∞

When she woke, Luna was standing beside her, dripping and shivering. "Luna, baby! You're freezing!"

"I had to get you, Mommy," Luna said through chattering teeth. "You needed to wake up. It's Christmas morning!"

Dee clasped her daughter to her, and held her, using both their warmth to thaw them from what had been a very long winter.

Luna looked up at her, still in her grasp. "Daddy's dead," Luna pointed.

On the bank, some feet from them lay a headless body, steam wisping off it.

"I'm glad," said Luna. "He needed to go. He was so unhappy. Things are right, aren't they, Mommy?"

Dee nodded her head.

"And we can be happy, can't we?"

"You damn well better believe it, Lunariffic."

∞ ∞ ∞

Early morning Christmas Day, 2019, Shelly and Rooster Cogbert unaccountably heard a rapping on the door of their ancient double-wide. When Shelly opened it, she saw something out of myth. Two savage river goddesses, one small, the other taller, stood soaked on the lim. The tall one threw into the snow-covered yard a branch that Shelly thought had been the goddess' staff. But it had been a crutch. In the background, Shelly heard "In the Bleak Midwinter" playing.

The taller goddess brushed Shelly aside, limping into the living room to the recliner in which a be-robed and bewildered Rooster Cogbert stared at her. The goddess bent down and gave him a peck on the cheek. "Merry Christmas, Rooster Cogbert. I never deserved you."

About the Author

Author of North Street Book Prize Finalist, How to NOT Know You're Trans, Bethany A. Beeler has penned thriller, fantasy, horror, and comic novels, short stories, and poetry. She lives in Colorado with Pam and three cats of disaster.

For information on her paintings and novels,
go to her website at
bethanybeeler.com

Other works by Bethany A. Beeler

TransQuality: How Trans Experience Affirms the World
Gods of Rome
The Smoking Inn (Vol. 2 in *The Chronicles of Diana Atestesso*)
Yanter
How to NOT *Know Your Trans: A Memoir*
The Fire Golem (Vol. 1 in *The Chronicles of Diana Atestesso*)
Mirrororrim
Maria (of the angels)
Above the Stars (forthcoming)
Brighton's Bluff (forthcoming)
L & the League of Short-Order Cooks (forthcoming)
The Engine of the Avenging Angels (forthcoming)
Freeland (Vol. 3 in *The Chronicles of Diana Atestesso*) (forthcoming)
Caerdwain (Vol. 4 in *The Chronicles of Diana Atestesso*) (forthcoming)
The Bishop Tripped (forthcoming)
Master of the Universe (forthcoming)

Made in the USA
Middletown, DE
04 October 2021